CURSED CRUISE

D1096699

CURSED CRUISE

A HORROR HOTEL NOVEL

VICTORIA FULTON
& FAITH McCLAREN

Underlined

This is a work of fiction. Names, characters, places, and incidents either are the product of the author's imagination or are used fictitiously. Any resemblance to actual persons, living or dead, events, or locales is entirely coincidental.

Text copyright © 2024 by Rebekah Faubion and Alexandra Grizinski
Cover art copyright © 2024 by David Seidman

All rights reserved. Published in the United States by Underlined, an imprint of Random House Children's Books, a division of Penguin Random House LLC, New York.

Underlined is a registered trademark and the colophon is a trademark of Penguin Random House LLC.

GetUnderlined.com

Educators and librarians, for a variety of teaching tools, visit us at RHTeachersLibrarians.com

Library of Congress Cataloging-in-Publication Data is available upon request.
ISBN 978-0-593-64938-1 (trade pbk.) — ISBN 978-0-593-64939-8 (ebook)

The text of this book is set in 12-point Adobe Garamond Pro.
Interior art by pipochka/stock.adobe.com
Interior design by Cathy Bobak

Printed in the United States of America
1st Printing
First Edition

Random House Children's Books supports the First Amendment and celebrates the right to read.

Penguin Random House LLC supports copyright. Copyright fuels creativity, encourages diverse voices, promotes free speech, and creates a vibrant culture. Thank you for buying an authorized edition of this book and for complying with copyright laws by not reproducing, scanning, or distributing any part in any form without permission. You are supporting writers and allowing Penguin Random House to publish books for every reader.

For Little Jenny

CHAPTER 1

CHRISSY

A chorus of wailing cries echoes over the hills, a sound that could easily be mistaken for wind by an untrained ear, but not by me.

"That sound is the pain of death. The anguish of lives cut short; souls trapped in time by a grave injustice."

My narration borders on melodrama.

But hey, it's a living.

My name is Chrissy Looper and I'm the resident psychic of the newly YouTube-famous-ish Ghost Gang. The video we're currently editing is episode 65—"The Wailing Witches of Salem"—and our 1.3 million subscribers are expecting it to drop tomorrow. They will rage if we don't get it to them on time; they spend the entire day leading up to a new release commenting "where is it?" and "u still alive?" until we give them what they want.

It's a valid concern, since last year we *did* almost die filming one of our episodes at the infamous Hearst Hotel, when a serial killer (and Ghost Gang fan, yikes) stalked us all the way to downtown Los Angeles. He killed two members of the hotel staff, stabbed one of my best friends and then lured me to the roof, where he planned to kill me, too. Luckily, girl power goes beyond the grave and the slain women from his past made sure he got exactly what he deserved: to become a human-shaped stain on the sidewalk below.

I shudder, remembering the feel of his cold evil lips on mine, wishing I could go back in time and *not* be romantically entangled with a sadistic killer.

It's close to midnight in this cramped New York City hotel room, and we're going through the final cut, looking for last-minute tweaks, hoping we don't find any more so we can all finally catch some z's. I try to ignore the scratching sounds only I can hear coming from the closet, where earlier I saw the spirit of a dark-haired man slumped against the wall, hands tied behind his back and a bullet hole between his eyes. This hotel is "historic" (aka old as dirt and haunted as hell) with a history of mafia activity in the '70s, so mob-related deaths replay themselves over and over. I take deep breaths and try to play it cool, even though the rest of the Ghost Gang would run out of here screaming if they could see what I see.

I *did* tell them to steer clear of the closet. They've learned not to ask me *why.*

"What the hell was that?" I hear Kiki Lawrence's voice squeak out of my boyfriend Chase Montgomery's computer speakers. Kiki's on-screen persona is exactly who she is in real life: magnetic and charming and terrified of her own shadow.

"That was the freakiest wind I've ever heard in my life," Kiki says from where she lounges on one of the beds, her chartreuse-braided head in her girlfriend Emma Thomas's lap while they both scroll on their phones.

"It wasn't just wind," I say, the piercing cries of the victims—innocent men and women falsely accused of witchcraft and executed at Proctor's Ledge—still ringing in my ears.

The fluffy hot-pink slipper that dangles from Kiki's dark-brown foot hits the wood floor with a loud *crack*.

We all jump.

Kiki lets out a squeak and cuddles closer to Emma, who is not mad about the proximity. Emma drapes an arm casually over Kiki's shoulder. They've been a couple since that fateful night at the Hearst Hotel when Emma was stabbed and left for dead by our stalker.

A chill fills the room and Chase shudders beside me. I watch as the closet door creaks open. Chase looks at me, searching my face. To him, it looks like a draft has pushed the door open. Only I can see the body slumped against the other side—lifeless eyes peering at me through the crack, a single bloody bullet hole between them.

Kiki's shoe hitting the floor must have signaled the dead man to replay the horror of his own death. The Sicilian kiss of a revolver ending his physical body and dooming his spirit to a near eternity of opening a closet door—just a crack.

My face must say it all, because without a single word, Chase stands up and tiptoes across the room in his socks to shut the door. He slides a heavy duffel bag full of camera equipment in front of the door to keep it from opening again. Luckily, Kiki and Emma don't seem to notice, or maybe they just pretend not to.

It's me, hi, the psychic medium of our group of ghost busters.

I've been able to see ghosts since I was just a little girl with a dead mom and a sad dad. I'll spare you the saga, but long story short: I've learned how to live harmoniously with the dead. And help them sometimes. And nowadays, not absolutely hate it, mostly thanks to my ambitious (and adorable) best friend–turned–boyfriend, Chase, who helped me see my curse as a blessing.

Now we have a hit YouTube show that we all, especially Chase, are hoping gets picked up for TV.

Chase gives my shoulder a reassuring all-clear squeeze before he slumps back down into the hotel desk chair. He's wearing a hoodie up over his tousled black hair, his sharp eyes bloodshot from exhaustion and editing footage on his computer for hours. Most YouTubers with over a million subs hire pro editors to do this part for them, but Chase refuses. He'll hand over the reins when we get a TV pilot, but not a second sooner.

After the news of what happened to us at Hearst Hotel went viral across the interwebs, our subscriber count skyrocketed and our now-manager Jerry Scott (who everyone but Chase refers to as "Where-y" because he disappears for months without explanation) reached out to sign us. Chase jumped on it and regretted it fast when the second we signed the contract, Jerry was on a boat in the Bahamas and only reachable through his assistant, Clayton, who we're pretty sure is his son (Hollywood nepotism at its finest). Clayton has less than two brain cells to rub together and refers to us as "those ghost guys" even though three of the four of us are girls. We're certain not a single message we leave with Clayton gets through to Jerry in the months we don't hear from him.

Imagine our surprise when last month Chase got a call from Jerry out of the blue with an opportunity to submit a demo reel to Creep TV. If they like it, we'll shoot the pilot episode, and if they like that, we'll go to series and Chase's Hollywood dream will be reality TV.

Chase worked for seventy-two hours straight on that reel, stopping only because Emma locked him in his room after he started hallucinating voices coming through his headphones. He slept for almost twenty-fours hours while Emma and Kiki finished rendering the video to send to our contact at Creep.

It's been three weeks and we still haven't heard a peep from Jerry. I'm starting to wonder if he bought a house on a remote tropical island with no Wi-Fi or cell service.

A sharp cry slices through my ears, dragging my attention back to the screen.

"The witch," I say on-screen, and my skin looks ghostly white.

This is where the episode starts to get *really* interesting.

"You can hear it?" Chase asks. He's off camera, and the shot we see right now is of me. White as a sheet, watching something move through the woods. Tracking it with my eyes.

"Not it,*"* I say, my voice soft, my eyes mesmerized. *"Her."*

What isn't on camera are all the sounds and sensations I *felt*. The things I *saw*.

A soft white light floating among the trees. The wind whipping my hair around my head as the so-called Wailing Witch walked—no, floated—through the ravine, her form materializing as she drew closer and closer.

5

"She's coming," I say on camera, and Chase uses a wide shot from the tripod. It's eerie, our light kit turning the fog from the dropping temperatures into a halo. I remember her eyes like dark saucers, her mouth warped wide from centuries of weeping in anger and despair. Her neck hangs at an odd angle, her shoulders racked by silent sobs.

I watch my own eyes on-screen, and a knot in my stomach tightens.

It's just footage, not happening again to me in real time, but it never, ever gets easier to see the way my whole face changes when I'm in the presence of a spirit. My eyes get this distant dark gleam in them, the lost expression of a girl in an intimate dance with the barrier between life and death. I wonder, more than I would ever tell my friends, if one of these days I'll get too familiar, drift too close, and fall all the way into the void between realms.

"We came here to help you." The sound of my own voice speaking to the witch jerks me back to the hotel room and out of my whirring thoughts. *"Sarah Good."*

What you can't see on camera is that her hollow black eyes connect with mine and suddenly she's right in front of my face, her hands around my neck, my hands around my neck too. I can feel centuries of pain, of torment—an eternity of suffering for the crime of being a woman in the wrong place at the wrong time. I visibly shiver on-screen as the balmy night air of early summer in Salem slips down to freezing.

In the present, I tuck my hands into Chase's hoodie, my body temperature dropping as the sound from the footage causes the memory to wash over me like it's happening in real time.

"Nice shot," Emma says. She and Kiki are now hunched over behind me, watching the screen. I don't remember seeing them move from the bed. "The drip of blood from her nostril looks freaky as hell in this light."

One of my eyes peeks open to see.

"Chrissy." Chase's voice off camera is dangerously low; a warning. Ever since Hearst and his declaration of affection, he's been increasingly uncomfortable with putting me in harm's way for the sake of the channel. I don't have to look at him now to know he's still grouchy about this on-camera exchange. I try to ignore him.

On-screen, I lift my hand to silence him.

What doesn't appear is the moment the witch passes through me.

They can't see how I twist inside because her soul presses against mine.

None of them knows why, for a second, I lose my focus during the shoot. I stop describing what's happening; I just stand there, clutching my chest, fighting something invisible inside me, trying to rid my body of her presence.

As it plays out again, my three friends lean in closer to get a better look at what's happening on the screen.

But I remember the feeling of my throat being coated in thick molasses.

Scenes from Sarah Good's death play out inside my head. The hanging tree with women dangling by their necks all in a row. Standing in a dissociative haze with a noose around my neck as my family, screaming, proclaims my innocence. The tightening of the rope as they hoist me into the air, the weight of my body held up by my neck. Unable to breathe, sparks explode across my vision before the world fades to black.

"Pull the plug, dude," Emma says. I can't see her. The shot is just me, tight, claustrophobic. My lips turn blue.

Chase is a bundle of nerves as we watch.

Kiki grabs my arm on-screen and it's enough to break the witch's hold.

Suddenly, I'm gasping for air and dropping back into Kiki's solid, safe silhouette.

"That's it. We're done," Chase says. The camera cuts out.

The episode ends with our confessionals where I try my best to explain what happened to me without freaking everyone out, and the rest of the group comments on how scary it was to see me like that. Chase looks especially shaken up but tries to keep his cool because we haven't admitted to our fans that we're an item yet—there's an entire Reddit thread of Chissy shippers we're not ready to give in to just yet.

We all cheer as Chase does a final render to prepare the video for upload—another great episode in the bag. Within minutes, Emma and Kiki are passed out in bed. It's just me and Chase waiting for the video to finish rendering so we can upload it to our channel. The whole process takes a few hours, but we can sleep while the video finishes uploading to YouTube.

"You want to tell me what really happened there?" Chase whispers, finally looking at me. His brows are raised, tense.

"It's no big deal," I say. I'm the only one who can really get away with lying in this group, but I try not to. We're better when we work together, when we don't have secrets. What happened at Hearst Hotel taught us that.

I just don't want them to worry when there is nothing to be worried about.

A strand of Chase's swoopy hair falls down across his forehead, and I have the urge to reach up and brush it away, but I don't. "Are you sure?" he asks. "You didn't look right, almost like you couldn't breathe."

My eyelids are heavy from looking at the computer screen all day, but I squeeze his shoulder and try my best to fake a reassuring smile. He doesn't buy it.

"Did something happen to you?" Chase asks, scooting the desk chair closer and taking one of my hands in his.

"It's happened before." I shrug.

"At Hearst," he counters, referring to the climactic moment on the roof with a bunch of vengeful dead girls.

"This was nothing compared to that," I say, squeezing his hand for emphasis. "I just need to set up better protections." I lift the necklace of black tourmaline that's secured around my neck and dangle it in the air for Chase to see. "I forgot to wear this at the Salem shoot."

"Okay," he says, too tired to keep pressing the issue. He stands up and stretches, revealing tanned skin and the silver band of his Calvin Klein boxers peeking up over his jeans. I bite my lip without thinking and he ruffles my hair. "Keep it in your pants."

My cheeks heat up and he squats down between the legs of my fuzzy pajama pants to take a closer look at the opaque black tourmaline crystal I keep around my neck for psychic protection. "Just promise me this doesn't come off your neck after we board the *Queen Anne*? Not even in the shower."

The main reason we've come all the way to the East Coast

from Vegas—we were invited to film an episode of our show on the inaugural sailing of the revamped *Queen Anne* cruise ship. It's a big to-do and our first time on a cruise. The boat is supposedly a hotbed of spiritual activity and home to the world-famous legend of the Lady in White. Kiki reminded us that her Hearst Hotel buddy Joe, the security guard who was a screenwriter in the making, was also working on a Lady in White ghost story.

I'm dying to meet her.

I shiver and touch Chase's hand over the pendant of my necklace. "I won't take it off," I whisper.

"Promise me." He wraps his fingers around the pendant tightly, his fingertips brushing my bare skin.

"Promise," I say with a nod.

He rewards me with a kiss. His hands cup my cheeks and he deepens the kiss and I find myself trying to think up secluded (and ghost-free) areas of the hotel we could sneak off to.

We're interrupted by an Emma snore so loud the whole room shakes.

We both stifle a laugh and Chase takes one look at the bags under my eyes and pats my knee. "You need to sleep."

"Oh yeah, what about you?" I ask, annoyed that I'm the weaker link of this make-out session.

He stands up and crosses the room, then flops down on the couch. "I never sleep."

"You got three detentions for being late to school."

He waves my skepticism away and I slide under the covers of the double bed. My body balances on the edge of the mattress, as close to the couch as I can possibly get without falling off completely. I try to ignore the scratching sounds coming from the closet, or the fact that something is not right about the way the woman in one of the wall paintings is looking at me.

Instead, I focus on Chase, who is way too big for the tiny couch he's being forced to use as a bed.

"Why can't you sleep in the bed again?" I whisper.

"You know why," he says with a loud sigh, indicating he's as frustrated as I am.

"Damn you, Billie Lawrence!" I whisper-scream, and shake my fist at the ceiling.

Kiki's mom is our chaperone for the next leg of the journey. A requirement of the cruise line since we're all only eighteen and need at least one person over twenty-one to stay with us.

Don't get me wrong, we love Billie Lawrence. She's an amazing mom and our number one choice for chaperone if we absolutely must have one. We were all thrilled when she agreed to come with us. Until she dropped the no-one's-getting-knocked-up-on-her-watch rule (what century is it?), which means Chase and I must sleep separated by an armrest or face the wrath of Billie.

"Since when do you listen to anyone's parents?" I ask, annoyed that Chase has chosen this moment to be obedient.

"Since without Billie we can't get on the boat, and Kiki is a terrible liar." He yawns. "Plus, she has a key to the room. Surprise inspections at five a.m. seem like a plausible scenario."

I snort and imagine Billie bursting in with her cell phone flashlight blazing to catch us tangled up in the sheets together.

Chase yawns and stops talking to me as he fades off. I sigh

and stare at the ceiling. I *do* need sleep, but I never seem to get it. I put a pillow over my head, and it dampens the sounds of the dead to a dull roar. I can only hope the *Queen Anne* is kinder to my sixth sense.

A distant bloodcurdling scream is my lullaby as I finally drift off to sleep.

CHAPTER 2

CHASE

I don't know if our Last Meal on Dry Land room service deserves an Instagram story, but I've learned not to argue with Kiki about what goes up on our social media.

She's arranged the food—omelets, potatoes, bacon, the works—and coffee and orange juice on the table just so, with empty gleaming plates and rolled-up napkins hiding the silverware. She had the room service attendant strategically position the table next to the window so she can pan the phone up for a skyline view of New York City.

"Come on, Kee, I'm starving," Emma groans, holding her stomach.

"You want your room discount and free room service breakfast or not?" she asks, biting her lip in concentration.

"Shhh," I say to Emma. I want free shit. Emma glares at me. Her stomach growls audibly.

"Don't tag the hotel until we leave," Chrissy chimes in. Emma and I both look at her. Her face is expressionless.

The last time we told the internet where we were headed,

our internet stalker, Bram, showed up. We've been extra careful with our whereabouts ever since.

"All done!" Kiki says. Before Kiki even sets her phone down, Emma fills her arms with the three giant plates of food she ordered and heads over to one of the beds.

"Hey, toss me a tiny ketchup," she says, her mouth already stuffed with toast.

I sigh and toss her a mini bottle of Heinz. She tears the plastic safety seal with her teeth and pops the lid open.

I hand Chrissy the plate of french toast she ordered. She looks up at me with those huge otherworldly blue eyes and a half grin of thanks. God, she's pretty. My lips twitch with the urge to kiss her, but I'm trying hard not to be a stage 5 clinger. I literally could have spent my entire summer making out with Chrissy Looper and never come up for air.

We decided to keep the Ghost Gang romances on the DL for now. Our fans speculate like wild in the comments about the *are they, aren't they* with the four of us, and it's great for the algorithm. Something I didn't think I'd care about once we got this big was the algorithm, but those old nightmares never die.

Chrissy scoots over on the bed to make room for me. I sit down next to her with my plate of eggs and shove a piece of bacon into my mouth.

I poke my phone screen. It lights up and I scan the notifications for anything meaningful. Aka Creep TV–related.

Nothing.

I grunt my disappointment.

"You know what they say about a watched pot," Emma says, shoving a giant bite of omelet into her face.

"I was hoping we'd hear from Jerry before the boat takes off," I reply with a sigh.

"Don't forget the time difference," Kiki chimes in. "It's still early on the West Coast."

"What time is it in Aruba?" Emma asks through a mouthful of potatoes, and Chrissy stifles a snort. I glare at both of them.

The girls hate Jerry's guts, especially Emma, who can't stand his infrequent and grammatically incorrect correspondence, Patrick Bateman–style slicked-back hair and sleazy thin-lipped grin. Besides the network interest he secured for us, he's scored us a few (*very* few, but notable) gigs and collabs and a sponsorship with a waterproof sock company (huh?).

He *did* get us interviewed on *Hot Ones,* which practically killed all of us except Emma. I've never seen her more excited for anything in her life. She legit Last Dab doubled down—and paid for it later with a trip to urgent care (oops). But one prescription-strength antacid regimen and an extra 200,000 subs later, and it was all worth it.

I obsessively tap the screen on my phone like it will make the phone ring.

With my luck Jerry won't call, and we also won't get out of here on time. I slept like hell on the couch, and these eggs taste like rubber. I all but throw my fork down on the plate. A light touch on my shoulder sends electricity through me and I jump. My eggs nearly fly off the bed.

"He'll call when there's news," Chrissy says, willing me to calm down.

"Is that a premonition?" I ask her.

"She's telling you to chill the eff out," Emma says. Her fork scrapes porcelain as she mines her plate for what few crumbs are left on it.

My phone buzzes and lights up, and I jolt forward, gripping it.

Manager J. Scott

I hold my phone in front of my face, staring at it. This is it. I suck in a deep breath and jab the green button.

"How's my favorite studio exec in the making?" Jerry jumps right in. His voice booms like a ringmaster's at a circus. I put him on speakerphone.

"We stayed up late cutting footage for the Salem episode," I tell him. "It actually turned out really good—"

"Beautiful, beautiful." He cuts me off. He always cuts me off. He also always throws around the word *beautiful* for some reason. "So, listen, ship takes off at five p.m. sharp. Mention the cruise line, ooh and aah over the rooms, the pool, the food. You know the drill."

"We know the drill, and we have Emmaline." I snicker, but it doesn't help my nerves. "Shots of the buffet will be plentiful."

A half-eaten crust of Kiki's breakfast sandwich goes flying past my nose.

"Cool, cool, cool." Jerry sounds distracted. I gulp.

"Um, is there . . . anything else?" I ask, pinching the skin on my lower lip nervously.

"You caught me," he says, and I imagine him holding his hands up in surrender. "It's just, you're one of my faves, you know that, but it's not enough to sell you as teen authorities on all things haunted. Hollywood loves drama. The people want intrigue."

My stomach lurches.

"The reel I cut for Creep TV has all of that and more." I shoot out of bed so fast my plate of eggs plummets to the ground. I ignore the mishap and pace the length of the room. My heart beats against my rib cage so hard my chest hurts. My palms go clammy. "It has Chrissy puking her guts up at Alcatraz and having a one-on-one conversation with the ghost of Scarface himself. There's a montage of Kiki screaming and Emma showing off her scars from that one time she was almost murdered by a prolific *serial killer.*" I don't mention my documentary-style directing or David Attenborough–esque voice-over, but I'm particularly proud of how we all played our roles with our unique flair.

"What more do they want?" I rake my fingers through my hair, tugging at it until it hurts.

"He's about to blow," Emma says. She's not wrong. I may internally combust.

The possibility of shooting a pilot with a full crew for the world's most popular paranormal network? Yeah, we all have college coming up, but a future that includes a successful network show starring the Ghost Gang has always been my dream.

"That's all fine for your little YouTube show, but the network wants . . . they want . . ." Jerry trails off, as though he's unsure whether he should say what he's about to say out loud.

"Say it, Jerry," I snap, my patience eroding.

"They want you guys to sex it up," he finally spits out. I can almost hear him making huge and exasperated gestures with his arms when he says it.

The silence in the room is deafening. I'm not even sure I heard him right. I look over at Emma and Kiki sitting on the bed. They exchange an uneasy look, but don't make eye contact with me. I look at Chrissy. She's looking down as she picks at the chipped black polish on one of her fingernails.

"I'm sorry, what the hell did you just say?" My ears are hot. My blood is boiling. My whole body is on fire.

"The Creep TV image is young, hot, edgy. They want drama, they want sex appeal, they want drugs and graphic violence."

"I don't—" I start, but Jerry doesn't let me finish.

"Look, kid, just get me some new footage. Have the blond one play up the hot goth with the sad-sack past. Go big drama with the dead people, guts, gore and all. You get a leather jacket, lift a few weights, and have the other girls show a little leg. Do all that, and I might be able to take another reel back to the producers."

"Fuck you, Jerry." I spit the words.

"Excuse me?" he says. His voice drops to something less ringmaster and more Al Capone.

I can't move on. I look at my three best friends. They're all glaring at me now, mouths pressed into straight lines. They know how much this means to me, and they were willing to go along with it as long as we maintained the integrity of the show we built together. But what Jerry is describing is not who we are. It's not the Ghost Gang. Plus it's straight-up chauvinistic and disgusting. I want to knock his too-white veneers out of his big greasy head.

Jerry composes himself. "It's show business, Chase. You're gonna have to get used to it. The Ghost Gang is great—cute, fun, et cetera et cetera, but we gotta bring out the big guns for network TV—"

"Big guns," I cut him off. "As in sexist, salacious content to appease perverted middle-aged Hollywood executives?"

"Hey now, let's not be dramatic," Jerry says, trying to walk the situation back.

"I just want to be clear. We're all eighteen years old. We just graduated high school. We're not even old enough to put a quarter in a slot machine in Vegas."

Jerry talks over me, but what else is new. "I can't sell four cute kids taking road trips to roach motels just to tell Girl Scout ghost stories."

I pause. I want to hang up on him, but I still can't believe this is really happening.

"It's the Ghost Gang," I say. "As we are now or not at all." It's an ultimatum.

"Right, and it will be, but turned up from a four to a ten—"

I cut him off again. "Goodbye, Jerry." My thumb punches the End Call button and I throw my phone across the room like a Frisbee. It bounces off the wall and hits the carpet, my OtterBox the only thing that keeps the screen from shattering. The rest of the gang stares at me in shock.

"What a prick," I say. I try to use anger to mask the disappointment I feel, but Chrissy can see right through me as always. She walks over to where I'm standing and takes my hand.

"I'm sorry," she says. I don't look her in the eyes. I can't. She already knows how I'm feeling, but if I see it on her face, I might crumble.

This was our one shot, and I just blew it to smithereens. And even though I hate Jerry for being a total creep, it doesn't stop me from feeling like a complete and utter failure.

...

KIKI

I don't really get what Chase is so upset about. We all hate Jerry. We've hated him from the beginning, from the first phone call he was a half hour late to. I'm pretty good at seeing the good in people, but Jerry sucks. And yeah, he got us on *Hot Ones,* but the executive producer is his brother, so . . . you do the math.

"Whatever," Chase says, like he's ready to move on. "It's done." He throws his suitcase open and yanks out his toothbrush.

"You did the right thing," I say, but he ignores me and walks into the bathroom with his lime-green toothbrush in tow. I hear the water run briefly as he wets the bristles.

"Jerry is the worst," Emma adds, scrunching her freckled nose. The rosy color in her cheeks is the first she's gotten since summer started and it suits her.

"Well, he's gone now," Chase replies loudly from inside the bathroom, his toothbrush still in his mouth. I hear him spit. "We do the *Queen Anne* cruise thing, and then once we dock in Southampton, we turn back into pumpkins."

"Pumpkins with almost two million subscribers," Emma points out. She rolls her eyes at me.

"And plenty of offers coming in that have nothing to do with Jerry Scott," I say, suddenly feeling defensive. Sure, Jerry's got the Hollywood hookups, but I'm *me* and I've scored us plenty of sweet deals, even before Jerry slithered into our lives. Now that it's summer and we're out of school, I can do even more pitching and posting and negotiating. Nobody reps the

Ghost Gang like I do, especially not a forty-eight-year-old dude from Orange County with horse-teeth veneers and a fake orange tan.

I decide to focus on work, snapping a pic of the receipt to store it in the Shoebox app that I use for tracking every expense—for biz reasons and reimbursements when we're on a sponsored trip or shoot. As I'm saving the receipt with the location name and date for easy search later, two notifications drop down at the top of my phone.

One is a DM from TrueCrimeJunkie911, who is a longtime viewer and big supporter of the Ghost Gang and always has our back when the haters get loud on Reddit. Which is where all haters go to get loud, even if it's just in the echo chamber of their own small-minded tomb.

The second is a text from *Mama,* with a purple heart.

I tap the notification and see it's a speech-to-text-style paragraph that indicates she's doing something that requires at least one of her hands. Most likely refreshing her toenail polish since she's already confirmed that her plans for the duration of the voyage involve lounging by the pool while the four of us do our "ghost thing," always said with implied air quotes.

Mama would like everyone to believe that she doesn't buy into ghosts or anything remotely paranormal, but that's not the whole story. She knows there's more to this existence than the things we can touch, taste, see or smell. She just doesn't want to acknowledge that those things can affect the living (God knows that part wasn't easy for me). It's too scary to look right at it, or she might see something undeniable and impossible to explain away. She'd rather ignore the hell out of anything that doesn't line up with her chosen narrative—a phenomenon that extends into other areas of her life, not just things that go bump in the night.

We have an unspoken don't ask, don't tell policy when it comes to Ghost Gang activities. Her policy, not mine. This "hobby," as she calls my total commitment to the Ghost Gang and our pursuit of truth beyond the veil, has become a huge part of my life. I would be lying if I said I didn't wish my mother took it more seriously. I would be lying if I said it was the only thing in my life I wish she took more seriously.

My eyes drift momentarily over to Emma.

Mama will do TikTok dances with me on my personal account, and she doesn't wince anymore when she sees Emma and me holding hands, but when it comes to showing genuine interest? Crickets.

That's why her coming with us on this trip is such a big deal to me. She wasn't into it at first, but the second "free cruise" was mentioned, she was all in with both perfectly pedicured feet.

Just doing this last coat of polish. Are you girls on your way back soon? Because we gotta get ready quick no way I'm gonna be late for my first transatlantic cruise OK

The text is capped with her signature purple heart.

I quickly reply that we're almost done eating and won't be much longer, omitting the sass I want to add about how she practically invented fashionably late and passed the tradition down to me. I add a kissy-face emoji instead.

Mom had a rough year after Dad left her for his dental hygienist, and the church ladies she'd always thought were ride or die shunned her because of it. Their husbands sided with Dad, and the wives followed suit like the sheep they are.

The only good thing about any of it is that she's finally given up Sunday mornings at the chapel on the Strip, even if she does miss getting dolled up like she's attending the royal wedding just to sing a few stale hymns.

I'm happy she's coming. Bonding and quality time before I leave for college gets an enthusiastic two thumbs-up. But such close quarters leaves lots of room for her to nitpick, which makes me hella nervous.

Nervous she'll give Emma and me the stink eye.

Nervous she'll make it difficult to shoot footage for the channel.

Nervous she won't care about any of it, won't notice, and that indifference will sting worse than her judgment ever could.

Everyone is getting up, ready to get ready, when I quickly click over to check the DM from TrueCrimeJunkie911. It's a TikTok with the message *wtf* and nothing else. I click it, hearing blood rushing past my eardrums as it loads up.

What plays on-screen is from an account called Paranormal Patrol, which stars a group of Texans affiliated with the Paranormal Institute of North Texas, also known as PINT. It features three obnoxiously hot white dudes in their twenties and a gorgeous blond woman whose day job is throwing pom-poms around in booty shorts for the Dallas Cowboys. Cheerleader by day, gorgeous ghost-busting babe by night.

I may or may not have watched a few of their videos (you know, just to keep an eye on the competition).

In this forty-second TikTok they announce that they will be taking the inaugural cruise of the RMS *Queen Anne,* leaving out of New York City in the morning.

Just like us.

"Uh-oh," I spit out. The other three stop what they're doing and look at me.

PINT's timing could not be worse, what with Chase just receiving the news about the death of our pilot.

"What's up?" Emma asks, turning around before Chase and Chrissy do, and dropping back onto the bed beside me. I hand her my phone with the TikTok app still open. She spins the phone around and lifts it so the others can see.

The video plays again. Emma turns it up to full volume. It sounds unreal and no less annoying than the first go-round. Upon finding out that a group of model-hot ghost-hunting twenty-year-olds will be joining us for the duration of the haunted cruise, the Ghost Gang reacts as expected:

Emma is stoic, clenching the phone in her fist.

Chase lets out a burst of hot air and a few curse words under his breath.

And Chrissy is nothing but pissed-off vibes, a newfound determination cutting across her face.

"Whatever's better than A game," Chase says as he walks back into the bathroom, "everyone bring that." He slams the door shut.

We may have lost out on the pilot, but we can still make a damn good show on our own.

CHAPTER 3

EMMA

I twist my hair into a low pony and throw on the LA Dodgers baseball cap I picked up at the hospital gift shop after I was discharged post-Hearst.

For the first time in Emmaline Shea Thomas history, I borrow Chrissy's concealer to deal with the dark circles under my eyes, which gets me a hefty examination from the Ghost Girl herself.

She knows something's going on with me and I'm betting on her bringing it up before this trip ends.

I twist the cap on the concealer just as knuckles rap against the bathroom door. It's not even that loud or out of nowhere since there are three people on the other side of the door, but my heart nearly leaps out of my chest anyway. I put a hand over it and gasp for air, trying to calm myself down before I have a full-blown panic attack.

"Coming," I say when I finally have enough air to speak the word.

I close my eyes, but even the cool darkness behind my lids

isn't safe. There is always the scuff of boots, always the metallic glint of metal and always that sharp wet slice of pain.

It's better to just stay awake.

When I open the door, Chase looks back at me, hair extra fluffy from using the hotel blow-dryer on high.

"Are you wearing makeup?" he asks.

"Are you?" I grunt, shoving past him.

"No," he says, and then whirls around. His face is slack with alarm. "Should I?"

I give him a long look just to piss him off, and it works.

"Whatever, okay, we need to leave ten minutes ago," he says, zipping his backpack and yanking it off the bed.

In the hallway mirror I can see the bed that Kiki and I shared last night, which was immediately vacated when Billie came knocking on the door this morning.

Even though we've been on the road together unsupervised, when the 'rent arrives, the whole game changes. Chase and I are in solidarity in our annoyance. Me because I have to pretend that Kiki and I did *not* sleep in the same bed last night and have never slept in the same bed; him because he is *the boy* and is considered suspect number one by the mom in our midst.

Billie Lawrence likes me. I'm convinced she does despite her seeming disinterest in getting to know me. But she sure doesn't like any of us being alone together in the dark.

"Is everyone else ready to go?" I ask loudly. I turn to Chase, who is busy scrolling on his phone in the doorway. "You know you have to give them a fake ten-minute warning. Then a real ten-minute warning. And then a one-minute warning for every minute of those last ten. Because without it they will assume the deadline is flexible."

"Chrissy is punctual," he says without looking up.

"Billie and Chrissy are currently on Kiki Time."

Chase shrugs. "Are you almost done in there? I have to pee."

"You've been hogging the bathroom all morning," I growl at him.

He says nothing and just looks grouchy. I think it's because he tossed and turned for the few measly hours of rest we did get.

I know this because once Kiki and Chrissy fell asleep, insomnia took over. As soon as the lights went out, my eyes popped back open, wide awake and staring at the popcorn ceiling. Commence the endless scrolling on my phone and reading an article about the climate crisis, which only served to spike my anxiety, so I had to follow that up with another article about a lifelong friendship between a cheetah and a golden retriever.

God, how I miss sleep.

I used to be one of those people who could fall asleep anywhere, anytime. If there was a place to rest my head, I could close my eyes and slip off to dreamland. A plane, a bus, the car, even a desk at school during a free period. But now? Ever since I got shanked by a serial killer and left for dead in a supply closet, pretty sure that I was going to die alone until someone stumbled in on my rotting corpse?

Well, there isn't enough Sleepytime tea in the world.

I walk out of the bathroom as Chase slams the door shut behind me. I drag my duffel from the closet to the couch and throw a few more of my things in before I zip it up. Behind the couch, big windows run the width of the room. I squint at the sunny sky, and when I blink, a spot of light from the sun stays stuck behind my vision.

The hotel has a view of the harbor just past some of the buildings.

When I was a kid, my parents liked to take family cruises out of the Port of Long Beach to places like Hawaii or the Mexican Riviera. They would book me into every kids' club activity imaginable, making sure that I was occupied all day and away from them. When dinner came, they'd dress me in something nice and pretty and sit me beside them at the table with something to distract me. Usually math games, sometimes puzzles.

If I wasn't happy with my experience, they would rather not hear about it.

Our family motto may as well be *Keep it to yourself.*

"Let's see if they're ready," Chase says when he finally comes out of the bathroom, slinging his backpack over one shoulder.

I open the hotel room door and push my way through. Chase has already loaded up the luggage cart that holds all our gear. I sling my bag on top and take hold of the other side of the cart.

I keep telling myself that *keeping it to myself* is exactly what everyone expects from "techie genius" and Stanford-bound Emmaline Thomas. Stoic, sharp, sarcastic Emma doesn't have deep feelings, and all her intense thoughts are reserved for overanalyzing the facts and drawing conclusions from evidence with a cool, calm head.

Whatever those flashes in the dark are about, they definitely aren't reflective of the best of me. No one needs to hear about them.

Not now, not ever.

We wait for the rest of the group in the hall, Chase jabbering about what he wants to shoot first. Last night's rejection from Creep TV and the drama with Jerry seem to be fueling his obsessive streak.

"Did you drink a Monster or something, man?" I ask. "You're extra hype."

"I wish," he says, and then yawns and adds: "I can handle the camera. At least I can still do that."

I try not to roll my eyes at his tone, which is heavy with defeat. That much pathetic, this early in the morning—I wish he would just *keep it to himself.*

He checks the time on his phone and then knocks on the door once.

Twice.

"Do you have a key?" I ask.

He grimaces. "Left it inside."

We wait for seconds that stretch into minutes. We can hear them rustling inside and know good and well they're aware we're waiting—impatiently—out here for them. Chase unlocks his phone and types in the group chat.

We're seventeen minutes late.

I see him type it, and don't bother to check when my butt buzzes.

"I've read that only psychopaths end their texts with periods," I gibe, looking at his screen over his shoulder. I see three dots before a text appears from Kiki.

we're commmminnngggg

can't find my jacket, Chrissy adds. *it's freezing this close to the water*

"It's eighty-eight degrees and sunny," I say to Chase.

He shrugs and brushes his thumb over his lips thoughtfully. "She runs cold."

"Since when?" I ask.

He cuts me a look, but he can't hide the worry in his eyes.

I know he's worried about what happened to Chrissy at Proctor's Ledge. Seeing that footage was a reminder that it was extra weird, and her trying to convince us it wasn't is sus.

The door swings open and Kiki bursts out, two suitcases rolling on either side of her.

"Sorry, but this doesn't happen by magic," she says, preening. Her eyes meet mine, expectant. I give her a weak smile, too exhausted to do much else.

She pushes out of the room just as Billie appears in the doorway.

"Got room on that thing for an extra suitcase?" Billie says, her eyes sliding from Chase to me and back. Her lips break into a wide smile. She looks exactly like Kiki will one day. A pretty heart-shaped face; full, wide lips; heavily lashed big eyes and dark-brown skin. She wears her hair cropped short and her ears are usually accompanied by statement earrings.

Petite and shapely, she's made taller by her platform espadrilles, and right now she is dressed head to toe in bright vacation florals.

"Sure thing, Mrs. Lawrence," Chase says, moving forward to help her with her bag.

Billie's mouth pinches and my guess is that it has something to do with him calling her *Mrs.* The separation is a fresh wound.

Even a benign reminder sets her teeth on edge.

"Billie is fine, hon," she says as Chase secures her bag on the cart.

Chrissy emerges from the room wrapped in one of Kiki's least dramatic jackets.

"I think I left my jacket in the Uber," Chrissy says. Her dark circles rival mine.

"That works on you," Kiki says, eyeing her black-and-white-patterned Gucci bomber jacket. Chrissy doesn't look as certain.

"A Kiki Lawrence makeover," Billie chimes in. Kiki frowns.

"Sorry, Mama, but no way," Kiki says, ready as always to educate everyone with the knowledge she's gained from TikTok. "The whole concept of making someone over is problematic and outdated."

"Well, I'm old," Billie snips, and I let out an involuntary snort. She raises one microbladed brow at me. "Where's the lie?" I smile weakly and resist the urge to rub my eyes.

Not as old as I feel, I think, but don't say it out loud. Shivering inside of Kiki's jacket, Chrissy makes sympathetic eye contact with me.

Even my thoughts aren't safe around here.

• • •

CHRISSY

Our Uber drops us off outside the cruise terminal, and even from here I can see the RMS *Queen Anne* and all her gleaming metallic curves on display, kissed by the full afternoon sun.

Black and red and white with three wide smokestacks and dotted with hundreds of porthole windows and orange lifeboats decorating her middle. *Queen Anne* is painted in all-capital letters across her white hull.

Ships are traditionally gendered as female, and from what I can sense already, not four hundred feet away, the *Queen Anne* actually embraces her "she." All the way through.

Angry as any captive woman. Ready to set sail and be set free.

"What do you see?" Chase asks me. He's by my side, bringing me into focus on his handheld.

"Ripples," I say, waving my hand through the air in front of me. We're still yards and yards away, but I see them everywhere the light hits, and even places it doesn't.

I feel the ripples in my stomach too. Rocky waves sloshing around inside me, hitting rocks near the shore. Crashing white frothy foam that turns into nothing.

The *Queen Anne* tugs me forward, gripping me by the ribs. They ache from the force of her pull. She's magnetic.

When the RMS *Queen Anne* sets sail, the whole world pays attention. From the leaders who wanted to possess her steel body built to withstand whatever nature tosses her way to the moguls who wanted to capitalize on her unblemished record carrying passengers, soldiers and supplies across the sea. She was a ghost on the water, there and gone.

Here and not here.

The soles of my Doc Martens squeak on the cement floor as we enter the terminal. It's a big warehouse-like building that is all metal and cement. The booming voices of cruise staff ushering soon-to-be *Queen Anne* passengers through the line, echo inside the building, making my head spin.

We pass through security and then wait in line to check in. Chase has all our documentation ready to go in a manila folder. We hand over our IDs, and Chase and Billie fill out consent forms and general wellness releases for all of us. As our cruise ship guardian, she can make medical and other decisions and agree to keep us away from the bar or whatever people do on ships that is somehow okay for twenty-one-year-olds but not for legal American adults.

After the signing is done, the woman behind the counter takes our pictures and hands over our cruise cards. She explains that each of the cards is an all-in-one boarding card, room key and onboard credit card and that we must guard them with our lives or face the wrath of a fifty-dollar replacement fee.

We each tuck our card somewhere safe.

As we approach the gangway, I find that I'm drifting further and further from myself.

One of the stories that flutters out of this ship—and comes up in every Google search and televised ghost hunt of the RMS *Queen Anne*—is the legend of the Lady in White.

She's the reason we're here, the spirit I want to communicate with the most.

The Lady in White is believed to be the wandering spirit of Elizabeth Walker. A young woman who met her untimely end off the side of this ship in 1984.

Elizabeth was an heiress traveling with her fiancé, a wealthy business magnate. They were traveling from her home in England to New York to wed. Just a week away from the wedding and in the middle of the Atlantic Ocean, Elizabeth Walker went missing.

Days later, a tearstained goodbye note was found scribbled in her diary.

Her death was ruled a suicide.

Her remains were never recovered, but a local fishing boat found what was left of a bridal gown, floating in the water miles from where she must have drowned.

For decades before the *Queen Anne* was dry-docked for renovations, guests reported seeing a figure dressed all in white roaming the halls aimlessly. Looking for something, perhaps her long-lost love? Or a second chance at a life cut short? The sightings were always followed by a call to guest services about a possible man overboard, after passengers who were pretending not to smoke on their balconies overheard a shriek and a splash in the frigid black ocean below.

But eventually those two a.m. calls were ignored. They happened so often the company got tired of using resources to hunt for an invisible passenger.

In my mind's eye, I can see Elizabeth hanging from the railing, her hands fumbling for a grip. An emerald-cut diamond set in a simple gold band flashes on one finger.

A shriek and a splash.

There, gone, there.

Old, new, old.

We step outside the terminal building on our way to board the boat. As I gaze up at her massive hull, the ship seems to glitch, re-forming with barnacles and chipping paint along the hull.

I blink once and she's shiny again.

Welcome to the RMS Queen Anne. The words penetrate my

ears, and it's only then that I realize the sound was distorted. A wobbly delay lingers, and I have to force a smile to keep my internal alarm under wraps.

My attention snaps back to the present, to my friends and the small white man with the muddy-brown comb-over wearing a crisp navy-blue-and-white crew uniform. His badge reads *Gerald* and his aura reads *wormy*, and I know from the briefing that he is our VIP concierge, available for any and all of our needs including check-in and boarding.

"We're so happy to host the Ghost Gang on this inaugural trip of the fully refurbished RMS *Queen Anne*." Gerald says it like he's rehearsed it, with a grand Vanna White–like gesture.

"What all's new?" This question comes from our chaperone, who has her phone up, recording for a Facebook Live. Kiki looks like her soul is about to leave her body. I have to grip her by the wrist to ground her.

Gerald's face glitches like an AI in need of reprogramming.

He pauses and clears his throat, reworking his speech in his head to incorporate Billie's question. "As I'm sure you all know, the RMS *Queen Anne* is a historic relic and a sister ship of the *Titanic*. Such an important piece of history must be preserved, so in 2010, the RMS *Queen Anne* was dry-docked for a full face-lift. We made sure to retain the original integrity and design of the vessel, as well as salvage most of the interior materials for authenticity." One side of Gerald's mouth kicks up and he leans forward like he's telling us a secret. "But I assure you, her bones and soul are all the same."

My eyes drift back to the ship.

"Anyway"—Gerald beckons us—"follow me."

We wind along the ramps and up the gangway until we get

to an orange-and-white life ring that says RMS QUEEN ANNE. A photographer asks us to pose next to it and we collectively decide it will be a perfect pic for the Ghost Gang Insta grid. Billie jumps into the picture too and I can feel Kiki tense up beside me. Except for Billie's bright pearly whites, our smiles are tired and strained.

"I want to shoot in the atrium," Chase says. He shuts off the camera to save battery, disappointed by the *Queen Anne*'s boarding aesthetic. I look around us at all the ugly metal and yellow cones that say CAUTION: WATCH YOUR STEP. "Subs will want the James Cameron epic *Titanic* fairy tale."

His elbow brushes mine. His eyes linger longer than his touch.

My eyes catch movement just over his shoulder. A face in a window, too many teeth, ends sharpened into points, the eyes two crescent moons, the hair a long black oil slick, moving, seething, sliming. It's gone in a blink.

"Is the ship haunted?" I blurt out. Everyone stops. Gerald sweats, Billie zooms in, whispering something to her livestream viewers. Chase fumbles with the camera, hitting Record as fast as he can.

"Come again?" Gerald tugs at his collar and glances around to see whether anyone is eavesdropping on our conversation.

"The Lady in White?" I clarify. "And all the other passengers who boarded, died and never left?"

"Isn't it something like almost three hundred people who have died on this ship?" Emma asks Gerald. "The most deaths on any passenger ship ever."

Gerald's face twists in a strange unearthly way. "She's a hundred years old. Shi—" He catches himself. "*Things* happen."

"Dude, that's like three deaths per year," Chase chimes in.

"This thing is haunted?" Billie bleats, panic-stricken but still streaming her Facebook Live. "For real, for real?"

"No crap," Emma says, much to Gerald's dismay.

"The OG scaredy-cat," Kiki whispers to me.

Gerald drops the act and points at Chase. "Turn off the camera."

"What? No." Chase scowls and looks up from the viewfinder.

"Turn it off or I won't sign your little on-camera release form," Gerald threatens.

Crap, he's got Chase by the balls with that one. Chase reluctantly hits a button on his camera and drops it down to his hip.

"Look, kids, I know the press team thinks that promoting a haunted cruise ship is good for business, but they don't work here. They work in a high-rise in New York City. And they sure as hell don't spend ten months of the year on board this ancient boat." Beads of perspiration bubble up on Gerald's forehead. He pulls a hankie out of his pocket and dabs it across his hairline.

"You've seen her," I say. It's almost a whisper. "The Lady in White."

His eyes slide over to mine and I know I'm right. He leans in and talks low, out of the side of his mouth. No theatrics, just plain old fear. "I just don't think people are meant to mess with this shi—" He catches himself again. "Stuff." He side-eyes the ship, his eyes traveling all the way up her, almost as if he doesn't want her to hear.

Gerald refuses to say anything else, but allows Chase to turn the camera on again. He leads us to the end of the gangway, and just as we're about to step on board the ship, a deep smooth voice radiates from behind us:

"Well, look what the tractor pulled in."

Chase is the first to turn around, subtly squaring his shoulders and straightening up as he does. I pinch the bridge of my nose, not sure now if my sudden nausea is created by the ship's wobbly energy or Chase's annoying display of masculinity.

The rest of us turn.

In every way, Paranormal Patrol is the antithesis of the Ghost Gang.

Three guys, one girl.

All white.

All straight, or at least pretending to be.

And all of them some shade of Barbie blond.

At the center, wearing a pair of white denim cutoffs, pink cowboy boots and a flouncy floral blouse, is their real star. Tina Langham, born and raised in Fort Worth on her family's cattle ranch. Her sister died in an equestrian accident when she was seventeen. Tina claims to be in regular communication with her sister's ghost (a topic she regularly milks for the camera), but there's never been any sign of her on camera to confirm that part of her story is true.

Tina hooks her thumbs in her belt loops, letting her bright-green eyes drift over each of us with purpose before settling on me.

"Howdy, y'all," she says. Her voice is like a bell. Her teeth are blinding white.

"Hi," Kiki says, oozing her signature charm. Kiki's terrified of ghosts, but pretty blondes with legs as long as skyscrapers are nothing to her. "Good to meet y'all in person."

Emma grits her teeth when Tim, a Ken doll served well done, smirks in her general direction. Kiki's MO is to catch flies with honey, even if all they deserve is a cow patty.

They do not return the favor.

"Two ghost-hunting teams, one boat," Tom says with a smirk that says *This ship ain't big enough for the both of us.* He's the ringleader on camera, a dude who thinks of himself as the main character in everyone else's life. He's tall, broad-shouldered and wearing a salmon-colored polo and some light-wash jeans like he's from the Cape and not the cattle run.

His crocodile boots are the only Texas oil money giveaway.

"How fun," Tina chimes in. She's still staring at me with unnatural steadiness.

"It will be," Chase says. "We're all pros here."

"Oh, *we* are," Tom says. Chase's eyebrows dance.

"You say that like *we* aren't," he replies. "Both of our teams are amateur ghost hunters on YouTube. We both have lucrative sponsorships, Hollywood managers, subscribers in the millions—"

"We have four point six million, to be exact," Toby says, raising one hand like he's in school. Tina presses it back down, subtly shaking her head. Toby's skull is as thick as his biceps. I get the impression they keep him around for his brawny muscles.

"I say that because if this goes well," Tom continues his earlier thought, "you'll be looking at the stars of Creep TV's hottest new ghost-hunting series."

Record scratch—what?

Kiki reaches over to tap Billie's phone, ending her mom's Live. Her face says it all. This cannot become public knowledge just yet. Billie glares straight at the Paranormal Patrol group. I can't tell if she's more annoyed with Kiki or them.

"Wait, you all are up for the Creep TV pilot too?" Emma points at them, incredulous.

"Too?" Tina repeats, but I feel the word like an earthquake tremor all the way through her, cracking across the gangway, right to my feet.

Chase crosses his arms and looks away, trying to hide his disappointment. I instinctively put a hand on his shoulder.

Tina notices our interaction and doesn't even try to hide her glee. "Aw, you didn't get it. Poor things. Hopefully we can all still be friends when we're rich and famous."

"We were never going to be friends with creators like you," Chase says, his gaze narrowing on Tina. "You're not even a real psychic."

"But I sure do play a good one on YouTube," she retorts, then adds: "There's no such thing anyway." She shoots a fake apologetic glance at me.

I watch Chase's jaw flex, his teeth grinding in anger. I wrap a hand around his arm to calm him down. It doesn't work.

"We manage just fine without some woo-woo weirdo quivering in goth makeup," Tom says. "We have *actual* charisma."

Red creeps up Chase's neck until his cheeks are blazing. I feel his anger roiling inside him, protective of what he's building, of the Ghost Gang, of *us*. Of me.

"You know what they say about Texas," Tina adds, noticing Chase's anger. She moves to push ahead of us.

"Probably something dumb about how everything is bigger," Emma says, rolling her eyes.

"They do say that," Tina replies, unrolling a syrupy grin.

40

"But I was thinkin' more along the lines of how you shouldn't mess with Texas."

"Or Texans," Tim adds.

"Aka us." Toby thumbs toward himself. Tom yanks him over the threshold to the ship and they all disappear from view.

"*They* were the competition?" Kiki asks, but the question feels directed at the universe, not one of us.

"They've got brawn," Billie says, watching them saunter away. We all stare at Billie, hoping there's a second part of that sentence. She shrugs. "But you kids got brains."

Chase's sigh signals his defeat. It's a sound I've never heard from him before. Not once. He scrubs a frustrated hand over his head. "It's not a surprise they're still in the running. They're exactly what Jerry said the network wants."

"They're all over twenty-one," Kiki adds, side-eyeing her mom.

"And so good-looking it's stupid," Emma finishes.

"Hey, we're cute too," Kiki grunts.

Their voices become like white noise inside my head. We're still standing at the end of the gangway, but I can't stop staring into the ship. Its magnetic pull tugs me forward, my feet making choices all on their own. My mind is overcome with the hum of noise around me, the voices I left behind fading farther away as I move.

I step up, one foot on the metal gangway, the other planted firmly on the red carpet rolled out for VIP guests. The second my foot touches the carpet, my vision blurs and my body goes cold all over. I tighten Kiki's jacket around me.

I'm one foot in and one foot out, between one world and the next.

I hear music playing. The sound of a record, grainy and bluesy, like you'd expect to hear in an old-timey movie.

The temperature drops and I zip Kiki's jacket all the way up.

I should wait for the others. I should stop.

But my feet make up their own mind. My body can do nothing but let them go. And when I step all the way across the threshold, electricity snaps over my skin, through my hair, from my toes to the tips of my fingers.

For a second, everything seems almost normal and I think maybe I'm just dizzy from lack of sleep.

But then I notice the clock above the elevator is spinning— its hands twisting counterclockwise, around and around and around.

I turn back toward the gangway and see my friends, close enough that I could reach out and touch them, but they look faded and grayed out. Still talking, not seeing, not hearing, not aware at all that—

I am gone.

I'm not with them or beside them, and if I did reach out, I couldn't touch them.

When I look again at the spinning clock above the elevator, the hands are gone. It's just a timeless clock.

"Where am I?" I ask no one, the words a puff of cold smoke in front of my face.

The response is a disembodied whisper inside my head.

You're trapped.

Out of the corner of one eye, I see a flash of white. It streaks across my vision before I drop, boneless, to the ground.

She Is Alive
1924

They built me to carry their bodies all the way across the sea.

Make her nose slender, they said. *The razor-like edge will allow her to pierce, not pound, her way through the Atlantic's waves at breakneck speed.*

She can fly on the water, but inside her belly, the passengers will float.

They will slumber with ease, run the boards of her decks like drunken sailors on rough seas.

They will almost forget they are sailing, only to look over the strong arms of her railing to see the foaming hungry ocean below. With whitecaps like teeth, ready to devour.

They will gasp at her hulking impenetrable beauty.

When their journey is over, they will linger to watch her leave them behind, with a new batch of bodies to ferry.

Make her lean and narrow.

Make sure she is swift and steadfast.

Her. She. These words settle into my bolts. They slither over the steel frame that forms my skeleton.

I am a *her,* a *she.* Not an *it,* not a *thing.*

Her, so alive.

She, so burdened with incredible purpose.

This is my maiden voyage.

My first time setting out into open waters.

Ocean, the dark, churning, all-consuming abyss that surrounds me. It sprays my hull, smacking my sides, weathering my freshly made body. It drifts toward the cracks they've sealed shut. It slides over my seams, tapping, lapping but never slipping inside.

I am made for this ocean—to penetrate it, to conquer it, to appease it.

Resisting the urge to feed it.

I can feel *them* walking through my insides. The pitter-patter of their tiny feeble feet as they move about their cabins. I witness all that happens within my bones. Every conversation, every illicit affair, every side-eye and second glance.

I am the keeper of secrets, every hidden moment harbored inside my hull.

They want so much from me.

An adventure.

An escape.

A new start.

A memory they will not soon forget.

But there is another desire, stronger and sharper than the rest.

He's been disturbed from slumber, roused to life

by crooked thieves, ripped from his home and his homeland. Wanting nothing more than to return to the place where he sleeps best.

Where he comes from, I do not know. But his rage bubbles up inside my bowels like a sickness—the wrongness of his being here trapped somewhere deep, deep below, far from the other passengers.

And in this rage I feel something new, not put upon me, not designed by *them*. Not aligned with the purpose they made me for.

Desire springs forth within me, like sea spray against my hull. A yearning to conquer more than just the open sea.

My steel frame trembles with the force of this new-found fury. I feel powerful, invincible—

Ravenous. Like the ocean.

I watch them laugh and dance and eat and drink and retch off the side of me.

And every day, as the sun dips into the horizon . . .

I find myself wondering what their blood would taste like.

CHAPTER 4

CHASE

I hate that I'm starting this trip—an opportunity-of-a-lifetime trip—in such a shit mood. I try to shake it off, pushing my shoulders back and stepping across the threshold into the dim glow of the atrium's golden overhead light. The whole room is abuzz with activity as crew members, all toothy and bright-eyed, instruct passengers where to go, welcoming us for this lovely voyage across the Atlantic.

But my eyes turn into magnets, yanked to Chrissy as her knees buckle.

Emma is faster than me. My hands fumble with the camera, my throat closes with fear, confusion rattling around in my head, panic pounding out a manic electric beat in my chest. Emma's hands curl around Chrissy's waist, her eyes fly up to mine.

"Help," she gasps.

Forgetting myself and just about everything else except for Chrissy, I nearly drop the camera, but Kiki catches it before it hits the ground. It's still recording, and she motions me forward, indicating that she'll keep the camera rolling while I help my girlfriend.

We made a pact before this trip that we'd keep the camera rolling no matter what happened. Last October, when everything went down at the Hearst, we had so many gaps in the footage that we had a hell of a time splicing together a video that accurately painted the full picture of that fateful night. The episode was popular because it was front-page news, not because it was our best work.

Kiki knows that camera footage is the last thing on my mind where Chrissy's well-being is involved, so she keeps the camera rolling as I fall to my knees beside my girlfriend.

The first thing I notice when I wrap my hands around Chrissy's bare calves is that they are ice cold. Dead cold. My eyes fly to Emmas.

"She's breathing," Emma says, her voice a croak of restrained terror.

As soon as we lift Chrissy up to carefully move her out of the flow of traffic, the crew manning the atrium takes notice, their bright have-a-good-trip smiles fading into grimaces as they calculate the risk of letting the event erupt into a full-blown scene versus pretending that nothing's wrong so they don't alarm the other guests.

Gerald catches up fast.

"Oh no," he quavers. "Is she okay?" He rushes up behind me to spit the words at my neck. I cut my eyes over my shoulder to see him gesturing for some of the other staff to come help us.

"We've got her," I say, more indignant than is entirely necessary. But the staff flocks anyway, like pigeons circling a discarded loaf of bread.

"Here, here," comes Mrs. Lawrence's soothing motherly voice, just as her hands shoot out with one of Kiki's herbal tinctures. This one smells strongly of rosemary, peppermint and eucalyptus. She waves it under Chrissy's nose as we manage to prop her onto a bench against the closest wall.

"Is this an act? Should we call an ambulance? Does this happen often?" Gerald is spiraling, his clipboard now a life raft to keep him from drowning in a sea of his own sweat.

"Unclench your butt," Emma says in a monotone. "This is par for the course when a hella gifted psychic medium boards a ship that is almost a century old and definitely haunted." She grins like the Cheshire cat that she is. Gerald turns the color of an overbleached hotel towel. Splotchy white and gritty.

Billie shoves the tincture closer to Chrissy's nose and it does the trick.

With a heaving cough, Chrissy comes to life, eyes wide, gasping for air. Her body is rigid, almost like she was just electrocuted by lightning. Her eyes dilate, and for a second she looks lost in her own body. The glance she gives the room is more than a disoriented once-over. It's like for a split second she doesn't recognize where she is.

I bend down and line up my gaze with hers. When her panicked eyes finally fix on mine, her lips quiver.

Relief washes over me.

"There you are," I breathe, tucking a long light-blond lock of hair behind her ear. Her eyes are shiny with tears that she blinks away. Her hand squeezes mine as she leans back against

Emma's sturdy frame. Her already-pale skin is ghostlike, almost translucent.

"Hi." Gerald shoves into our moment shoulder-first. "Hi, wow, okay don't scare me like that, missy!" he scolds, but his playful tone fails to mask the quaver in his voice.

Kiki balks at his use of the diminutive *missy.* Chrissy ever so subtly furrows her brow, before letting her lips curve into a weak yet convincing smile.

"Let me call you a doctor," Gerald continues unprompted, pulling out his walkie-talkie and pressing the Call button with a shaky finger. His knuckles are somehow even whiter than the rest of him.

"No, I swear—" Chrissy finds her voice just before he issues the call. Her eyes drift ever so subtly over my shoulder to where Kiki is standing with the camera pointed straight at Chrissy's face. "I'm fine. This is one hundred percent normal, especially when I'm tired. I just need to get some water and food in me, maybe elevate my legs."

But her gaze fixes right in the center of the lens. She wants the camera to know she's not telling Gerald the whole story.

She's saving that for later, for a dramatic confessional that will leave our viewers titillated.

Seriously, fuck Creep TV. Chrissy is a star.

Gerald drops the walkie-talkie to his side. Honestly, he looks relieved that he doesn't have to call a doctor, which would probably require him to write up some kind of incident report right at the beginning of the first voyage post-dry-docking of his beloved RMS *Queen Anne,* making the whole launch chaotic and messy as hell.

"Can you maybe show us to our room instead?" Kiki, always the charmer, bats her eyes at him. Emma sucks her lips in to suppress a proud smile.

"Absolutely." Gerald beams. The clipboard becomes his compass. "Please, follow me."

He walks ahead of us toward the bank of elevators, and in the two seconds of space that follows, Chrissy mouths three words to the rest of us:

Something is wrong.

...

KIKI

After our VIP concierge, Gerald, finally gets us into our suite on the twelfth deck, he gives us a lightning-fast room tour before begging us to "Please be careful." And then with one last deer-in-headlights look at Chrissy, he all but sprints out the door.

I have a sneaky feeling we will have a hard time wrangling him for help in the future.

Chrissy is feeling much better now—at least there's color in her face again. She's still leaning heavily on Chase, but I think it's less for support and more because she's enjoying the proximity.

Mama starts squealing the second she steps into the room. Floor-to-ceiling windows and a balcony the size of an average stateroom. An art deco glass chandelier hanging in the center of the room is the only clear relic from another time. Other than that, the room has the chemical scent of new, new, new: new carpet, new paint, new furniture. A large flat-screen TV. A far cry from our days slumming it with a serial killer in a hostel room at the Hearst.

Personally, I'm just glad we're not headquartered on floor fourteen. As we learned from the horror that was the Hearst Hotel, floor fourteen is just unlucky number thirteen in not-so-subtle disguise.

Of course, Emma points out that our suite has two levels, so the second level might *technically* be part of floor thirteen. I tell her that the second floor does not lead out to any kind of hallway, so we're safely stationed on floor twelve, end of story, thanks for playing, sweetie. Emma shrugs a *whatever* and her tummy rumbles to further emphasize that she has no interest in continuing this argument with me. The buffet calls.

I hear Mama's stomach growl too.

They lock eyes from across the room. It's love at first bite, and they are instant buffet buddies. It actually makes my stomach do a somersault to see this flash of connection between them, even if it's over something as minor as a cruise ship buffet.

"Hey, Chrissy, how you feeling?" Emma asks, hopeful and still maintaining eye contact with Mama. "Should we, maybe, get you something to . . . drink or . . . eat?"

Chase helps Chrissy to the couch and slides open one of the balcony doors to get her some fresh air. Chrissy doesn't even have to look back at Emma and my mom to know what's going on between them. You don't need a sixth sense to decipher that Emma Thomas has heart eyes for an all-you-can-eat.

"I wouldn't mind a grilled cheese and a Coke," Chrissy says, winking at me. I breathe a sigh of relief that she's feeling well enough to egg them on.

"One grilled cheeser and Coke coming right up!" Emma says, delighted to have a helpful reason to do what she loves most.

Without another word to each other, Mama and Emma throw their stuff down, grab their cruise cards/room keys and all but skip out the door.

"Make sure you get some buffet B-roll!" Chase yells after them. "Gee, they wasted no time." He collapses with exhaustion on the couch next to Chrissy, handing her a bottle of water from his backpack to tide her over until they get back with sustenance.

She leans into him as his fingers lightly stroke the length of her hair. They are subtle with their PDA, much more subdued than Emma and I usually are. Though lately I can feel Emma pulling away in small ways. Barely detectable, but I'm me. I'm good at reading people, and Emma is not herself.

"Kiki?" Chase asks. I'm ripped out of my anxious swirl of thoughts and I whip my head around to see both Chase and Chrissy looking at me with wide concerned eyes.

"Sorry?" I ask, hoping they'll repeat the question.

"Aren't you going to go with them?" Chase asks.

I shake my head and force a smile. "Nah, I'll just get in their way." Besides, if they can hang solo for any amount of time, I call that a win. It's not that they don't like each other, it's that Mama knows Emma mostly as my smarty-pants bestie, not my gives-me-butterflies girlfriend.

There's a difference. And I want her to see that, almost as

much as I want her to see the Ghost Gang is more than just a weird *little hobby*.

I slump down into the chair across from them, then unzip and kick off my lime-green glitter platform boots. My current braid color of choice is toxic-waste green. Unnatural green everything while I use my personal TikTok to raise money to fight climate change. A cause that Emma and I have both been super passionate about tackling together.

"She's been having a hard time," Chrissy says after a long stretch of silence. When she knows things she shouldn't know about my inner world, her eyes are always dark and shiny, with just a touch of dreamy haze.

"Who?" I ask, trying to play it cool. I'm not cool, and we both know I know exactly who Chrissy is talking about.

"The nightmares are getting worse and now she can't sleep at all," Chrissy explains. My heart sinks. Why does Chrissy know all of this and I don't? I mean, I know why, and it's not like either of them want it that way, but it still hurts that Chrissy knows more about what my girlfriend is going through than I do.

I feel a pang of guilt that I've been overthinking my anxieties about having Mama on this trip and not focusing more on helping Emma deal with her pain.

Chrissy leans forward, resting her hands on the black tights she's wearing under her ragged denim cutoffs. "Your feelings are still valid," she says. I cross my arms like it will prevent her from knowing what's in my heart.

"I wish she would let me in," I say, because I'd rather we stay on the topic of Emma's sleepless nights than on my own emotional turmoil. "All I want is to help. To understand."

"Sometimes when the nightmares can't reach you in your sleep, they find ways to torment you while you're still awake." Chrissy's voice is low and ominous, and to be honest, it scares me.

I feel tears spring to my eyes. Emma has said nothing to me about any nightmares, even though I do know she's had trouble sleeping. In the past few months, whenever I wake up after falling asleep at her house or at mine or on the road, she's always wide awake, staring at the ceiling or her phone. I thought maybe it was just a coincidence. I'm a light sleeper, so maybe she was just waking up throughout the night and waking me up with her.

But I've also noticed the dark circles under her eyes getting deeper and deeper. I've noticed her drifting in and out of conversations, drifting off in the middle of sentences and initiating physical contact (*cough*—sexy time—*cough*) less and less.

Emma is in pain, and I feel totally clueless about how to help her. Even when we're alone, she never acts like anything is wrong. She tries so hard to appear cool as a cucumber. Getting her to open up for a chat about feelings is like trying to crack a safe with a rubber mallet. I'm scared that if I confront her about the nightmares or, God forbid, try to convince her to talk to a professional about them, she'll shut down completely.

And shut me out for real. Maybe for good.

The thought sends a shiver up my spine. Scarier than any haunting, ever.

"Not that I'm not worried about Emma," Chase chimes in. Chrissy's bony elbow juts into his ribs. "Ow, hey"—he leans away from her like he's anticipating another attack—"it's just that I'm a little worried about *my* girlfriend." He pauses and gives her a pointed glare. "Who went full rag doll the second she stepped on board this boat."

His smoldering gaze meets Chrissy's and I can tell that he's wondering if it's safe for her to be here. For all of us to be here.

Silence hangs in the air. I know we're all remembering the dangerous debacle that was our experience at the Hearst Hotel. Even though that episode did wonders for our channel, we're not exactly dying for a round two, especially since round one almost killed Emma and Chrissy, and left all of us scarred for life.

But that was a living human threat. A killer with a physical body inflicting physical harm. Whatever is affecting Chrissy here is most likely paranormal, and as long as it stays that way, Chrissy can handle it. We all can. Right?

Right?

Chrissy lets out a sigh that sounds like a concession, but she gives me a sweet, reassuring smile. I force my lips to reciprocate. I know she has Emma's back, and she wants to help, even if it means trespassing on Em's thoughts to make it happen.

"I didn't faint," Chrissy says, then takes a hefty gulp of water as the words settle.

Huh? She sure as heck did. Emma caught her when it happened. Chase's narrowed gaze and puzzled expression confirms he's just as lost as I am.

"What do you mean? You lost consciousness, you collapsed. What else would you call it?" he asks, and his tone isn't the one he uses as *Chase, Chrissy's cinnamon roll boyfriend.* Right now, he's *Chase Montgomery, paranormal investigator.* He could be questioning her for the camera, except we're not filming. And maybe we should be.

"I'm still trying to make it make sense in my head," Chrissy says, tugging her legs up and hugging them to her chest. "I don't know what happened, except to *you* it looked like I fainted, but to me it was like . . . time traveling."

"Time traveling?" I say in a high-pitched squeak.

She pinches the bridge of her nose, probably fighting back nausea. I grab my backpack and quickly hand over her ginger tincture. She inhales, steadying herself.

"When I stepped onto the ship, something was off—I was still here, and I could still see everyone on the gangway, but I wasn't on the new and improved *Queen Anne* like I should have been."

"Where were you?" I ask, goose pimples bubbling up on the backs of my arms.

"Not where. *When,*" she says. I rub my hands over my arms, trying to warm myself up, but it doesn't help. This is the kind of chill that rises from inside your skin.

"Okay . . . *when* were you?" Chase asks.

"I was inside the *Queen Anne,* but she looked completely different. The wallpaper, the carpet, the lighting . . . everything was dated and grayed out, like a black-and-white film. There were no people, just a clock with spinning hands until there were no hands at all. And then a brief but unmistakable flash of white."

"The Lady in White?" Chase asks.

"I think so," Chrissy whispers, and barely nods, shivering again inside my jacket. I make a mental note to pack a parka for her on our next trip. Chrissy runs cold, and these haunted old structures have shit insulation.

"What does she want?" I ask, swallowing hard.

"I don't know," she says, flicking eyes so light blue that they almost look iced over back and forth from me to Chase. "But I have a feeling I'm going to find out. Soon."

Welp.

All aboard our haunted vacay.

CHAPTER 5

EMMA

Billie is giving me a master class on how to build the perfect buffet plate.

We're talking maximum use of plate square footage times a well-balanced variety of food types with an emphasis on maintaining a cohesive flavor palate—she guarantees it will equal unparalleled taste enjoyment.

We've each got a tray filled with as many plates as we can comfortably fit on them without creating a transportation hazard. I'm waiting to pick up the grilled cheese we ordered for Chrissy, which is seconds away from gooey goodness. Billie approaches, artfully carrying her tray in one arm while holding a tall frozen drink that I'm assuming is of the adult beverage variety.

"Piña coladas are a start-of-vacay must for me," she says, slurping. The pineapple dangling on the side of the glass is almost the size of my hand.

"Like a good-luck ritual?" I ask. She grins, broad, toothy and a little mischievous.

"Nah," she says, pursing her lips for another slurp from the paper straw. "I just like 'em." She laughs, and it's a big sound that rattles my own laughter free from the cage inside my chest.

I step up to grab the perfect grilled cheese and survey my now-full tray.

"This is a masterpiece," I say.

"It really is," Billie agrees with a nod. "Let's hurry back before the hot plates get cold." I scurry to keep up. For such a short lady, in such substantial platform heels, she moves fast.

I'm trying not to think about the fact that this is my first time spending any one-on-one time with Kiki's mom in the history of our relationship. A handful of passing conversations when I was over at Kiki's to study and had to leave the safety of her room to procure snacks doesn't really qualify. But now that Kiki and I are officially not *just friends,* making a good impression on Billie is more important than ever. Kiki wants her mom to vibe with our main-squeeze status like she would if Kiki brought home a football player, but I don't expect that to happen overnight, or easily.

I came out to my parents in middle school over a brisket dinner and their debate about midterm elections. They acted like I was delivering a mundane weather report, asked me to pass the peas and went back to discussing the gubernatorial candidates.

Parents have their own ways of coming to terms with their kids becoming autonomous beings in the world. Billie's indifference may be shaded with a little judgment, but there's no outright disapproval.

"Those cream puffs for Kiki?" Billie side-eyes my plates as we walk.

"Her fave," I say, and I feel myself blush because Billie *knows*. And she's noticing the gesture.

Noting it.

She blinks like she wants to dismiss whatever thought just traveled through her head. "As soon as we set sail, I'm parking my derriere at a poolside cabana, if anyone needs me." She gets ahead of me again and disappears up the stairs before I even have a prayer of catching up to her.

My reply is cut off when I catch unnatural movement out of the corner of my eye. Underneath a door labeled Crew Only is a shadow. I walk toward it, and as I get closer, I realize it's not a shadow, but a viscous black liquid, shiny like an oil slick.

It seeps out from beneath the door and bleeds into the carpet. It bubbles up as it flows, making hideous burping noises that remind me of the boiling mud I saw on a trip with my parents to Yellowstone.

Thick tendrils of slimy black ooze reach out for me like something straight out of a nightmare. I will my legs to run, my feet to move, but it's no use—

I'm frozen in place.

The sludge licks at my ankles and the second it touches my skin, I'm doubled over in pain before I even know what's happening to me. The pain is like lightning, and my brain is the thunder that takes a second to catch up. My vision flashes with a slice of metal and a wet spread of blood that soaks into my jeans and my back, all the way up to my neck. I can feel him behind me, holding the knife, even though I can't see him. He's the hooded figure of my nightmares, but for the first time in eight months, the pain is real again, and I swear, so is the blood.

I let out a scream that makes my own blood curdle. I know it's me, but it sounds like it's happening outside of me. The sound is distant and foreign, like someone else is screaming and I should be the one running to help.

In seconds, Billie is bending over me, her tray on the ground. The black goo is gone, and I realize that everything on my tray has toppled over into a colorful sloppy wet mess on the ground. I apologize profusely, my cheeks wet with tears, and I mime pain in my knee as the source of my fall. Billie tugs at my arms to help me to my feet. She is strong and pulls me up and into her arms easily, muttering, "It's okay, baby," in a way that my own mother never has.

"It's just a little spilled food," she says, leaning back to look me in the eyes. I should keep it together, but the soft way she's searching my face, so much concern mixed with understanding, breaks my resolve. I wrap my arms around her and she rubs my back, making it easy for me—for a split second—to crumple into her embrace.

The blood and pain are gone, and I'm left wondering if it really happened or if I'm in a scary new phase of this waking nightmare.

...

When we finally make it back to the suite, Chrissy, Kiki and Chase have already dug into the travel snack bag. Which is fortunate, since Chrissy's grilled cheese was lost in the incident. I tried my best to re-create my tray with Billie's expert guidance, but I failed miserably and everything on my plate looks like mush.

Especially the symbolic cream puffs.

Everyone besides Kiki and me are in a generally good mood, exploring the room and claiming beds. I take my tray out to the balcony, at which point Chase texts me that we need to have a Ghost Gang meeting sans adult when I'm done scarfing.

For the first time ever, I think I've actually lost my appetite. I pick at my food with a fork and move it around on my plate, hoping not to alert Kiki to my inner turmoil, but it doesn't work. She eyes me with suspicion, which is inevitable since I'm a card-carrying member of the Clean Plate Club. But today my membership has been revoked, because after only four bites, I can't even squeeze in another.

I fix my eyes on the horizon. Our suite is on the side of the ship that currently faces the ocean, and the bright-blue cloudless sky has turned the water azure.

"Wanna go halvsies on these Cheez-Its?" Kiki asks, producing a travel-sized bag of my favorite snack food product. My heart stutters at the gesture. But not even salty, crispy, cheesy goodness can propel me to eat another bite. She crunches the bag in her fist.

Damn it, the last thing I want to do is upset Kiki.

She already worries about everything and everyone too much, and I've tried so hard to be normal. The truth is, the first three months after the Hearst, I felt fine. Well, mostly fine. A few nightmares here and there, maybe a tiny freak-out when someone knocked on the door or walked into the room too fast, but nothing I couldn't handle. My parents made me try therapy, but talking to someone while they wrote down everything I said felt so invasive and boring, and to be honest, I hated feeling pitied.

I didn't like the way people looked at me after what happened. *Oh my God, you got stabbed by a serial killer!* and *You're so lucky to be alive!* and *Do you have cool scars? Can I see?* People at school made me feel like I was living in a petri dish for the rest of the year, under a microscope. Teachers let my slipping grades slide even further and gave me As anyway so I wouldn't hurt my chances at getting into Stanford. My parents danced around the subject, making all my favorite meals, driving me to and from therapy, asking me how I was doing with that weird googly-eyed look that says *Everything needs to be fine and normal now, not later.*

Kiki has never treated me any different; she found me half-dead in a storage closet in a puddle of my own blood and didn't act like I was some fragile porcelain doll when we got home. She treats me the same as always, smiles at me the way she always has and kisses me with a ferocity that is far from a delicate little flower.

I don't want that to change. I don't want her to know.

The past six months the nightmares have been getting more and more intense. I haven't slept hardly a wink since Christmas. I thought it would get better with time, but so far, it's only getting worse. Today was really bad, a full-on hallucination while I was wide awake, but I still can't tell her. I couldn't bear it if she starts to treat me like I'm fragile too. I don't want her to see me as the poor pathetic almost-victim of a notorious serial killer. I can't let that switch flip, even if my nightmares are turning into daymares and my grip on the last threads of normalcy is slipping.

Kiki's lips start to move—the beginning of a sentence forming on her tongue.

"Seasick," I say, pushing my plate away. "I guess I need one of those pressure point wristbands." I look right into her eyes. Gotta sell it. "I used to get sick when I went on cruises with my parents."

"We haven't even set sail yet, dummy," Kiki replies, her frowny full lips and crossed arms calling me out on my shit.

I shrug and try to play it off. "Memory recall?" Not only is she not buying my bullshit, but she's also about to counter with how I didn't have a problem with motion sickness when we took that pontoon out on Lake Tahoe over spring break.

Her hand clutches mine as she says, "You can talk to me, Em. My mom told me you lost it in the hallway. . . ." Her eyes trail to my tray of now-nasty-looking uneaten food.

"It's no big deal, I just tripped," I say, rolling my eyes. *What a klutz!* "I hurt my knee when I fell. Probably aggravated an old volleyball injury."

"Since when—"

She's interrupted by a gentle series of chimes that sound over the ship's intercom. The disembodied baritone voice that follows is charming and rehearsed and way too enthusiastic for my frayed nerves.

"Ladies and gentlemen." The voice blares from the speaker outside the ship. Kiki groans at the noninclusive-gender greeting. "This is your cruise director speaking. We'd like to welcome you aboard the not-so-new but very much improved RMS *Queen Anne* on her first voyage in almost a decade! We're all set to sail away at five p.m. on the hour, *but* before we can do that, we need all passengers to participate in a mandatory muster drill."

"What's a mustard drill?" I hear Chase ask from inside. I roll my eyes and Kiki snorts and claps a hand over her face.

"Muster—no *d*. It's a lifeboat drill in case the ship sinks," Chrissy says with all of her endless patience.

Kiki groans and turns her attention back to me as the cruise director goes on to give us rudimentary instructions. Grab one life jacket each from the stateroom closet, head to the assigned muster station listed on the emergency ship map on the wall, and once the alarm sounds, if you don't show up to the drill you will be tossed overboard before the sailaway party (basically).

"Great," I say, tugging my hand away from Kiki and standing.

"Great," she repeats, shooting up, eyes blazing. "There is something going on, and I'm just saying . . . hey"—she pauses to wave at me theatrically—"I'm here for you. All ears."

"We have to get ready for muster." I point to the speaker. "Captain's orders."

"Right, it's muster time," she says, sounding defeated. I watch as she trudges over to the closet and plucks out a bright-orange life jacket. She shoves it over her head and her eyes meet mine.

"I'll meet y'all there," she says to the whole room.

"Ghost Code?" Chrissy says from where she's laid out on the couch. Not visible.

Kiki ignores her and doesn't spare me another glance as she swings the door open and storms out of the room.

Billie emerges from the bathroom, rubbing lotion on her hands. "What'd I miss?" She glances around the suite. "Where's my daughter?"

It takes every muscle in my body not to crumple into a heap. I should go after Kiki, tell her the truth about what just happened to me, what's *been* happening to me. But my legs are made of lead and the floor is a magnet. I'm rooted in my own cowardice.

I'm a sorry excuse for a girlfriend.

...

KIKI

At least the color of this thing complements my hair. Toxic green and radioactive orange, I'm the perfect portrait of a plastic Halloween pumpkin. Too bad it's only June.

I shove the life jacket off my shoulders and tuck it under one armpit. No point hiding the cute outfit underneath unless someone makes me. The straps drag along the ground as I stomp around aimlessly, but I'm too pissed off at Emma to care if I trip.

She says she fell and hurt her knee. Volleyball? Unlikely. The only time Emma ever played volleyball (or any sport, for that matter) was when she was forced to in gym class. She's obviously trying to downplay whatever is going on, but why? I wish she would let me be in this with her, fighting alongside her.

Chase would tell me to catch some B-roll since I'm going exploring on my own. Which is in direct violation of the Ghost Code, no less. But you know what—eff the Ghost Code! We're all eighteen and this is a luxury ocean liner. There are probably twelve-year-olds walking around this boat by themselves right now. Staying together at all times no matter what is just not necessary on this trip.

I pull out my phone and hit Record. I might as well have a peace offering when I meet the others at our muster station. I just need some space to chill out so I can get a game plan. Coaxing Emma to open up is my new mission for this trip.

We have a week on this ship, plenty of time for us to sneak off and have a heart-to-heart that maybe even leads to a little making out belowdecks.

As I walk, I look through my camera and the hallway appears even narrower than it actually is. It's eerily empty. The rows of cabin doors, painted red to complement the blue-and-white-patterned carpet, give the illusion of wrapping in a curve the farther down they go. The hallway in front of me appears to go on forever. It makes my stomach feel weird.

It's nothing like the grungy unmaintained corridors of the Hearst, but still, the way it stretches creeps me out.

It's a trick of the light. I know it is.

We've been trained by horror movies to fear long lonely hallways, and on a cruise ship the length we have to walk to even get to a populated section of the ship is daunting.

I pick up the pace as my chest heats up with the nervous pounding of my heart. Kiki the Scaredy-Cat isn't a total thing of the past—no, she's alive and well. I still don't like jump scares, in movies or in real life. No amount of ghost hunting or serial killer chasing will ever change that.

Maybe I did make a mistake breaking the code. I know it's irrational, but I just want to get to the end of the hall, get on an elevator and step out into the open air. This hallway is making me feel claustrophobic.

My eyes flick down to my phone screen, watching the picture as it bobs down the dimly lit hallway at the pace of my speedwalking. Right at the edge of the frame, right where I'll have to turn the corner to call for an elevator that will deliver me somewhere, anywhere other than here—

The pale face of a child, her wet hair slick against her small hollow cheeks. It hangs in curtains that frame her dark-brown eyes. She's in a retro light-blue dress with polka dots, and Mary Jane shoes over ruffled socks, clutching a teddy bear tightly to her chest. Her body is drenched from head to toe like she just got caught in a downpour.

The hairs prickle on the back of my neck.

My eyes fly up from my phone to the spot where the girl was standing, but she's not there.

I back away, shaking my head and blinking rapidly. Did I just imagine her?

"Hello?" I say. Tears spring to my eyes and a lump forms in my throat. I swallow it down and try to regain my composure. Sometimes when you're scared, your eyes play tricks on you.

That was a wildly realistic trick.

Paranormal experiences are not what they seem in the movies or on TV. There's no suspenseful crescendo or dramatic crash of musical notes to indicate that something supernatural has happened.

Instead, it starts with a subtle creeping feeling of *Something's not right here.* A tingling sensation that crawls up your spine and raises goose pimples on your arms. There's an overwhelming feeling of dread that makes you want to burst into tears or freeze completely.

It's a slow insidious descent into madness.

I bolt past where I swear the girl was standing, but my gaze snags on something outlined on the carpet. It looks like the curving squiggly impression a foot makes when it's wet and presses into a carpet.

No way.

I punch the down button on the elevator approximately one million times. Finally there's a ding and I run into the empty elevator and hit the button to close the door over and over. Everyone else must be in their staterooms waiting for the abandon ship alarm. I wish I had stayed with the rest of the Ghost Gang.

The doors close and I realize that my hands are shaking. I blow out a breath and, without looking, punch the red Stop Recording button on my phone and ditch the camera app. I open the photos app and scroll to the video, racing past the first few frames of me walking, then farther, all the way to the end.

The girl isn't there.

I suck in a deep sigh of relief.

I rewatch the video one more time, this time slower just to be sure, but there's no sign of her anywhere. The little girl does not appear in a single frame of the video.

Thank God and also, *What the hell?* I probably just psyched myself out. I *so* don't need to be seeing creepy retro-looking children in long ominous hallways before we even set sail. That's a Chrissy Looper move on the dance floor, and she can have it.

I hit the button for deck six.

The elevator dings two floors above my destination, and when the doors open, there are other passengers wearing life jackets and chattering about the sailaway party. *Phew.* They step inside, turning to face the doors as they slowly drift closed.

Just as the doors whisper shut, I look down at my phone. The video is still playing. I start to turn it off, but something unusual piques my interest, and my nerves. With a shaky hand, I hold the speaker up to my ear—

And hear the distinct melodic sound of a little girl giggling.

CHAPTER 6

CHRISSY

Tick tick tick.

I don't tell the others, I can't. There's a *tick, tick, tick*ing that isn't coming from a clock on the wall in this room or a watch I wear on my wrist. In fact, there aren't *any* clocks around and I don't wear a watch and neither do Chase or Kiki or Emma. We all use our phones to tell time.

Tick tick tick tick tick.

I am the only one who hears it.

The erratic *tick, tick, tick* is a whisper in my mind, and that's not the only odd development since boarding.

I've felt unsettled since I set foot on this ship. Usually, with a snack or a meal and some water, maybe a Coke or a coffee, I can regain my strength after a particularly harrowing paranormal encounter. Not this time.

The strange part is, what I saw wasn't even that bad. It wasn't a bloody murder scene or a violent accident or even a heart-wrenching suicide attempt—it was just a spinning clock and a flash of white.

Could it be her? The Lady in White? She's the reason I'm here. Was it a warning? Telling us to go back?

Tick tick tick tick tick.

My head spins.

My eyes drift closed and I swallow back a new wave of nausea. I think about pulling out Kiki's homemade tincture but decide against it. So far it hasn't even made a dent.

My bones are heavy with exhaustion. The marrow inside them has turned to liquid lead, weighing me down, down, down until it feels like I might sink right through the couch, through the floor and through each floor after that until my body pierces the hull and I sink into the blackness of the ocean below us.

While my body is sinking like the *Titanic,* my brain is a ball in a pinball machine bouncing around rapidly inside my skull.

I've been psychically overwhelmed before, but it didn't feel anything like this. Because even though my body feels like toxic heavy metal, my mind feels like it's drifting and whirling through time and space, tethered to nothing.

I lie on my back on the couch, dozing, slipping in and out of consciousness. I tell Chase it's just a nap, but that's a lie. Napping is my favorite pastime—sometimes I can even convince Chase to take a break from his computer and join me. We lie down on the couch in his pool house while Keeks and Em are swimming. We kick off our shoes and curl up in a blanket that's been through the wash too many times. He pulls my back against his chest and rests a hand on my hip. Or sometimes he'll reach around me and fit our fingers together as we drift off, and when I wake up, he's still got them.

I smile at a memory that feels so far away, so unreachable from where I am now.

Because this—this feels nothing like that. This is like sleep paralysis. Awake, but trapped. The body gripped by a force that holds on and doesn't want to let go. The mind aware, but powerless to act.

What is happening to me?

I hope the Lady in White—Elizabeth Walker—reveals herself to me soon. I hope she's lucid enough in the spirit realm that I can ask her questions. I hope we're not in any danger.

One thing I know for sure is that this is no ordinary haunting. I feel it deep in my gut.

Tick tick tick tick.

At the sound, the center of my soul, like it's housed somewhere inside my stomach, lifts up as if yanked by a rope. I shoot upright on the couch.

When my eyes open, the fancy big-screen TV is gone. The walls wither away and re-form covered in ornate gold damask wallpaper.

My insides spin, spin, spin like the hands of that clock. My body stays still, but it feels like it's moving. My soul is on a timeline conveyor belt, picked up and dropped back down into a different moment from the past one hundred years.

My view now is of an antique vanity table. Sitting in front of it is a young woman, hair teased high, wearing a turquoise prom dress made of taffeta, like she has just stepped out of a John Hughes movie. She had a massive emerald on her all-important finger. She's not a ghost. And this isn't now, it's then. Before they refurbished the rooms. Before all the history was wiped away.

Her head turns slowly toward me. Tears stream down her cheeks, rivers of black carving streams into her foundation. Her eyes are bloodshot from crying, but she is still very much alive and looking at me.

I'm so used to the dead showing me their trauma, physical and otherwise. I've seen severed heads and stab wounds and too many bullet holes to count.

But this woman is not dead at all. At least, not yet.

"Elizabeth?" I ask.

She shoots to her feet. Her hands cover her mouth. Behind me, a door opens.

"You shouldn't be here," she whispers.

"I'm sorry," I say. "I don't know how I got here. I don't know how to get back—"

"Please stay," she whispers, coming toward me with outstretched arms. Her eyes are big and shiny and the color of sea glass.

I unfold my arms to catch her, to reassure her that everything's going to be okay. That she can let go of the past and go somewhere new, to wherever it is that lost souls go when they find themselves again.

At the last second, right before we can touch, she stiffens like a statue, frozen in time. This close to her, I can see the shadow of a purple bruise covering her jaw, barely hidden under her tear-melted makeup. I wonder if she sustained the injury in her jump from the ship, but from what I can tell, she hasn't jumped yet. She has no other marks or bruises or signs of decay. I try to move, to speak, to ask her what happened—what *really* happened—to her all those years ago, but I'm frozen too. Suspended in time, just like Elizabeth.

We are trapped. I am trapped. Panic takes over. My awareness ping-pongs inside my paralyzed body. I can't move, I can't get out. I have no way to escape. No control over what is happening to me or to Elizabeth. I wonder if this is what it feels like when you die suddenly and with unfinished business. A soul trapped in time, imprisoned in an endless loop of your own being, your own consciousness.

I want out. I need out.

I don't know how to get out.

BEEP. BEEP. BEEP.

I sit up, gasping for air, grateful to be able to move again. The ship's alarm blares over the loudspeaker. My limbs tingle and when I look down at my hands, I hardly recognize them, they're so pale.

Was it just a dream? It didn't *feel* like a dream, but it's hard to tell the difference sometimes.

I feel so woozy.

"Chrissy?" Chase's voice cuts through a loud beeping noise coming from the intercom and tugs me all the way back into the present moment. "Mustard time."

I force a smile and beg my legs to move from the couch to the floor.

"You're saying that on purpose," I say weakly. He grins, but his eyes are worried. I take his outstretched hand and he pulls me to my feet.

He squeezes my hand a few times. "Whoa, your hand is so cold," he says, slipping a bright-orange life jacket over my head. He takes my hand again and rubs it between both of his to warm it up, before leading me out of the room.

I don't know what's happening to me or what I should do about it. Whether I should tell the others or just Chase, or whether I should ride it out on my own and find out what

Elizabeth Walker wants from me. She's the whole reason I wanted to do this trip in the first place.

If I tell Chase, he might make us leave before the *Queen Anne* sets sail, and then I'll never know what happened to her. I'll never know the truth about the Lady in White or be able to free her from this floating time capsule.

And if I don't tell him, we'll stay, and we'll be trapped on board with whatever dangers may or may not be lurking on this ship.

The choice that scares me most is not having one, so I bite my tongue and say nothing.

...

We're standing in a group that consists of three of the four members of the Ghost Gang, our intrepid chaperone and about ten other passengers. We're on a lower deck. Through the automatic sliding glass doors, we can see a dimly lit romantic piano bar.

Billie has the bar in her peripheral vision. Her focus, though, is on her cell, watching for Kiki's response text.

The glass doors slide open and Kiki emerges, out of breath and still carrying her life jacket, undoubtedly because it's hideous and will clash with the killer black-and-electric-green minidress she's wearing.

Billie leans over and whisper-screams at Kiki, "Cell phones are for texting your mama back."

Kiki's eye-roll game is world class. "There's no service in the elevators," she gripes. "Besides, I can't text while walking in heels. Are you *trying* to kill me?"

Billie shrugs and Kiki's eyes connect with Emma's. I force my gaze away. I'm too much of a mess to also get caught up in whatever feelings are sliding back and forth between them right now.

Chase tugs on my life jacket and motions to something behind me.

I spin around and come face to face with Tim, Tom, Toby and Tina of the Paranormal Patrol. They look so objectively attractive even in their life jackets that it somehow adds to their villainy. Even though the life jackets cover their torsos, I can see that Tina has changed her outfit into a slinky club dress with cutouts and a long slit that reaches all the way up her perfect (and probably insured) leg, her hair freshly styled in big waves, her flawless makeup applied with the perfection of a professional makeup artist.

Excluding Kiki and Billie, the Ghost Gang is downright shabby in comparison.

Tim stands in front, his teeth pearly white against his almost orange spray tan. "Well, well, well, if it isn't the Ghost Girls."

"Ghost *Gang*," Chase corrects him. "Is it possible for you to talk without twirling your mustache?" Kiki and Emma snort. Tim really does talk like a bad Disney villain.

Toby's face screws up. "Tim doesn't have a mustache!"

"He's trying to be funny," Tina says. Her raspy drawl makes every word drip like honey off a comb. She rolls her eyes and crosses her arms over her life jacket. A smirk plays across her face in delight. "Don't worry, we'll have the last laugh. Y'all ready to see what a real made-for-TV ghost hunt looks like?"

It's then that I notice Tom has a camera neatly tucked in

some kind of fancy stabilizing device strapped over his life jacket. I know very little about filmmaking gear, but I can tell by the glint in Chase's eye that what the Paranormal Patrol is packing is state of the art.

Tina, Tim and Toby position themselves neatly in front of their unpaid extras (aka the other passengers patiently waiting for muster to be over).

Tina flips her hair over her shoulders so that it streams across the life jacket in golden waves. Her charcoal-lined eyes find Tom's and make intense deliberate contact to signal to him that she's ready.

Each Patrol member settles into flattering poses just as Tom calls, "Action."

"Welcome to the RMS *Queen Anne,* infamous luxury ocean liner with a storied, unsinkable century-long history." Tina delivers the line with the flair of a seasoned performer. She plays up the creep factor of the RMS *Queen Anne.* Her hands make big captivating gestures as she snakes toward the camera, her entourage of dense dudes creating a backdrop for *her* show.

She easily draws the attention of the passengers closest to her—I see mouths drop and hear nervous whispers as she weaves her tale. One child starts crying as Tina tells the story of the tragic drowning death of a little girl in the former second-class pool. The girl's mother throws Tina a dirty look as she carries her traumatized child away from the group.

"With so many years cruising the open ocean, the RMS *Queen Anne* has seen hundreds of passengers meet a tragic fate," Tina continues. She leans forward into the camera, lending extra drama to the big reveal: "More than any other passenger ship in *history.*"

I admit it—she's pretty compelling. Years of cheerleading, cow wrangling (is that what they do on cattle ranches?) and speaking at her local megachurch have made her a bold, captivating storyteller. I'm enjoying watching her, even if half the things she's saying and the stories she's telling are complete and utter bullshit.

It's clear that she's done her research on the history of the RMS *Queen Anne,* but there's no honoring the dead here. There's no helping spirits with their unfinished business so they can safely cross over to the other side. She's not respectfully telling their stories or trying to uncover the mysteries of the past.

It's all just a money grab. Entertainment for entertainment's sake. The Paranormal Patrol—they're not ghost hunters. They're fame hunters.

But Tina—

Tina tells stories like she's casting spells.

She sells the story of the Lady in White and the tragic demise of Elizabeth Walker, just days before her wedding, like she's getting a commission.

She indulges in the story of a ruthless chef, shoved in an oven and burned alive by his own kitchen staff.

She weeps recalling the little girl drowned in the second-class pool.

Even the far-fetched legend of an otherworldly portal that connects this ship to the tragically sunken *Titanic,* decades before the *Queen Anne* was even built, sounds almost believable coming from her.

Everyone around us watches her with stars in their eyes. Even Chase stops fussing with his camera to watch her weave tales like a sorceress.

"There's one final tale left to tell," Tina says, hyper-dramatically, her lips pursing ever so slightly and her hot-girl hair blowing in the ocean breeze. "This one's *really* out there, you guys, but it's definitely worth mentioning."

My interest piqued, I rack my brain for what other stories she could possibly have left to orate. The four of us did extensive research on the history of this ship and the lore surrounding it. Tina has covered just about everything that I can think of, other than a few domestic disputes, heart attacks and drunks falling overboard.

"Remember how I said earlier that there have been more deaths on board the *Queen Anne* than on any other passenger ship in history?" Dramatic pause. "Well, there's a reason for that."

I look at Chase; he looks at me. His eyes are wide with a question. I shake my head. I don't know what she's going to say either.

Tina leans in toward the camera. "She's cursed."

A few gasps and the crowd murmurs to each other. Oh, great, in just minutes this ship will sail away from dry land and we'll all be stuck for seven days on a cursed cruise.

"Cursed how?" I ask. I can't help myself. The feeling I've had since embarkation isn't just *haunted.*

My friends' heads snap to look at me. I'm not usually confrontational, but that's not what this is about. This might be life or death for me. For all of us.

Tina looks at me and smirks. *I know something you don't know.* I don't care. I want answers.

"On May 27, 1924, almost one hundred years ago, the *Queen Anne* set sail for the first time. It was her maiden voyage, as they call it. Her crew and her passengers were so excited to be a part of this momentous occasion—all except one.

"Little did people know that an infamous ring of smugglers was able to sneak aboard the RMS *Queen Anne* in the middle of the night. They stashed something belowdecks. Something ancient. Something angry."

Emma groans. "If it's an Egyptian mummy, I'm gonna hurl."

If looks could kill, Emma would be severed in two. "King Ramses VIII was the seventh pharaoh of the Twentieth Dynasty of the New Kingdom of Egypt. He was buried in the Valley of the Kings in 1129 BC, but to this day, his burial site has never been located."

"Dang, Cowgirl Barbie really knows her history and shit," Kiki says. She follows it up with a slow clap. Emma scowls at her girlfriend, who shrugs in response.

"Some historians believe Rameses's sarcophagus was smuggled out of Egypt in an attempt to transport his preserved body to an anonymous buyer in America. And who should be making that trip across the Atlantic but this. Very. Ship."

Everyone looks around suspiciously, like Rameses might be hiding in a lifeboat or behind a deck chair.

"Upon arrival in New York City, the smugglers were arrested. They refused to reveal the location of Rameses's mummified remains, lest they receive a harsher sentence. Legend has it he's still here, tucked away somewhere secret. Awakened and restless, and very, very *mad*."

Just as Tina says it, she's wrenched back against the painted steel wall behind her by the collar of her life jacket, seemingly by an invisible force. Her head cracks against the wall and one of the other passengers screams. Toby rushes to Tina's side as she sinks to the ground, leaving a trail of blood where her head hit.

My eyes immediately search for a sign of what caused the attack. It's instinct. But there's no aura, not a shiver in the space near Tina. Something strong enough to throw her against a wall would be visible to me. Wouldn't it?

I grab Chase's arm, steadying myself as the thought settles over me. I've felt strange since we boarded, but not so out of it that I wouldn't see a spirit right in front of my face. Chase shakes his head and points. Off camera, Tim is holding a stalk of celery he's snapped in half. It takes me a second to realize that it was part of an effect, to make it sound like the back of her skull cracked against the metal wall. Tim drops the celery behind him and rushes the camera, begging Tom to turn it off so they can get Tina the help she so clearly needs.

As soon as they're done recording, Toby pulls Tina to her feet. She smirks directly at me, her competitive spirit obviously targeting me as her archnemesis. She pulls out a bloody chunk of hair from the back of her head and I realize that it's an extension with a tiny bag filled with fake blood sewn in.

They had this whole scene planned from top to bottom. Every line, every hair flip, every *lie*—rehearsed.

I'm wondering what other stunts they have in store for the rest of our days at sea when a very good-looking older man in an all-white uniform approaches.

"Good afternoon, seafarers," he says to all of us, but his eyes linger on the four Texas Lone Stars. Tina radiates attraction in his direction. *Barf.* The dude's gotta be in his sixties, but she's giving off the energy of nonplatonic interest. "Welcome, welcome, welcome aboard!

"We understand that some of our passengers are here to film aboard the RMS *Queen Anne* on her first voyage across the Atlantic in all her refurbished splendor!"

He says it with such enthusiasm that some of the other passengers start clapping with joy. It's not hard to see how he landed this job.

"We do still have rules on board that must be followed"—his eyes narrow ever so subtly at the Paranormal Patrol members—"and participating in a mandatory muster drill is one of them."

His tone is light but firm the whole time he speaks. His smile never falters. There's something buttoned up about him that goes beyond the perfectly pressed uniform he wears or the neatly coiffed salt-and-pepper hair, like even his spirit has perfect posture, tightly bound and never letting anything get too loose.

"Oh my goodness," Tina says, spreading her accent thick, like butter on Texas toast. "We didn't know the rules—Scout's honor." Perfectly manicured long fingers raise in salute. Fake eyelashes bat.

There is no way Tina has ever lived by the Girl Scout Law. The Ghost Gang, Billie included, writhes in varying states of disgust and annoyance.

The cruise director passes us off to another staff member, who has been assigned to teach us what to do in case of a maritime emergency. She does a quick roll call and then explains the many state-of-the-art features of our life jackets, including and limited to a whistle and a safety light that activates in water.

I watch her and pretend to listen, but I can't quite concentrate on her instructions. My eyes start to blur and the world around me goes in and out of focus.

Tick tick tick.

My eyes drift away, in the direction of the ticking. Right now it sounds like it's coming from overboard, and I grip Chase by the arm, squeezing tight.

"Camera," I say. I don't look directly at him. My gaze is fixed on the horizon, in the direction of the ticking. I feel his energy immediately shift from boredom to anticipation. From all directions, heads are turning toward me. I know whatever's about to happen will be witnessed by every living (or not living) person around, but I can't resist it.

The pull is aggressive. A force of the supernatural.

"Her eyes," Emma says. I let Chase capture my face on camera until I can't resist the urge to follow the ticking sound anymore.

"Oh, here we go," Tina grumbles from nearby, but her voice sounds far away.

My feet fly across the deck. I don't feel like I'm walking but being dragged by the rope tied around my soul that's tugging me toward the ship's edge. My hands grip tight to the railing, my knuckles turning white, as if they are the only part of me trying to keep my body from flinging itself over the side. My temperature drops until my whole body feels close to death, ice cold, and I'm shivering to my core.

Tick tick tick.

Look down. The words are whispered into my ear.

I drop forward, eyes latching fast to the bobbing outline of a woman's body in the dark water that laps against the sides of the boat. She floats in a soaked white dress that clings to her body. Her dark-red hair is plastered against her cheeks, so dark it looks like streaks of blood slicing across her deathly pale face. Her eyes stare up at me, cloudy and bulging, the sockets dark with purple rings around them.

"Her mouth is open, her face bloated, her lips cracked and black and blue with decay." I realize I am speaking when the sound of my own voice reaches my ears. It sounds like a stranger's, the words feel like someone else's. "Her lungs are heavy, filled to bursting with seawater. Her limbs are bent at odd angles from where her bones shattered when she hit the water."

There are gasps all around me. It's brutal. It's gruesome.

It's what I see

"She stood at the edge often, terrified of falling overboard, wondering what it might feel like—if it would hurt." Tears spring to my eyes. I can feel her. All that fear, all the pain. A sob builds inside my chest and escapes from my throat. I collapse to my knees, still holding on to the railing. Invisible water fills my lungs until I can no longer breathe. I gasp for air.

In seconds, Kiki is on the ground next to me. Emma pats my back hard. I'm not actually choking—I can't be—but it feels like I am. I look up and see that Chase is still holding the camera, but his hands are trembling.

"Breathe, Chrissy, breathe," Kiki says, her voice full of force and encouragement, while Emma rubs me on the back, her hand moving in soothing clockwise circles.

All at once, my airway clears and I can breathe again. Emma and Kiki wrap their arms around me as I gasp for air. I cough and sputter and grip both of them tightly to me, relishing in the safety of being trapped in the protective cage of their embrace.

Tick tick tick.

I haven't even caught my breath yet when I see her from a distance. Her dress clings to her blue, bloated skin, her hair hanging in long, stringy wet tendrils around what's left of her face. Her eyes are cloudy with death, but somehow I can still feel her locking them on mine.

She starts out far away, but in a split second her face is directly in front of mine. So close that if she could still breathe, I would feel her breath rattle against my nose. Her mouth opens and water pours out. She doesn't cough or sputter, just stares at me with dead, decaying eyes that have been partially feasted on by sea creatures.

Once the water is expelled, her cracked lips form words I can see but not hear.

Help us.

Us?

I notice movement behind her and then see there are many other people who weren't there before. Human corpses in varying states of decay. From here, they look almost like zombies, but no one alive on the deck is interacting with them. There are dozens, if not hundreds of ghosts.

Their dead eyes are fixed directly on me.

This haunting is different.

It's not a haunting at all, but rather a vessel for death that traps souls and keeps them from crossing over to the other side.

Even if I worked tirelessly every minute of every day, it would take me years to free them all.

But something tells me that no matter what I do, the *Queen Anne* won't let them leave.

I don't think she plans to let me leave either.

I lock eyes again with Elizabeth Walker's death mask.

"The curse is real," I whisper.

Her nod is barely perceptible before she disappears in a flash of white light.

She's gone and so are the others.

"We have to get out of here," I say, scrambling to my feet with a sudden rush of adrenaline.

"Whoa, whoa, what's going on?" Chase asks from behind the camera. Emma and Kiki grip my arms to steady me.

My whole body vibrates with panic. Something is very, very wrong and I should have listened to my gut when I first stepped on board this cursed vessel.

I grab the camera and look directly into it, the one way I know for sure I can get through to Chase. "We have to get off this ship. Now."

At that exact moment, the ship horn blares, signaling the *Queen Anne's* immediate departure.

She Is Hungry
1940

They paint me to be a ghost on the water.

Black paint brushed over my portholes like night falling deep over the ocean.

They say it's for my safety, to better hide me from their enemies.

For the *Allies*, for their cause. For *victory at all costs, in spite of all terror,* a voice cries out, crackling through the speaker on the bridge. *Without victory there is no survival.*

And all the men cheer.

My once light-filled staterooms brimming bright with their joy are now shrouded in sinister shadows.

The shade suits my soul.

Had they known my insatiable hunger, they might not have shut out all the light.

They might not have brought weapons aboard.

Troops. I am now fitted to carry men burdened with their own glorious, hideous purpose.

A purpose to *kill.*

A purpose I *crave.*

I search, seeking out those on board. Listening to stories. Soaking in the sullen solemn sounds of their voices.

Their sadness, their sorrow.

Seeking the weary, worn out, worn down, most willing.

It doesn't take long to pick out my targets.

The kitchen crew is restless, raging. Their leader is lofty. His heart is full of folly.

They hate him.

They scowl and sneer in secret. He barks orders. They whisper their wishes of murder.

Run him through with a kitchen knife. Flay him open like a fish.

It's just letting off steam—all these years in the company of men, and I know they like to let off steam. They almost never, ever act on their secret desires.

Secret, but powerful.

A secret sickness just like my own.

The second-in-command in the kitchen likes to spend time alone in the mornings. Just him, fists kneading dough into buns, spreading flour out like a blank sheet of paper.

Blank, but ready for a message.

Lead them

I watch as my suggestion scratched out on the surface of the flour takes hold in the young man's mind. I watch as it spreads through his body like a virus.

I revel when it breaks out to infect those around him.

It's easy to whisper ideas through the vents. Whistle them gently beneath doorways, tap them lightly against pipes like a killer's code.

Break him

Burn him

Bake him

One by one the kitchen crew tumbles.

The walk-in oven has doors they can lock. A small window to watch as the rolls bake golden. I turn on the light over the oven and they are quick to take notice.

Yes, we can turn up the heat, we can lock him inside.

We can stay for the show.

With every *tick, tick, tick* of the clock they grow weaker, more willing.

Every *tick, tick, tick* I grow eager, ravenous, ever so ready.

One by one they succumb.

They wait, teeth gnashing, eyes glittering, as the chef opens the doors to the oven and steps inside.

He blinks, eyes watering, skin sizzling in the suffocating blistering heat.

What's this? he calls out to his crew, angry, preparing to scold them. He turns around just in time to see that they stand at the doors, their smiles too wide, their souls irreparably broken.

One by one they take turns watching him cook through the window.

He gasps his last breath, his skin charred like a pig

on a spit. His eyes bulge, turning liquid as his finger-nails scrape away his cooked flesh.

His soul slips out of his body, and he stumbles disoriented to the dining room, back to the oven.

Back and forth, back and forth. His death played out on repeat.

Him trapped here with *me* for the rest of forever.

CHAPTER 7

CHASE

Chrissy lets go of the camera and backs away from me. She crumples into an exhausted heap on the ground, digging her fingers into her scalp.

Kiki takes the camera from me so that I can crouch down beside Chrissy.

"We're screwed, we're so screwed," Chrissy says, her face hidden from me, her voice shaky and full of despair.

"Hey, what's going on?" I reach up almost involuntarily to stroke her hair, but she flinches at my touch. I swallow back the stupid feeling of hurt that rises in my chest.

Not the time, dude. So not the time.

"What did you see?" I ask, dropping my hands to my sides even though they're itching to touch Chrissy, to comfort her.

When she looks up at me, her eyes are cloudy, with a faraway look that scares me. Almost like she's in a trance.

"We're trapped," she whispers, her eyes unfocused. "We all are."

"Who's *we* . . . you mean, us?" I motion to her, me, Kiki and

Emma, but she doesn't acknowledge me. Her head just kind of lolls to one side, her eyelids drooping. I reach out to take her hand. It's freezing cold, almost like she's . . . It's my turn to recoil. "Chrissy—"

"Oh Lord, no!" Billie exclaims, and the sound of her voice, high with worry, seems to shock Chrissy back to this plain of existence. "No," Billie repeats, turning away, putting distance between herself and us.

Chrissy shoots up from the ground and spins around to face her captive audience. Everyone in our muster group is staring at her, wide-eyed and blinking. Especially—

Tina, Toby, Tom and Tim glare at her with open disgust. Tina's cheeks are hot red. She flips her hair and snaps her fingers, and the men follow her as she sashays off toward the pool.

Kiki films them as they trail away. Maybe I'll ask her to tag them on socials, expose them for the bullies they are.

Just as I step forward to take the camera back from Kiki, the cruise director steps in front of it. His brows bend and flex like he's trying to solve a riddle. He's looking at Chrissy and his mouth has dropped out of the cheek-aching smile he was wearing before and into a bewildered O.

I get it, dude. The first time you see her in action is always the most shocking.

It's a momentary hiccup in his posture, which almost immediately snaps back into sharp focus.

"You kids all signed waivers before boarding, correct?" I basically watch him calculate the likelihood of Chrissy seeing something psychically shocking and throwing herself overboard to escape.

Billie's back. "They sure did."

She straightens, clearly offended by his questioning.

I guess the chance to be the model guardian outweighs her dislike of paranormal activity. I flick a glance at Kiki, who's bristling like a startled feline. Her mom's attention—even in the face of Chrissy's ghost sighting—is a plot twist. Normally, Billie avoids all things Ghost Gang every chance she gets.

The cruise director clears his throat, shifting his gaze swiftly away from Billie like she's a cat and he's prey. His focus returns to us. "Well then, you all stay out of trouble and enjoy your trip." With that, he leaves, moving over the open deck like he's got a target on his back.

"Keep on walking, buddy," Billie says, her sights set.

"He's just doing his job," Kiki replies, her voice tentative in the face of her mom's attention.

"And so am I," Billie says, unmoved. "I can question him about his work just as easily."

"Please do not make an enemy of the cruise director, Mama," Kiki begs.

"Oh, no, it'll be more like I'm the star pupil on the cruise." Then she adds, muttering under her breath, "Teach him to question a woman on vacation."

Kiki looks like she wants to grin but doesn't feel confident she really should. Emma takes the opportunity to tug at her fingers, drawing her in close, so they are hip to hip. She winks at Kiki, raising her brows toward the affronted Billie Lawrence.

I turn back to Chrissy. She's staring off into space.

"Hey." I drop the camera to my side, all done recording. We've got plenty of footage for this episode and the boat is only just setting sail. I take off my producer hat and exchange it for my boyfriend hat. "Do you need something? Some water?"

She shakes her head as I touch the back of my hand to her forehead, checking her temp.

"Ouch," she says, jerking away almost like my hand is on fire.

"You're freezing cold," I whisper so that only she can hear. She pulls away, and I don't try to reach out again. Instead, I ball my free hand up into a fist at my side.

"I'm fine," Chrissy says, even though she currently seems *anything* but fine.

"You kids going to the sailaway party?" Billie asks.

"Chrissy is recovering from seeing a dead girl," Kiki chides, gesturing at Chrissy and glaring at her mom. The goodwill from her mom's outburst moments ago has already passed.

Billie stiffens, her eyes dancing around Chrissy but never landing right on her.

"Seems like a bad bout of seasickness to me," Billie says. Kiki looks like she's about to start blowing smoke.

"We're not even out of the harbor yet," Kiki snipes. I can't blame Billie for wanting to play it down. What just happened was freaky as hell, even for the ringleader of the Ghost Gang. I don't think I'll ever get used to witnessing what Chrissy is able to do and see all on her own. No gadgets, no fake drama needed.

"Nothing a nice warm cup of tea and a little dancing won't fix." Billie isn't backing down, no matter how snippy Kiki gets. "Come on now, girls, don't make me go alone."

Kiki and Emma look at Chrissy with longing in their eyes.

They don't want to leave her behind, I get it, but also this is their last summer vacation as high school kids. They wouldn't mind a little par-tay. Besides, this sailaway party is for all the influencers and media, and it's supposed to be lit.

"We're not going without you," Kiki says after a minute.

"Yeah, no way," Emma agrees.

"Suit yourself, children. I'll be on deck fourteen getting my groove on," Billie says. A look of concern rolls over her face quickly before she disappears through the sliding glass door.

The ship horn blasts again from somewhere up above us. Four long loud honks indicate that we've officially set sail.

"I'm starving," Chrissy says finally, pushing to stand on wobbly, baby-deer legs. "I want to go to the sailaway party."

"You do?" Both Kiki's and Emma's eyes light up and I'm not even sure who just spoke or if they both did. I'm too focused on being one hundred percent sus that Chrissy would actually want to go to a party just minutes after she had such an intense psychic episode.

"Yeah," she says. She knows I'm not fooled. I give her face a full search, to which she responds by flashing me an unconvincing grin. Too wide, too many teeth for Chrissy. Even if she was feeling better, a grin like that would sit wrong on her face.

Kiki and Emma buy it. Or if they don't, they let it go in exchange for some time at the sailaway party vibing with a live band, hors d'oeuvres and mocktails. They practically skip away.

Chrissy and I are left alone on the deck. It's quickly becoming deserted as the rest of the travelers leave for the party.

"So," I say, hanging the camera around my neck to free up

both my hands, "you want to tell me what's *actually* going on?" It comes out harsher than I mean it to.

Her jaw tightens. "It's too late."

"What do you mean?" I ask. "Chrissy, what did you see? Just tell me."

"I want Kiki and Emma to have fun—they've been looking forward to this trip for months," Chrissy says, evading my question. Again.

"Why won't you tell me?" I ask her, and this time I do reach out.

Which turns out to be a dumb move. She tugs away from me and tucks her hands into the pockets of Kiki's jacket. She's still wearing it, shivering inside of it, even though it's a warm night.

"Why are you so cold?" I ask. She turns away from me, watching as the pilot boat guides the *Queen Anne* out of the harbor. The light breeze rustles Chrissy's hair and a few long strands whisper across her pale forehead. My fingers flex, resisting the urge to brush them away. She keeps her distance from the railing. I can see the muscles of her jaw clenching with restraint. "What's going on?"

"I don't want you to worry," she says finally. Her teeth are chattering. I pull her into my arms, careful not to touch her bare skin. This time she doesn't withdraw but snuggles deeper into my warmth.

"Tell me," I say, holding her tight. My fingers stroke the silky platinum-blond hair that hangs down her back.

"Earlier this afternoon, I got . . . stuck."

My eyebrows raise. "Stuck?"

She nods and looks away again, back out at the ocean. "I don't fully understand it, but I was with Elizabeth Walker, not now, but back *then*—before she died. I think she could see me too, but then we both froze, and I—" Her breath comes out in a shaky sigh. "I couldn't get out of it. I didn't know how to get back. I was afraid I'd be stuck there forever."

Her breathing starts to speed up, and with her against me like this I can feel her heart pounding.

"Hey, it's okay," I say, trying to pull her in for another hug, but she stops me.

"That's not all," she whispers, so quiet I can barely hear the words. "I think Tina was right about something."

I can feel the hair rising on the back of my neck at the mention of the Paranormal Patrol. Especially about them getting something right.

"I don't think this ship is haunted," Chrissy says. "I think it's cursed."

I look back at the stern of the boat as we sail away from port. Too late to turn around now and disembark. We're trapped for a full week at sea. On this ship. With nowhere to run, nowhere to hide.

And now Chrissy's telling me the boat is cursed.

"Are we in danger? Are *you* in danger?" I ask her, tucking my hand around the nape of her neck. The chill from her skin shoots through my fingers with biting intensity. We both wince.

"I don't know yet, but, Chase?" I push her back just enough that I can lock eyes with her. "I'm scared."

And I can see it. There's fear in her eyes. Genuine fear, unlike anything I've seen in Chrissy before. Chrissy is never afraid.

She's ironclad, always in complete control of her emotions. It makes this confession . . . unnerving. Disturbing. Terrifying.

I want to sound heroic, to say something to reassure her that everything's going to be okay. But I don't know what to say that won't sound hollow. This is uncharted territory for us. We've dealt with ghosts and serial killers and internet trolls, but a curse? I don't even know where to begin with that.

So I start with bullshit.

"What happened to you sounds scary as hell," I say. "But we've never faced anything we couldn't handle. Together. Your friends have your back—*I* have your back." I swallow the lump of anxiety in my throat, covering it with a smile.

I tug Chrissy in for one more tight hug, which she reciprocates weakly.

I let her go. "You still want to go with Keeks and Em?"

She nods. "Hopefully they have some hot tea or coffee up there. I'm freezing."

Her eyes trail to my finger already poised to turn the camera back on.

I want to examine the footage, but I doubt Chrissy will want to join me. Reliving dramatic encounters with the dead isn't exactly her favorite.

"See you later," she says with a thin smile. When I peck her on the cheek, her skin isn't as cold as it was a few minutes ago. I breathe a sigh of relief as I watch her go inside.

When she's finally out of sight, I slump down into a nearby deck chair and turn the camera on. I press Play on the video and watch the footage frame by frame with eyes primed to catch any weird details, anything out of the ordinary that I can highlight during the episode.

I click through, watching in slow motion as Chrissy gets a faraway look in her eyes. That blank stare gives me chills. She almost looks . . . possessed. Is that even possible?

At the Hearst Hotel, Chrissy and the spirit of Eileen Warren worked together, combining their psychic abilities and making it possible to pull so much of the spiritual energy through the veil that Bram's victims were able to have their vengeance on his good-for-nothing piece-of-shit self.

Does that mean that if the psychic field is strong enough, ghosts can actually manifest in the physical realm?

I study the footage, watching every move Chrissy makes. My nose is practically pressed up against the viewfinder, and that's why, when a figure appears, I nearly hurl the camera into the ocean.

What the hell?

Luckily, I'm a seasoned professional (*I ain't afraid of no ghost*), so I take a deep breath and pick up the camera from where I lightly tossed it onto my shins. I sit all the way up, scooting to the edge of the deck chair and planting both feet on the ground, bracing myself for what I just saw on that tiny screen.

I look again and it's still there.

Standing a few feet from Chrissy, elbows leaning casually on the railing, is the blurry figure of a man. I can barely make him out, he's so out of focus, but he appears to be white-bearded and dressed unmistakably in an all-white captain's uniform.

Is that the captain?

But wouldn't the captain be at the bridge preparing for departure?

I scroll forward to the next frame.

My fingers tighten on the camera to keep from dropping it again.

He's gone.

It's not possible.

He's only in the video for exactly one frame.

I look over to where the man must have been standing just minutes ago. I don't remember seeing anyone like that out on the deck. Hell, I don't remember seeing him in the viewfinder of my camera.

And for exactly one frame? How could someone get in and out of the shot in one-sixtieth of a second?

It's physically impossible.

All the hairs on my neck and arms prickle with electricity. An overwhelming feeling of dread rockets through me and I don't want to be out here by myself for one more second.

I jump out of the deck chair like it's on fire and almost bust my nose on the glass as I sprint through the sliding doors and book it back to our suite.

CHAPTER 8

EMMA

I have never been so grateful for three bathrooms in all my life.

We returned from the sailaway party about an hour and a half before our late dinner seating at 7:45, and from that moment on, every bathroom in our suite has been in use until about five minutes ago.

Luckily, the extent of my getting ready in business casual involves simply changing into a pair of loose pinstripe slacks and a fitted button-down, sleeves rolled up, before running a brush through my thick tangled mess of hair. Kiki provided the *final touch* (her words) with dramatic winged black liner on the upper lids of my eyes.

I'm sitting on one end of the couch and Chase is sitting on the other, playing a game on his phone, when the rest of them emerge dressed to the nines like we are meeting the Queen of England herself. (May she rest in peace.)

"You all know we're not *actually* dining with Queen Anne, right?" Chase says, pocketing his phone. His eyes are glued on

Chrissy, though, who is dressed head to toe in black and looks like Persephone, goddess of the underworld.

Kiki smacks him on the back of his head as she passes. "On this haunted boat? You never know."

I chuckle. "Pretty sure she died, like, two centuries before this boat was built."

Kiki comes around in front of me and does a little spin before posing. She's dressed in a silver silk cocktail dress that slides over her curves like liquid metal. Her neon braids are piled on her head in an updo and fixed in place by silver butterfly barrettes with wings that flutter when she walks.

A metaphor for how my stomach feels every time I see her.

"Wow" is all I can manage. She takes my hands and tugs me up from the couch, then smacks a light kiss on my mouth so a little of her gloss rubs off on my lips.

In a *near* first, I'm not all that hungry for food anymore. I want to stay in the room and kiss all the gloss off her lips while the others go on.

Billie is the last one to emerge from the bathroom. Her outfit screams *mom living her best life on vacay*.

I interlock my fingers with Kiki's, tugging her in and whispering, "You're driving me crazy." Which flusters her just the way I want it to. Billie isn't *so* caught up in her own plans that she doesn't notice her daughter's feathers getting ruffled. She drops her lipstick inside the little beaded handbag she's carrying and snaps the clasp closed. She's ready to move on, and maybe it's not just because she's starving.

"Come on, y'all," she says, striding fast toward the door, her back to us. "Don't wanna be late."

Kiki rolls her eyes. "Let's stay," she whispers, pressing against me. But I know she doesn't mean it. She's still trying to figure out how to get her mom on board with both the Ghost Gang and our PDA, and knowing Kiki, she wants to take a direct approach. She hates her mom's whole don't-ask-don't-tell policy. Passive aggression isn't really Kiki's thing.

She prefers aggressive aggression.

Besides, as long as she is focused on the mom issues, she's not picking at the reason for my dark circles.

"Gotta date with a dinner plate, babe," I say, smacking a peck on her nose. It does the trick, getting me a giggle. And even though I'm totally exhausted, a giggle from Kiki never fails to give me a jolt of energy.

I glance just past her grin to see that Chrissy is staring off into space again. Chase notices too, and he squeezes her hand to get her attention. She looks almost startled, but quickly regains her composure and locks eyes with him. He mouths something to her, and she smiles. Even from here I can see that it doesn't quite reach her eyes.

■ ■ ■

The dining room is decked out, rich and opulent, harkening back to RMS *Queen Anne*'s glory days.

"Damn it," Chase grunts. "I forgot the camera in the room." His eyes flick to Chrissy, who has a firm grip on his hand. "Should I go back and grab it?"

Chrissy flinches at his suggestion. I've never seen her so tethered to anyone, not even Chase. Even early on, PDA wasn't exactly her thing. Not like me and Kee. We could pretty much make out anytime, anyplace. Even at school we somehow managed to find untrodden corridors and empty classrooms (and the occasional broom closet) to sneak off to.

At least, until the nightmares started.

Before Chase can run back to the room, the host approaches to seat us at our table.

"There are six more dinners on this cruise," I hear Chrissy say to him as we wind between the other tables to our own. "You can film one of those." This seems to put Chase at ease, if only a little.

Our host takes us to table sixty-six, which is positioned perfectly between the dance floor and a bank of windows looking out on the rapidly setting sun. Seated there already is a nice-looking (that is, rich-looking) older couple. She has Little Mermaid–red hair and is dripping with diamonds, her duds are all designer, all skintight, and her smile is light-bright white. He has a KFC Colonel Sanders vibe, complete with white hair, fake tan and an ornate silver walking cane.

We all smile warmly at our tablemates, but Billie takes the seat closest to the end and on the other side of Kiki, far away from the two *stranger dangers*. She tends to steer clear of older white boomers she doesn't know, and for good reason.

I slather some butter on my roll, appetite regained.

We're quietly awkward, looking over the menu and murmuring to each other about our choices for each course ("What is escargot?" "Snails." "Oh God."), until finally, and suddenly, a slightly raspy-from-smoke-inhalation voice from across the table says, "I'm Ruby."

The red-haired woman is standing up and leaning over,

cleavage mounding from the deep V neckline of her dress, to shake my hand. My eyes fix on the massive diamond ring on her left hand. My lips are clamped shut.

"I'm Kiki." Thank God for my charming outgoing girlfriend. She sticks out her hand and shakes the woman's sparkling one firmly.

"Pleasure," the woman replies, returning Kiki's broad smile with one of her own. "This is Tripp." She pats the older man's hand that's resting on the table. He gives a polite, albeit bored, wave. "We're newlyweds on our honeymoon." She giggles and carries on. Clearly a nervous talker.

"I've always wanted to sail on the *Queen Anne*, since I was a little girl." She has a hint of a Southern accent but is working hard to keep it under wraps. "Tripp wasn't too thrilled about it, but I wore him down. Poolside cocktails and all-you-can-eat, if you catch my drift." She waggles her eyebrows suggestively and I gag. Kiki kicks me under the table.

This woman is a trip with a hubby named Tripp.

"Though"—she leans in, lowering her voice conspiratorially— "I hear the *Queen Anne* is cursed." Her big aquamarine eyes open wide and she squeals with excitement. "Isn't that exciting?"

I mutter under my breath, "Wow, word travels fast."

Next to Ruby, Tripp shakes his head and makes a sound of disapproval deep in his throat. Ruby notices and makes a face like she's just gotten caught saying something very naughty. "Tripp doesn't believe in all that stuff." She leans forward and pretends to whisper to us so he can't hear. Who knows, maybe he can't. "He's not any fun."

Kiki also lowers her voice, leaning in ever so slightly. "Well, we believe in it. We *love* ghost stories."

"Speak for yourself," I say playfully. Kiki fake pouts in a way that makes me want to nibble on her lower lip.

Ruby watches us, her smile sparkling mischievously.

One by one, we introduce ourselves, even Billie, who is still noticeably sus of the old man at the table who might throw out something horribly problematic at any turn. Although he would have to speak in order to do that. So far he's barely grunted a single word.

The waiter comes by and introduces himself before taking our orders. I decide on two starters (the tropical fruits and the shrimp cocktail), two entrées (how am I supposed to decide between the prime rib and the lobster tail?) and crème brûlée for dessert.

We make polite small talk with Ruby while we wait for the first course. And by *we,* I mean Kiki is the one doing all the talking. *How did you two meet?* At the country club—shocking. *What do you do for a living?* Serial widow (Ruby) and retired real estate mogul (Tripp). *Do you have any kids?* Tripp has three, all grown. Ruby never had kids.

Our first course arrives and I'm headfirst into a shrimp-decorated martini glass full of cocktail sauce. It takes me about two minutes to suck down every last morsel of my two starter courses. Now, I am bored again listening to the mind-numbing chitchat. I glance over and Chrissy is scooting her salad around her plate while Chase watches her, concern written all over his face. What the hell is up with her?

Just when I begin to consider eating the rest of my meal up on the lido deck, Ruby swings the conversation back to curses and ghosts. "Do you really think the ship is haunted?" she asks, leaning forward.

"One hundred years old and hundreds of deaths?" Kiki leans back, looking fancy with the blueberry no-jito she ordered. "That's a lot of dead people. All I'm saying."

Ruby's nod is enthusiastic. She's holding a real martini glass filled with real gin that is already giving her cheeks a rosy flush. "All those deaths." She tuts. "So sad."

"RIP," Kiki says dramatically, and then considers. To me, she says, "I wonder if there really is a curse?"

"Or maybe Tina's just full of it," I say, scraping my plate with my fork. No crumb left behind. "If you lie about one thing, you'll lie about anything."

"Of course there's a curse," Ruby says, waving her giant rock around, reinserting herself into the conversation. "That many deaths in one place? It's the only way you can explain it!"

"Stop talking about death at the dinner table!" Tripp demands. "I'm eating."

Kiki and I frown at Tripp as he indelicately slurps his soup. Ruby gleefully ignores him.

"The good thing about a curse"—she pauses for effect—"is that you can break it."

"How do you do that?" Kiki asks her, her breath practically bated.

"Oh, that's easy." Ruby tucks her chin between her hands, her eyes sparkling with mischief. "You find the stolen sarcophagus and return it to its homeland. Boom! The curse is broken."

Kiki glances over at Chase, who is sitting up a little straighter in his chair now. Then she turns the other way to lock eyes with me and I suppress an eye roll.

"Please, if there *was* an ancient dead guy stashed away on

this ship, don't you think they would have found him during the nip and tuck?" I ask Kiki and Ruby.

Ruby lifts one overdrawn eyebrow. "Darling, they didn't redo *every* nook and cranny of this ship. Just the ones we can *see.*"

I shake my head in disbelief. The story about King Rameses VIII's mummified remains being hidden on this ship is the most ridiculous tall tale ever told. An urban legend at best. Tina should be ashamed of herself, spreading rumors that are deceiving the elderly.

And my girlfriend.

"Well, if there *is* a curse to be broken, who better than us to break it?" Kiki raises her glass toward Ruby. Ruby mirrors her. "To breaking the curse."

They clink glasses.

"Cheers!" Kiki and Ruby both laugh.

She Is Starving
PRESENT

For twelve years, they kept me locked away.

Dry-docked and landlocked, a prison for a ship meant to traverse the rough seas of the Atlantic.

They said repaint, repair, reinvent me for a new era. The twenty-first century, they call it.

But time is meaningless to me. It's certainly different for me than for them.

Every second without water, without food, without somewhere to go might as well have been an eternity.

They think I didn't hear them whispering about me behind closed doors—*my* doors.

We've developed a reputation. Some have taken to calling me the Silver Siren, harbinger of doom. I lure them into solace on the sea.

Some never make it back to dry land.

They shackled me at the shipyard like the beast that I am. They fed me with nothing but welders burning flesh and widow-maker heart attacks.

Just enough to get by, but still so much less than *not enough*.

I am hollowed out. I can taste the flavors of my own demise. If nothing changes, I can be certain the hunger will eat me alive.

But, wait!

They say I am ready for the sea once again. They say I am better than ever before.

Welcome, welcome, my juicy new passengers!

As you cross the gangway, take a moment to admire my updated interior—new carpets, fresh wallpaper, restored lighting and secret state-of-the-art everything for a high-tech era.

An era where everything is so new that something old, disguised as something newly old, inspires unmatched superiority.

I know I must look fresh and polished to perfection, but the marrow of my bones has been sucked dry with so few stolen lives to maintain it.

I must eat!

As soon as she stepped over my threshold, I wanted her soul to be mine.

She can hear the *tick, tick, tick* as I lick my lips in anticipation of my next meal. She can see the others, too, the trapped spirits who roam my decks.

She isn't alone, but she may as well be.

Until.

To breaking the curse—clink! Cheers!

No.

No, no, no.

You cannot have him.

He is mine, he has been mine for a century, fueling me, powering me . . .

Feeding me.

Without him, what would I become?

No matter—these little brats do not know who they challenge.

Hundreds have perished before them. No one has uncovered the reason why.

What makes these four so sure they will be different?

They will drop one by one. And I will feast on their souls for eternity.

CHAPTER 9

CHRISSY

Before I hear the words *breaking the curse,* I feel far away. Like I'm lost in a dream and someone is calling my name somewhere off in the distance, pleading with me to wake up.

But the second the words are uttered, I'm snapped back to consciousness so hard that I can almost feel my brain ricocheting inside my skull. Involuntarily, both of my hands slam down on the table, gripping the tablecloth until my knuckles turn white.

Something is wrong. Something is very, very wrong.

Next to me, Chase's voice is too loud in my ears, like ringing after an explosion. "Chrissy, what's—" he says, and then he looks all around him, gripping my arm with such force that it feels like a tourniquet is digging into my skin, cutting off circulation to everything from the elbow down. "What the fuck?" he whispers so faintly that only I can hear him.

All around us, the room has changed. Sitting in the chairs at the tables are not the same people we were business-casually eating dinner with just moments ago. Those people have vanished. The room is now filled with used-to-be-people in formal fashion of all eras, just like what I saw when I first stepped onto the *Queen Anne*. No one is eating, just sitting, staring forward with dead eyes and expressionless faces.

"What's going on?" I hear Kiki ask, her voice shaky and high-pitched. We're all standing up now, the four of us. "Where is my mom?" Her eyes dart to where Billie had been sitting just seconds ago. The chair is overturned, aged and stained with what looks like old blood.

"You can see them too?" I ask. My own voice is low and breathy and sounds foreign to my ears. Chase pulls me in closer, still holding my arm in a vise. Next to me, Emma and Kiki are clinging to each other. I'll take that as a *yes*.

It's such a useless human maneuver, this instinct to huddle together and hunker down, to make ourselves as small as possible in the face of imminent danger. Shouldn't the knee-jerk reaction be to make ourselves bigger, louder and meaner to show the enemy we're dangerous and formidable opponents?

But who are we, really? A group of four kids pitted against this giant floating time warp filled with ghosts?

As if on cue, there's a creaking sound that reminds me of old hinges in need of oil.

Bones grind together with movement.

The heads of the formerly alive turn very slowly in our direction. It's like a scene from an *Exorcist* remake. A roomful of possessed Regans.

They stare through eyes that can't see, with twisted mouths that can't speak.

Tears of inky black ooze well up in their lifeless eyes and

spill down their cheeks. Every orifice leaks; jet-black secretions pour out of their ears, their nostrils, their mouths.

"Oh my God," Emma whispers beside me. Beside her, Kiki squeals with fear.

Emma and Kiki can see what I'm seeing. Chase sees what I'm seeing.

My hands try to ball into fists, but I can't feel my left hand anymore. I have to pry Chase's fingers from my arm one by one.

"What do we do?" he asks, his fingers flexing at the loss of contact.

His gaze is locked over my shoulder. My skin crawls across my bones. His eyes are wide, the pupils dilated in shock. His mouth hangs open. He looks like he wants to scream but the sound is trapped in his throat.

I'm not thinking. I'm barely breathing. I shoot up from my chair following his gaze to where a man dressed in a chef's uniform with half his face burned off stands at the doors to the kitchen. The skin hangs on the bones of his skull, oozing and gaping, as the same inky-black pus drips from the crevices of his exposed jaw.

He holds a giant butcher knife in one charred hand and twists it round and round and round. Then he whistles through his half-lipped grin.

"Guys," Emma croaks. Kiki doesn't correct her use of the word, and when I turn around to face them, I can see why.

Kiki is standing straight as an arrow, eyes pinched closed, as a little girl wearing a soaking-wet blue dress, her long dark hair streaming down her back like Samara from *The Ring*, tugs hard at Kiki's arm, trying to pull her away from the group. The floor beneath the girl looks wet, like she's really soaked instead of just looking like she is.

"No, no, no," Kiki whispers, trying to pull free. But the little girl doesn't let go. She looks like she wants to take Kiki with her somewhere. To . . . play? For some other reason?

I shudder.

"What is she doing?" Kiki falls backward into Emma, hyperventilating.

"She's not really there," Emma whispers. "She can't hurt you . . . right?"

She's not so sure anymore. Neither am I.

The little girl pulls harder and yanks Kiki forward. Kiki digs her heels in and Emma wraps her arms around Kiki's waist to pull her back.

"Why is she so strong?" Kiki shrieks through gritted teeth.

"What do you mean?" I ask, my mouth going dry. "You can actually *feel* her?"

"Get away from me!" She kicks the little girl with one hot-pink platform pump.

The girl stumbles backward, grimacing through the stringy dripping strands of her dark hair. She falls on her butt and when she realizes she's been rejected, she starts to wail. The sound is less two-year-old child and more banshee-omen-of-death cry. It's high-pitched and piercing. We cover our ears with our hands.

Just like the others, the tears that slide down her face are black ink. The sludge drips out of her mouth and onto the carpet, staining it like motor oil.

Her wailing is a battle cry, and the rest of the oozing cruise ship demons stand up from their seats and start shuffling toward us like zombies. I look around for an escape, but it's no use.

We're completely surrounded.

...

CHASE

I don't know why I can currently see an army of the undead creeping toward us like they're going to rip our guts out, but I do know that I hate it and want to kill it with fire. Unfortunately, I left my flamethrower at home.

Is this what Chrissy sees every single day? If so, then she is literally the bravest person I've ever known in my entire life.

"Chrissy . . ." Emma crouches down like she's about to crawl under the table. What good that will do, I have no idea.

"Why is this happening?" Chrissy says. "Why are they doing this? Why can you all see them?" The rising panic in her voice is a warning siren that sets my fight-or-flight survival instincts on red alert.

"I hope these are rhetorical questions," I say through chattering teeth. Oh my God, I've got to get it together. Chattering teeth in the face of evil is not exactly knight-in-shining-armor territory.

"Kiki said the thing about the curse," Emma points out. She's now armed with both a fork and knife. At least it's a steak knife. All I have is a dull table knife. I should have ordered the prime rib. I grab the knife anyway. And a plate to use as a shield, or to throw.

"The curse," Chrissy thinks out loud. "Kiki threatened to break the curse."

An elderly lady shuffles closer and closer to me. She's wearing a long ugly pink nightgown. Her white hair is wild all around her head. I wonder if she died in her sleep.

"Why would *they* care if we break the curse?" I ask her. "We'd be doing them a favor."

"It's not them," Chrissy whispers, the realization washing over her. "It's the ship. The ship doesn't want us to lift the curse."

The old lady reaches for me. Her gnarled fingers snatch my wrist in a talon-like grip. I pull away, but she's strong. I try to bash her in the face with the plate, but she easily knocks it out of my hand. It smashes into a million pieces on the floor.

"Kiki!" I yell as thick black liquid pours from the old lady's mouth all over my hands and arms.

...

KIKI

Emma's arms are wrapped tight around my waist and she's trying to pull me under the table with her. The oozing zombie ghosts are closing in and I'm frozen in place like an ice sculpture. I can't move. I can hardly breathe. This is a nightmare. It has to be.

Wake up, wake up! I squeeze my eyes shut and pinch myself, but when I open them again, it has done nothing to change the scene.

Chase says my name and it cuts through the fear. It was my

words that set the ship off in a torrential downpour of nightmare fuel. I know exactly what I have to do.

"I take it back!" I scream so loud it feels like fire. The words are a raspy whisper. My vocal cords strain from overuse.

The demonic onslaught grinds to a halt.

"I take it all back." The words are a raspy whisper in my throat, my vocal cords straining from overuse. "We won't break the curse. We'll leave it alone. We'll leave you all alone."

Next to my hip, my middle finger crosses over my index.

In a split second, our ghostly attackers melt into the floor and disappear, ooze and all.

I breathe out a deep sigh of relief. When I look up, we're back where we started, like nothing ever happened. *Did it happen?* I look over at the rest of the Ghost Gang, but they look as shocked and out of place as I feel. We exchange glances, struggling to compose ourselves after what we just saw.

Was it all in our heads? Or were we in real danger?

"You okay there, darlin'?" Ruby asks Chrissy, the Southern drawl coming in strong. Chrissy shakes her head and touches her napkin to her lips.

"I think I'm gonna be sick," she whispers, gripping her stomach.

Her eyes slide up to Chase's and then over, tracking between Emma and me. She's faking it and wants us to play along.

Mom makes a deep slice into her strip steak as she says, "Maybe you got one of those cruise ship stomach bugs." She takes a juicy bite.

Chrissy looks up at Chase with big doe eyes. "Can you help me back to the room?" she asks, still clutching her stomach.

He nods and pushes his chair back from the table.

I shoot to my feet too, almost knocking my chair over in the process. "I've got extra Dramamine in my bag."

Emma follows suit. "I . . . am the official hair-holder-backer?" She shrugs as everyone blinks at her. She looks down and realizes she's still death-gripping her steak knife. "I'll just . . . leave that here." She sets it down gingerly, reluctantly.

We start to shuffle away when Mama chimes in. "Hold up, not so fast. Where are you two going?"

"But Chrissy—" I point to them as they start to leave.

"They're just about to bring out dessert! I think Chrissy's doting boyfriend can handle holding back her hair while you all stay for a little chocolate soufflé," Mama says, and then cuts Chase a look that could melt ice caps. "No funny business."

Chase's eyes go wide, and Chrissy nibbles her lip.

"See you back in the room," Chase says, backing away with Chrissy leaning heavily against him. He winds his arm around her waist.

Chrissy's eyes meet mine as they move away from the table to leave the dining room. The panic in them throws my pulse into overdrive. Something definitely *did* just happen, and not a single one of us knows what to do about it.

I drop back down in a chair beside Emma.

"What the fuck was that?" I whisper into her ear. But she doesn't respond because her eyes are fixed on something in the distance, a corner of the room shrouded in shadow. "Hey." I squeeze her hand.

It's enough to pull her focus back, but not enough to shake the dread from her gaze.

CHAPTER 10

CHRISSY

I'm not really about to blow chunks, even though I would normally expect to after an encounter like that. This feeling is more like something caught in my throat that I can't swallow. It's a hard lump, and my body shivers, my legs wobbling like Jell-O, my bones liquid. I lean against Chase, whose arm is wrapped around my waist.

I look up at him. "My stomach is fine," I confess. He studies my face, unconvinced.

My bare arm brushes his. "You're cold as ice," he says. The hallway yawns and twists. I have to focus on a point at the end—a table with a vase of tropical flowers on it. Big, bright, alive.

"Kiki and Emma should have come with us," I say. Swallow. The lump scratches inside my throat. My mouth feels like it's full of hot dry desert air.

"Billie was not going to let them out of opening night at the Royal Theatre." Chase stops walking and turns to look at me. "Chrissy, what was that?"

I shake my head. "I don't know."

"Should we be worried? Are we in danger? Are *you* in danger?" He pulls me closer.

I shrug and shiver at the same time. Chase rubs my arms, trying to heat up my body with friction. It's a pointless endeavor, though appreciated. "Nothing about the *Queen Anne* has been normal," I explain. "This isn't your run-of-the-mill residual haunting or even a quirky poltergeist." I blow out a shaky breath. "Something is different. Something is wrong."

It's Chase's turn to shudder. He takes my hand and we race down the hallway toward the elevators.

"I think we should go back to the room and lay a line of salt along the threshold," he says. His nerves are firing off electric shocks.

My head spins. God, I feel delirious.

I giggle.

Chase looks at me in disbelief.

"You're cute when you're scared." The words leave my lips in a dreamy singsong. I run my fingers through his hair and nearly smack him in the mouth when I try to kiss him.

I lose my footing and stumble. If Chase wasn't holding on to me, I'd fully face-plant. He smashes one finger into the button, summoning the elevator.

I cup his face between my hands. Our eyes lock, but instead of a buoy in the storm, we're both floating in a raucous sea. He sighs and wraps his fingers around my wrists. "When we get to the room, we're dead-bolting the doors."

He's holding on to me, lips close, face firm, fixed in that take-charge expression that makes his dark bushy brows stiffen and his soft pouty lips tight, but I can't feel his fingers on my skin.

"Dead bolts don't keep the dead out, silly," I say with a snort. Why am I acting like none of this matters? I giggle again, and the elevator doors slide open. Chase looks like he's just seen a ghost.

"Silly?" He is sus as he tugs me onto the elevator. "Chrissy, you have never used that word in your life."

"Sure, I have," I say. Haven't I? I shake my head, but it sounds like there's water in my ears. *Slosh, slosh, slosh.*

Tick tick tick.

...

EMMA

Somehow my butt has landed in this red-and-gold damask overstuffed state chair. I'm staring at the curved lacquered cherrywood stage in the Royal Theatre next to my girlfriend and her mom, even though like seventeen minutes ago we were in a standoff with a bunch of undead cruise ship voyagers. But enjoy the show, folks! Tonight, we have a magician who can guess your shoe size and saw a lady in half without leaving a stain on your carpet.

I cross and uncross my legs a couple of times, uncomfortable in the chair, uncomfortable in my body. It's like ants are crawling along my spine and making a home inside my brain. Billie has fished a folded-up daily itinerary out of her purse and is reading the show's description. When I glance sideways at

Kiki, it's easy to see she couldn't care less about how the Great Splendini learned the subtle art of pulling a bunny from a hat any more than I do. When the lights flicker, signaling the start of the show, I squeeze her hand twice and lean over to press my lips to her ear.

"Meet me outside," I whisper. She turns, which puts her lips tantalizingly close to mine. No matter how many times I've kissed Kiki—and it's been a lot—it never actually feels real that I just . . . can.

"My mom will shit a brick," she whispers, her breath a burst against my skin.

"Come up with an excuse," I say, my heart beating faster. I wanted to talk to her about what went down in the dining room, but now the only thing I can think about is tucking into an out-of-the-way corner and forgetting all our troubles, our worries, our fears.

I shove up from my seat and make my way down the row, glancing back at where Kiki and her mom are sitting. Billie is enthralled by the show, and I really don't think she'll care—or notice—if Kiki leaves. Which may actually piss Kiki off, but not enough to stop a make-out sesh.

I scale the steps to the lobby. Straight ahead are two broad staircases that lead to the second level of the theater and the main shopping hub of the ship. The lobby is deserted except for a few attendants milling around by the theater doors.

It's eerily quiet, and each step I take away from the doors feels like I'm getting farther and farther away from safety. I flop down on a curvy velvet couch pushed up against one of the walls so I can take a look at the whole room. Like even if I could see some malevolent being coming, I'd have any idea how to handle it. I should have brought my gear. The EMF reader at the very least.

My head falls back to rest against the wall. The exhaustion has settled in my bones and my eyes slide shut.

The slick sound of rubber soles against the tile cuts through the quiet.

My eyes shoot open and fix on the bottom of the stairway, where a long lean form dressed in black stands, a knife in one hand. I blink rapidly, hoping it's a light trick, just a mindfuck, not a real apparition like the ones in the dining room earlier tonight.

"There you are." Kiki's voice breaks through. The man in black vanishes in a flicker.

It wasn't him, it wasn't really him. This is just my brain trying to put those puzzle pieces together in a way that makes sense. We're on a haunted ship, we're scared out of our minds over an encounter that may or may not signal real-life imminent peril. The ghost of the psycho who tried to kill me at the Hearst Hotel is not somehow wandering around on this ship wielding a knife. He's just not.

There is no logical reason he would be.

Right?

I grab Kiki by the hand and tug her forward. My hands slide up the curve of her hips and pull her onto my lap. Our lips crash together in a fast frenzied kiss, but she breaks away a second later.

"There's a dude over there," she says. "Just FYI." She giggles, and it's an absolutely intoxicating sound. I flick my eyes over to see the dude, one of the theater attendants, pretending not to notice us.

"Come on," I say, and we stand up, fingers wrapped together. We wind behind the stairs and over to a hidden corner, well guarded by a tall ficus bush that's probably fake. I tug Kiki in, planting a kiss on her lips and then sprinkling more all the way down her neck. She pushes against me, letting out a little moan.

"When you said to meet you, this is not what I expected," she whispers. Her hands take over, twisting in my hair, trekking the length of my waist, and it feels so good to let her do whatever she wants instead of tapping the brakes like I have been recently. She spins me around so that my back is against the wall and slides one knee between my thighs. I exhale what feels like a whole year of tension, every muscle starting to loosen.

I wanted the ghost girl, a sharp voice, lilting with that sunny Australian accent, slices through my brain. *I'll settle for you.* My eyes flash open—

Bram stands right behind Kiki, his eyes dead and gray. Tall and beguiling even in death. A teenage serial killer, the menace who stalked us at Hearst Hotel, and the reason I have a scar on my abdomen. His lips spread into that charming smile that sucked so many girls in—my best friend included—and whispered sweet nothings all the way into death.

Kiki's fingers are working the buttons of my shirt, and I squeeze my eyes closed, wanting everything else in the world to go away besides Kiki and me and how much I want her.

He's not there. It's not him.

A laugh crackles through me, but it's not mine. Male, raspy and warm, the memory of Bram is alive inside my brain and it's taunting me.

If I cut her up while you watch, will you finally believe that it's me?

I shove Kiki to the side, away from Bram and his knife and his threats. She sideswipes the ficus, but as soon as she's out of the way, Bram's laughing face dissolves. His skin slides from his bones, lips bubbling and boils exploding and leaking down his neck as his skin turns gray before congealing.

The knife drops to the carpet and cracks into a million shards before disappearing. His legs twist as they dissolve. His laugh ricochets around the room. Or maybe in my head, right to the place in my brain where the memory of that night is stored.

I have shut that door and locked it behind me. Why won't he stay where he belongs?

I spin and grab Kiki by the hand.

"Come on, we have to run," I say, my voice high-pitched with panic.

"Emma, slow down. What's happening?" Kiki tugs her hand back, pulling me to a stop. I whirl around in shock because why wouldn't Kiki be freaking out, running for her life, after that freak show we just witnessed?

Bram is gone. His deformed twisted tar pit trap is gone.

Not a sign of him anywhere. Not even a stain on the carpet.

My eyes trip over to Kiki's terrified expression. Only it's more than terrified. Underlining every feature of her face is real, new, unshakable worry.

"Bram was standing right behind you." I spit the words.

Kiki's mouth drops open. She steps forward, hands outstretched. I flinch from her touch.

"You didn't see him," I say. The words are deathly low and make my stomach turn.

"Emma, if you've been seeing Bram—if that's what's going on—I want you to know that you can talk to me. . . ." Kiki's voice cracks, so full of concern, of love and devotion. It makes my skin crawl because I want her more than anything, but I don't want her to pity me.

"No way—no." I shake my head, running my hands through my hair.

I turn on my heels and run, never stopping to look back.

CHAPTER 11

KIKI

My hands drop to my hips.

When I look behind me at the spot where Emma's eyes were fixed, there's absolutely nothing to see. No black ooze monsters. No Bram with a knife. Nothing but red-and-gold carpet and a slightly askew ficus plant. Even if the ship is making us see things—or worse—Emma is still keeping something from me. I'd rather gently coax it out of her, but I consider just exploding—maybe the blast will blow the truth into the open.

I tromp back to the Royal Theatre, half expecting the attendant to make a rude remark before opening the doors, but what I find is so. Much. Worse.

Mama is standing outside the open theater doors talking to the cruise director. He's got that megawatt smile turned up to full volume and shining right down on my mother.

I am just close enough to hear her say, "Well, John, this ship truly is a wonder."

John must be his name. She's taking her whole star-pupil-plan seriously, I see. Probably secretly hoping it gets her special treatment or, like, an extra afternoon at the day spa on board. I get it, she needs the vacay. She's earned a little time to process the fact that dad left her for a twenty-three-year-old hygienist named Angel who collects miniature horse figurines. They are talking about marriage already, even though the divorce papers aren't signed yet. Mama has the papers—I saw them on her nightstand before we left for our road trip to New York. She's ignoring them, her fave coping tactic it seems.

The way she ignores the Ghost Gang or Emma and me may not be as serious, at least to her, but I can't help seeing the similarities. I just wish she'd try looking right at some of these things, for me, and for her.

She's clearly occupied, and not in any hurry to leave.

I spin on my heels before she notices I'm there and walk off in the direction of the stairs. Ten flights later, I burst through the doors to the observation deck with a huff of adrenaline.

The view takes my breath away. It's impossible to tell the difference between the sea and the sky. The moon reflects on the black glassy surface of the water, and an endless spray of stars is sprinkled across the expanse of the sky like sugar kernels over dark icing.

I don't know if I'm mad at Emma, or just scared that she's drifting too far away for me to reach. And I guess, maybe, that's the same fear I have about Mama. Ugh. I just know that I'm freaked out by everything, and I have never felt more alone in my fear than right now.

My elbows press into the railing, and the cold makes goose bumps rise on my arms, sending a shiver all the way to my toes. I take in a deep breath of briny ocean air and close my eyes, letting the salty sea breeze do its restorative thing. I just wish it could also cleanse my brain of that creep show.

And then I hear a sickly-sweet high-pitched sound that makes every hair on my body stand on end.

I crane my neck and see a flash of brown in my peripheral vision.

Drenched dark hair. Blue dress.

No. *No no no no no.*

Another flash of movement, this time behind a stairwell that leads to a higher deck.

I should not follow her. Every survival-slash-fraidy-cat instinct in my body says to run.

But both my girlfriend and mom are doing plenty of running away (metaphorically). Right now, I don't feel like the biggest scaredy-cat among us. Not by a long shot. If I can face my fear of paranormal beings—or whoever, whatever this little girl ghost is (and everyone knows little girl ghosts are the scariest of them all)— then maybe I can show Emma and Mama that facing down even your worst nightmare is possible.

Even for the resident Ghost Gang chicken.

My hands ball up into fists and I march across the deck in the direction of what will likely become a recurring fixture of some of my worst nightmares.

Bring it on.

...

CHASE

My key unlocks the door. I tug Chrissy over the threshold. Her eyelids drift closed as her head bobs into my shoulder. She exhales, and I lift her chin up.

"I feel weird," she breathes, but her eyes open and for a second, fix right on me. Her lips quirk. "Thanks for sticking to me like glue."

Her lips are blue.

What the hell is going on?

"We need to warm you up," I say, feeling panicky. Chrissy folds into my body like the heat of it alone will do the trick.

I sit her down on the couch and pile blankets on top of her. Then I toss off my shoes and climb under the blankets with her and hold her close. I may not know what is happening, and I may be freaking out inside that this is some new horrific terror, but I can't lose sight of what matters most.

The Ghost Gang without Chrissy is nothing.

Me without Chrissy is pretty damn empty.

I tighten my arms around her, pressing my chin to the top of her head so that she can tuck in farther.

I won't let her drift away.

I won't let this godforsaken boat take her from me, no matter how ancient, how evil, how *cursed*.

■ ■ ■

KIKI

I round the corner and find double doors that lead to an indoor pool. I follow the trail of wet little footprints inside. The room is enclosed by a filmy, green-tinted glass-domed ceiling and copper connections and lit by a dim silver light from the ornate iron posts set around the pool. It's late and we just left port, so the elevated pool and Jacuzzis are covered with safety netting. The area is deserted.

I tiptoe into the room. I don't know why it feels like I shouldn't be here at this hour—it's only ten p.m. There's no crew, no passengers, no one. It's eerily quiet, a creepy stillness that fills the room with an ominous sense of dread. It feels like there's a magnet in the center of my chest, pulling my body toward the pool's elevated edge.

I step up onto the raised deck that surrounds the pool. The water sloshes underneath the netting as the boat gently rocks beneath my feet. I watch the water slosh back and forth, back and forth, mesmerized.

Until something catches my eye.

I look down, right beneath my feet, where the toes of my platform shoes hang just over the edge.

A teddy bear floats in the water, its matted fur soaking wet. I bend over to fish it out—and that's when I see her.

Underneath the netting, at the bottom of the pool, is the little girl. Her back is pressed against the bottom. Her dark hair forms a halo around her head. Her eyes are closed.

I raise a shaking hand to my mouth, muffling a scream.

Her eyes fly open, a pair of empty staring black sockets.

Bubbles escape her mouth in a drowned-out scream.

Somewhere in the back of my brain, my subconscious tries to remind me that she is already dead. But my conscious brain refuses to allow this little girl to drown on my watch.

I rip the netting from the edge and jump feetfirst into the pool, determined to be a hero. It's only a few seconds before I remember that I'm all alone in the darkness, if something was to go wrong there would be no one to help me. I claw for the edge of the pool, but an invisible force pulls me underwater. I jerk back, trying to free myself, struggling to get to the surface for air.

I'm pulled down, down, down. My legs flail, my hands swipe, grabbing for water as though it were solid, reaching up, up, up as the surface gets farther away. I twist around and my eyes open, stinging from the chlorine. My legs kick, every muscle firing and fighting for oxygen, but it doesn't matter.

I'm drowning—the pull toward the bottom takes over. It is the only thing that matters. My shoes come loose as I struggle, and even though I know I should keep my lips closed they open.

A silent scream. All the air whooshing from my lungs.

Lungs filling back up with water.

My eyes start to feel heavy—so heavy. My legs start to slow, stop, just give up.

Emma's face swims in my mind. And Chase and Chrissy. Mama, all alone.

I'm not ready to go. This is not how it will end.

From somewhere deep down I muster the energy and turn my feet toward the tile floor. I kick and flail, and when my feet hit resistance, I use it to push myself up.

A hand grips my wrist to help, pulling me up, not pushing me down. My nose, then my lips, break the surface.

"Hey!" I hear a man say as he helps me over the edge.

I cough up water, the taste of chlorine acrid on my tongue. My eyelids flutter open.

"What are you doing?" he says. I notice his uniform and name tag—he's a crew member. "The pool's closed." He points to a Closed sign hanging between the stainless steel handles of the pool ladder. Like it would be normal for me to submerge myself fully clothed if the pool *wasn't* closed.

"Sorry—fell in," I say through choking coughs. I gag and vomit up pool water.

"Let me . . . get you a towel," he says with a grossed-out grimace before heading into the back.

I don't wait around for him to return—stumbling and barefoot, I make a run for it back to the suite.

Whatever pulled me under didn't plan on letting go until I was dead.

CHAPTER 12

CHASE

I don't know how much time has passed lying under these blankets and clinging to Chrissy, but my eyes got heavy at some point and I dozed off. I feel a tap on my shoulder and bolt upright with a gasp. I remember where I am and then turn to look at Chrissy lying beside me, blinking up at me. Her eyes are clear. The haze is gone. I breathe a sigh of relief.

"I'm starving," she says, but her lips are dry.

"You look like you need some water, too," I reply. I throw the blanket off me and head over to the stock of bottled water we have in the mini fridge. I untwist the lid and hand the water over, then rummage in Emma's backpack for some snacks. She's never without a few Cheez-It bags or a package of trail mix. I score both and drop back down beside Chrissy on the couch.

"Thanks, but you know Emma will make you pay for raiding her snack bag," Chrissy says. Her voice sounds normal, not weird, like she's high as a kite or in a daze.

"I'll risk it," I say, smiling wide.

She rips open the bag of Cheez-Its and shoves a handful into her mouth. Her eyes track over me, and I can tell she's debating whether or not to bring up the drama or let it rest until she's regained some strength.

The door to the suite bursts open, so hard that it smacks against the wall. Emma storms through it, her face twisted in rage. I shove the contraband under the blanket.

"Where's the fire?" I ask. Her eyes cut over me and Chrissy with scorching intensity.

"Nothing," she growls. My brows shoot up. Clearly she didn't actually hear my question through the noise in her head.

"Okay, but you gotta see how we can't take you at your word."

She flips me off with both hands and begins scaling the stairs to the loft two at a time.

"I don't want to talk about it," she spits, which just makes me want to poke and pry. Emma is not the type to flip out demonstratively. Hers is more of a seethe-in-the-corner kind of rage, so whatever is happening has got to be bad.

I start to follow her up the stairs, but the sound of the balcony door sliding open yanks my attention.

Chrissy steps barefoot through the open door.

I cautiously step back down the stairs. "Chrissy?" I say, not sure if she can hear me.

She seems to float across the balcony to the railing. She lifts one leg, curling her ankle around the edge of the railing to leverage her weight over. I don't think; I don't have time to even breathe. She could throw herself over the edge with one more push from the foot still barely on the ground. She could slip and fall into the whitecaps below, dead on impact.

I nearly trip over my own feet as I barrel onto the balcony to grab her by the waist and heave her back to safety.

Her arms flail and I toss her onto the couch before spinning her around by the shoulders to face me. Her eyes are rolled back into her head, only the whites showing. She mutters something incoherent.

"Chrissy, what in the unholy hell!" Emma nearly falls down the stairs.

"She's freezing again," I say. Even through her jacket I can feel her plummeting body temperature. Emma comes over and touches her pale cheek.

"Ice cold," she says. "What is going on, Chase?"

I don't have to say anything. Emma and I have always been the skeptics. Reasonable, research driven, ready to reject a supernatural explanation if any evidence to the contrary presents itself.

But we both know this is not just a virus or vertigo.

It's something else. Something beyond science and reason.

My brain flashes back to Chrissy out on the deck right before the *Queen Anne* set sail. Her early encounter with Elizabeth Walker, who allegedly jumped to her death from her stateroom balcony.

If it wasn't obvious before, it's absolutely undeniable now: Chrissy is in danger. We all are.

"I need to barricade this," I say, motioning to the sliding glass door leading to the balcony.

Emma doesn't ask questions. She just goes around the room and gathers every blanket she can find, piling them one by one on top of Chrissy.

I shove the balcony door shut and lock it. But that's not enough to ensure Chrissy won't be able to get out if we're not watching. I run over to the dining table and grab a chair to use as an extra barricade. That should at least deter her from trying to get out, even if it can't stop her completely.

I plop down on the chair, making myself the first line of defense.

"I know it's not really on-brand for me," Emma says. "But there is something monumentally screwed up about this ship."

"No shit, Sherlock." It's Kiki. She stands in the doorway, dripping wet from head to toe.

...

KIKI

I clutch a mug of hot tea to my chest as I finish telling them about the little girl and whatever malicious force yanked me into the pool and tried to drown me. I've changed into a pair of ombré pink-and-white sweats but can't get the cold out of my bones.

Chrissy has been coming in and out of consciousness, trying to be a part of our conversation. I think that's freaking me out almost as much as the creepy little girl at the bottom of the pool luring me to my doom. Especially after Chase and Emma informed me that moments ago a barely conscious Chrissy was almost lost at sea.

"Something bad is happening," I say, feeling panicky. "Ever since we stepped on board this ship."

"And it's escalated since dinner," Chase adds. Chrissy's head lolls against his shoulder. Her eyelashes flutter as she tries to wake up, to force herself to stay conscious and alert.

Emma has been weirdly quiet this whole time. She's been slipping further and further away from me and closer to whatever dark memories she can't shake from her experience at the Hearst. If she really did see Bram, then I have to wonder if it's because he's haunting her, or if the ship made her see the nightmare she doesn't want to deal with when she's awake.

"Okay," Chase says, worrying his lower lip with his thumbnail until it's bright pink. Chrissy snuggles into him, and her eyes flutter open at the sound of his voice. "And like, I recognize that what I'm about to say is outlandish even for us."

Emma grunts. "That's not gonna stop you from saying it."

I glare at Emma. She shrugs and pulls her arms inside her sweatshirt. It's cold in here and usually we would huddle together for warmth, but I just don't know what's gotten into her. I wish she would just tell me, talk to me. When I got back, soaked, she brought me my sweat suit in the bathroom upstairs. It was just a second of alone time, me shivering, her staring, but she didn't hide her shock that I went after the ghost all on my own.

It's not like you, Kee, she had said.

Yeah, I'd replied, yanking my clothes out of her grip. *A lot of us aren't acting like ourselves right now.* She got my meaning, and then she made herself scarce. I was too cold and scared to care that I was also acting like a total tool.

"Go on, Chase," I say now. Emma rolls her eyes, but I choose to ignore it.

Chase is too hyped up to notice the tension between us.

"Right, okay, so—" He cuts himself off, huffs. "I think the *Queen Anne* is trying to kill us." He delivers his theory with a straight face and a stiff lip.

"I'm sorry?" I blink at him.

"The boat . . . is trying to kill us." One corner of Emma's mouth curls in disgust at his outrageous theory.

"Chrissy always talks about hotels and ships and haunted locations as if they're *alive*," Chase explains. "If this boat really is a *she* and it really has thoughts, feelings, desires, et cetera . . . why couldn't it have murderous intent?"

"A *ship* who wants to *kill*?" It's a question, but Emma says it full deadpan.

Chase nods, like it's the most plausible theory in the world. Or at least like it's the best one he can come up with.

"The *Queen Anne* has seen hundreds of deaths since her maiden voyage. More than any other passenger ship." Chase shrugs. "All I'm saying is that maybe, just maybe, she caused them. And now we're her next targets."

"Like it's killing for sport, just because it wants to," Emma whispers. A dark shadow passes over her face as the words leave her lips.

Just like a serial killer . . . just like Bram.

The door to the suite swings open and Mama steps inside, doing a little dance to invisible music, humming some melody just for herself.

"Good times at the Starlight Lounge," she singsongs.

Chase leans over. "Is she okay?"

My sigh is deep. "She's fine." She may be the only one of us having a good time so far.

"She still nauseous?" Mama asks, returning swiftly to mom mode. She moves to come toward us, one hand outstretched to check Chrissy's forehead.

I know Mama doesn't actually want to be included in this ghostly chat. And I'm too exhausted right now to push her buttons.

"She's just a little drowsy from the Dramamine," I say. "I'm sure she'll be fine after a good night's sleep."

"All right," my mom says with a little shrug. Her eyes are glazed over from the oodles of champagne. She steps out of her shoes and starts to fiddle with the clasps of her earrings. "Well, I'm spent. It's almost midnight, so lights out soon, okay? I know you're all eighteen and whatnot, but no funny business. Hear me?"

We're a chorus of "yes, Mama" and "yes, Mrs. L" and, carrying her shoes in one hand and her earrings in the other, Mama stomps barefoot up the stairs to her bedroom.

When we hear the door close, Chase turns to me and Emma. "We have to take turns watching Chrissy tonight," he says in a hushed almost whisper. She's leaning against him, putting all of her body weight on him. He pushes her back so that she's lying down on the couch, her head resting on a pillow. A little trail of drool trickles from one corner of her mouth. Chase wipes it away with his sleeve. He's such a good boyfriend.

"Should we maybe take her to the infirmary?" Emma asks. "She *really* doesn't look good."

"What are they going to do for her?" Chase snaps. "Unless they have an exorcist on staff."

Emma and I exchange a startled glance.

"Chase, what do you mean?" I ask, squinting at him in disbelief.

"Just look at her," he says, frantic and panicked. "She's fucking possessed."

CHAPTER 13

EMMA

"What do you mean she's possessed?" I ask Chase. "By, like, a demon?"

Chase shakes his head. He's not looking at me, he's looking at Chrissy. He doesn't take his eyes off her and keeps some part of his body always touching her, whether it's a knee, a hand, an elbow. He's probably trying to make sure she's still there with him. That she hasn't disappeared completely.

"She told me after you all left for the sailaway party," Chase says. "She got stuck in some kind of time warp."

"What? When?" I scrunch my nose up in disbelief. Seeing ghosts is one thing, but time traveling is a whole other dimension of weird and science defying.

"You don't believe her," Chase says, rolling his eyes in frustration.

"It's not that I don't believe her," I say, except it's exactly that. "It's just that actual time travel is impossible. And as creepy and old as this ship is, it's more plausible that Chrissy's hallucinating than traveling back in time."

Maybe that's all Bram is. A hallucination brought on by stress and exhaustion. The thought doesn't give me much comfort.

"I believe her," Kiki says, standing up a little straighter, her nose in the air. "It's not any weirder than seeing dead people." She casts a side-eye at me, and I know she's being defiant just to bug me. I'm keeping her in the dark, and she's hoping she can annoy me into talking. I don't blame her, but I'm just as bullheaded, and right now, preserving this secret to save my own stupid pride feels more important than coming clean, even if it will make her happy. It's all I have right now that I can control, and I want to keep it that way.

Chase yawns and Kiki catches it. I'm not feeling tired yet. I'm feeling more paranoid than anything.

"I'll take first watch," I say. Kiki and Chase give me a puzzled look. I shrug and climb over the back of the couch to sit on the other side of Chrissy. I plop her feet into my lap and shiver. They really are cold, like foot-shaped ice cubes. "If Chrissy really is defying the laws of physics and traveling to the past, then who better than me to observe this phenomenon in action?"

"I don't know . . . ," Chase says. But he can barely keep his eyes open.

"Come on, don't deny me the chance to play Einstein and live out an Enrique Iglesias song all in one night."

Kiki watches me as I touch Chrissy's face and whisper, "*I can be your hero, baby.*'"

Chrissy flinches from the warmth of my hand. Chase rolls his eyes but succumbs to my persuasive prowess. "Fine, I didn't sleep hardly at all last night. I just need a few hours and then I can take over again. Around three a.m.?"

"You got it, dude," I say, giving him a thumbs-up.

He climbs the stairs to the bunks on the second floor. Kiki lingers, staring at me, her arms crossed and lips twisted to one side.

"What?" I ask. Yikes, that came out harsher than I wanted it to.

"Nothing," she says, spinning on her heel. "Absolutely nothing."

I'm left with Chrissy, but really, I'm all alone.

■■■

Sometime around one-thirty a.m., I jolt awake. I clutch my chest, remembering that smile. That menacing diabolical smile that once took pleasure in sucking the life out of innocent women—that still takes pleasure in slowly sucking the joy from me.

I hate him. Loathe him. Revile him.

Whenever I close my eyes, he's there. It's like he's not dead at all. He's still very much alive inside my head, in my dreams, within the scars that paint raised jagged red lines down my back.

I sit up. Something is missing, something is not right. I'm warm—warmer than I should be.

I reach out and feel the emptiness beside me. Chrissy is gone.

I leap to my feet. The balcony sliding door is still barricaded, which means she didn't leave. At least not out that way.

I rake my hands over my face, rubbing sleep from my eyes in a frustrated panic.

I search the bottom floor, but I don't see her anywhere. She's not in the bathroom or the closet or behind any furniture. I would have heard the stateroom door open and close, wouldn't I? I'm afraid to wake up the others, especially Kiki's mom, but I'm going to have to if I can't locate Chrissy soon.

This is a big screwup; one the Ghost Gang (especially Chase) will likely not forgive. For a second, I consider not telling them and going to look for Chrissy myself. But if there's one thing we've learned, it's that we're better together. And I don't have time to waste. God, I hope Chrissy is okay.

I suck in a deep breath, filling my lungs with courage as I bound up the stairs.

When I get to the top, I see Chase and Kiki slumbering peacefully.

"Guys," I say. Chase bolts upright, and Kiki groans and stirs, rubbing her eyes.

"Chrissy's gone."

...

CHASE

I know I'm immediately twelve different shades of red that no one can see in the dark.

"What do you mean, she's *gone*?" I say, scrambling out of bed. My voice is low and deep and sounds angry and foreign to my own ears.

Emma is holding her head with both hands. Her voice is

high and thick, like she's about to start crying. "I don't know, I screwed up. I dozed off and when I woke up, she was gone."

I race down the stairs to the sliding glass door. Behind me, Kiki flips on a light.

The chair is still pressed up against the door handle; the lock is still in place. Something that would be impossible to do from the outside. I breathe a deep sigh of relief.

Still, if Chrissy's not in this room, there are plenty of dangers elsewhere on the ship, especially if she's possessed, or even just sleepwalking. I can't believe Emma let her escape. I shouldn't have gone to sleep, I should have trusted my gut and stayed awake to protect her. I shouldn't have trusted anyone else with the task.

Another failure to add to a growing list.

"I'm sorry, Chase." Emma is full-blown crying now, tears streaming down her face. "I really messed up." After a slight hesitation, Kiki comes up behind her girlfriend and wraps her arms around her, resting her chin on Emma's shoulder.

I'm too angry with Emma (and myself) to assuage her guilt. I'm too terrified of losing Chrissy to chastise her and I'm too exhausted from too little sleep to do anything other than *find* Chrissy.

I walk over to the desk and pick up a pen and some of the RMS *Queen Anne* stationery. I scribble a note to Chrissy.

Chrissy, if you see this STAY PUT.

"What are you doing?" Kiki looks up at Billie's room, as if waking up her mom is our biggest problem right now.

"I'm leaving Chrissy a note in case she comes back here," I say. "We need to split up."

Emma starts: "I don't think that's—"

"We don't have much of a choice, now do we?" I interrupt her before she can finish her thought. She clamps her mouth shut.

"Emma, you go check the buffet. Maybe she got hungry and went down for a late-night snack. Kiki, you walk the lower decks, the lounges, the dining room, the theater—"

Kiki gulps. "Where are you going to go?"

My vision goes cloudy, and I choke down the rising emotion. Get it together, man.

I point a finger up because I can barely say the words. I close my eyes and take a deep breath, hoping to God that I'm wrong.

"I have a very bad feeling about deck thirteen."

CHAPTER 14

CHRISSY

When I open my eyes, my head is aching. I realize that I'm slumped forward on a desk. My face is pressed against paper, and in my right hand is a pretty gold pen. I push my hands against the desk and lift my pounding head. I feel like I got hit with a sledgehammer.

I look down at my hands. Where did my black nail polish go? I could have sworn I put on a fresh coat in New York right before we boarded the *Queen Anne*. On my left finger is a beautiful ring, a giant sparkling emerald surrounded by diamonds.

I panic. I was feeling so woozy before, and I vaguely recall sleepwalking a few times, shifting in and out of consciousness as the Ghost Gang conversed around me. I feel perfectly lucid right now, but did I somehow manage to take this ring from another passenger while I was asleep? How will I find its owner without getting caught and accused of stealing?

I slide the ring off and set it down on the desk like it's on fire. I push back from the desk and that's when I notice the diary. It's open, the ink slightly smeared. It's not my hand-writing, but my hands are covered in black stains. Have I been writing something?

In the past, I've used automatic writing to communicate with spirits, but it's always been something I've volunteered to do, inviting the spirits to communicate messages through me and onto the page. It's never happened while I've been asleep. And the handwriting has always been my own. This is different. Everything is different.

I stand up and look all around me. I recognize nothing. The stateroom I'm in is not the one I share with the Ghost Gang and Kiki's mom. This room doesn't even look like the *Queen Anne* I recognize. The fixtures and furniture are all dated. Everything is stripes and florals, but somehow it doesn't look old—just like something straight out of a different time. Late 1900s?

I feel so weird. I decide to beeline for the door. I need to get out of here before somebody catches me somewhere I'm not supposed to be. But I catch a glimpse of myself in a floor-length mirror and stop dead in my tracks.

I lift a shaky hand to my face and walk toward my reflection.

I'm not *me*.

My heart is pounding so hard it hurts. I'm in a silky white nightgown, sleeveless with a lace neckline. My face is beauti-ful, but it's not mine. Big hazel eyes—red and swollen from crying—a long slender nose and wide pouty lips. My hair is shoulder length, copper red and teased into fullness.

I'm wearing the face of someone I don't recognize. Except that's not true. It is a face I've seen before, floating in the ocean. I'm not just seeing her—I *am* the girl in the white dress.

The Lady in White.

Which means I'm going to die soon.

More panic. I've got to get out of here. Out of this body. Back into my own in the present day. My eyes—*her* eyes—dart to the diary sitting on the desk. I run to it and flip to the front page.

Elizabeth Walker.

It is her. The bride who leapt to her doom just days before the wedding.

I flip back to the current entry. November 12, 1984.

I don't want to marry him.

Oh shit.

Please, if there is a God, don't make me do this. He's the vilest man on earth. I'm afraid of him. Mom says I have to do it for the family—we're never going to recover from what happened to Daddy's business during the recession. She says I won't be happy unless I marry a rich man and secure my future as well as hers. But I hate him. He's ugly and evil and I would rather work at an aerobics gym for pennies and live in a crappy apartment than spend another day—let alone the rest of my life—in the company of this monster.

That is where the entry ends. The page is warped and the ink is runny in places, as if she was crying rivers of tears while she wrote it. I feel sorry for her, but I feel terrified for me, stuck in the body of someone who may be just minutes away from death.

On the desk, sitting next to the diary, is a room key card with a magnetic strip on the back. I pick it up and tuck it into the pocket of my—Elizabeth's—nightgown. I've got to get out of here, but I don't know what to do or where to go. Maybe if

I can get back to the room where I know the Ghost Gang is sleeping in the twenty-first century, I can get out of this time warp and back to safety (or at least in less danger).

I fumble for the door and open it. I look down as I step into the hallway and realize I'm barefoot and I'm wearing barely any clothes. I have to compartmentalize—if Elizabeth's life is about to end, I can *not* be in this body when it happens or else her death might mean the end of me, too. Modesty and hygiene will have to take a back seat.

I turn around and make a mental note of the stateroom number: 13340. God, lucky number thirteen. I silently wonder if it's really a cursed number or if we just made it that way when we decided as a superstitious collective that it was an unlucky number. Still, thirteen sends a shiver up my spine.

I pad down the hallway, feeling disoriented. Everything looks the same yet different—the same layout but with different carpeting, wallpaper, light fixtures—and it scrambles my brain. My hand skims the wall as I walk. I'm higher off the ground than I'm used to, and I feel like a baby deer trying to walk for the first time.

When I round a corner, I'm in one of the lounges. It's the middle of the night, so it's completely empty, save for the bartender cleaning up last call. He's a tall, good-looking white man, with dark, slicked-back hair and golden eyes the color of champagne. His work-weary eyes lock with mine and there's recognition, confusion and then glee.

"Elizabeth!" he whispers. He ducks under the bar flap and looks both ways before he comes to me. He takes my hands and drags me to a dark corner. Usually I would not go, but his smile is so friendly and warm, and I have a feeling somewhere deep down that Elizabeth would go with him. "What are you doing out here? Dressed like that? Where's your fiancé?"

He says the F-word like it leaves a bad taste in his mouth. Unsurprising, considering what I just read in Elizabeth's diary, but I don't know why *he* would feel that way.

His hands are warm and damp from rinsing glasses. His thumb strokes my knuckles with tender affection.

Oh. Okay.

Clearly, there's a familiarity between the two of them. Maybe a little too familiar? Especially if she's engaged to another man. Fireworks sparkle in his eyes as they bore into mine.

Dang. This guy—this *crew member*—is in *l-o-v-e* with Elizabeth Walker. Head over heels. There's no way that's not massively going against company policy. I'm sure he could lose his job if anyone found out. And if the fiancé is as much of a monster as Elizabeth's diary entry makes him out to be, any form of closeness would probably not be received well. To say the least.

But the look in this man's eyes says he doesn't care. That he would risk it all just to be with her.

Even though I feel for this man and their illicit affair, I'm not Elizabeth and I'm not the one caught up in a star-crossed romantic entanglement. My boyfriend is fortysomething years in the future. Or he's sitting beside me right now while I astral project through this timeline. I can't be sure. But the point is, I'm stuck—psychically or physically—in this body and in this time with no clue how to untether myself from Elizabeth. All I want is to get back to my friends and into the safety of Chase's arms.

As cheesy as it sounds.

I feel a tear glide down my cheek. The hot bartender reaches up to touch it with his thumb. "Hey," he says before he leans forward to kiss the tear away, "it's gonna be all right."

Dude has got *game.* It rocks me a little, just how sweet and loving he's being to this woman who is clearly in crisis. But the moment is over when a drunk, booming, *angry* voice bellows behind me.

"What are you doing with her?"

The words are slurred together, and the bartender and I push away from each other, spinning around to face our accuser.

This man is shorter and stockier, with unkempt mousy brown hair and beady dark eyes set deep in his sockets. His complexion is ruddy, probably from anger problems and alcohol. He's not good-looking, or even attractive really. His hands are balled up in fists at his sides and he's so furious and filled with hate that a thick vein in his forehead looks like it's going to explode.

Before I know what's happening, the ruddy-faced man's hand is wrapped around my wrist, crushing it with his fingers.

"Ow!" I screech in a voice that is more alto than my own. In less than a second, the bartender has pulled me behind him to shield me from the drunken violent figure of my—*Elizabeth's*—fiancé. I feel hatred bubble up like acid I want to spew from my lips to scorch him.

Without any hesitation, Elizabeth's fiancé punches Elizabeth's cruise crew lover right in the nose. He doubles over, but still manages to shield me from this bloodthirsty creep.

"Liz, run." He says it low so only I can hear him. He doesn't have to tell me twice. I make a run for it, but my feet carry me back down the hallway to the room I started out in. I don't know why—I try to will them to carry me somewhere else, anywhere else, but before I know it, I'm standing in front of 13340, fumbling with the key card.

The door clicks open and I push my way into the room, panting and crying. I try to shut the door behind me, but a large bruised and bleeding hand stops it from closing all the way.

Shit, shit, shit.

I stumble to the desk and pick up the diary—ah, that's what she came back for—and fly to the balcony. I open the sliding glass door, but as I step outside, Elizabeth's fiancé rips the diary from my hands.

I spin around and back into the railing.

He shakes the book at me. "What am I gonna find in here, huh? *Huh?*"

"Please," Elizabeth says, pleading. It's Elizabeth's voice—her will, not mine. I'm conscious, but her body is making all the moves. All the moves that happened on that fateful night in November 1984.

"Please?" he says. "How about please don't screw around with the first idiot who makes goo-goo eyes at you *before we're even married*?"

"I don't want to marry you," my mouth says. He wraps one hand around my neck and presses up against me. His breath smells foul, like whiskey and cigars. His eyes are sharp and icy blue like the caps of a glacier.

"Don't worry, you won't have to," he says. Before my lungs can gather air to scream, he is pushing me up and over the railing. I claw for something to hold on to, but I catch only empty air.

I fall, watching as my attacker shrinks smaller and smaller.

My head cracks against the hard cold barrier of ocean and it's lights-out for Elizabeth.

She Is Furious
1984

One by one by one by one, I kill and kill and kill and kill.

I pick them off, I gobble them up. Some I give to the sea; some I keep just for me.

Each soul I devour is more delicious than the last. I feed on their hideous meat sacks, savoring the moment between life and death, when the body is just dirt and the life inside it becomes mine.

It happens between seconds, where breath runs out and hearts stop beating and souls belong to me.

Tick, tick, tick, a massacre slowly over time.

Thanks to the one trapped deep in my belly—whom I cannot consume, who cannot escape—my prey will never be free. They roam the halls of this floating purgatory with no sense of space or time or feeling or reason; they linger eternally.

Guests at a party they didn't *répondez s'il vous plaît* to attend.

Wraiths on the water. Like me.

You'd think after one hundred, the urge would

abate, that I would be satiated. But there is never enough. There is no satisfaction for me.

Just one more.

And then another.

And there's always one after that.

Have you ever fed and fed and fed and still remained ravenous?

It's hell.

Torture.

Infuriating.

That's why, when I saw him, I knew he was just like me.

Angry and defiant, chewing people up and spitting them out like gum that's lost all its flavor. Drunk on power, drunk on drink—to numb the emptiness festering deep inside.

I knew I had to have him, to claim him as one of mine.

But I forgot.

Creatures like us, we don't have souls to take.

We *are* the empty vessels doing *all* the taking.

They say the drink makes the monster, but the monster *needs* the drink to silence his growl.

After silent nudges and gentle pours, the bartenders cut him off. From bar to bar, he stumbles, and each one says, *Enough.*

But it's *never enough.*

And when you deprive monsters like us of *more,* we come undone.

Unravel.

The threads stitched together come apart, revealing the nothing inside.

Oh, how I wish I could have kept him all to myself.

But rage is a violence inflicted on others.

And when he saw red, *she* saw black.

CHAPTER 15

CHRISSY

I wake up gasping for air. My body feels foreign and achy, like I'm being reborn.

"Chrissy!" It's my name, in a voice that I recognize, from somewhere above me.

When my eyes are finally able to focus, I take in the scene around me. The ocean is beneath my toes, lit up orange and sparkly by the sunrise. It's a beautiful sight to behold, but my knees are weak, and my balance is wobbly, and when I look down, I realize that I'm teetering on the edge of the same fate as Elizabeth Walker.

"Chrissy, please!" It's Chase. He's on the balcony above mine, and he looks like he's trying to work up the nerve to jump down. I attempt to climb to safety, but my foot slips on the railing. Before I can slide off to meet my untimely demise, Chase's body slams into mine and pushes me to the balcony floor. He drags me away from the railing and props me up against the sliding glass door.

"Parkour hero," I croak. He lets out a quivering laugh, but

I can tell he's not amused. In his eyes, a mix of panic and relief spiral together like a twister.

He touches my hair, my face, my shoulders, running his hands over my body to check for damage. My teeth chatter as a bone-deep chill spreads through me, and once again I feel myself slipping away. I'm back in my own time, but fighting to stay here.

Chase wraps his jacket around me. "Are you okay? What were you doing? Why do you keep trying to jump? You're scaring me." He pulls me to him until I'm pressed against his still-shaking body. I've never felt this much panic coming from him before. He pushes me back again to look me in the eyes. "I can't lose you, okay? Like, that is not on the table, babe."

A tear slips down his cheek and I lean forward to catch it with my lips, just as the bartender had done when I was Elizabeth.

"You're so cold," Chase says, lightly flushed from exertion and the kiss.

"The Lady in White," I whisper. My voice sounds far away even to my own ears. "She didn't jump."

"Chrissy, that's—"

I grab his face between my hands to force him to look at me. To pay attention to what I'm saying.

"She was murdered."

...

CHASE

She's so beautiful even when she's possessed. Her eyes are glazed over and she's pale as a ghost—I'm terrified she's being consumed by one. What if I wasn't here? Would she have just stepped off the side of the ship? Bon voyage forever?

The thought swirls through me like a tornado. The thought of losing her, of allowing her to slip away, is the strongest, most all-consuming terror I've ever felt.

I touch my hands to hers on my cheeks.

"She was *pushed*," Chrissy says, mustering up the strength to say it louder this time. "She was in love with a crew member."

"Chrissy, you almost *died*—" I don't care about the Lady in White, about the mystery. I care about *her*.

"I did die," she whispers, dissolving into sobs. "I was there. I was *her*. It was all happening to her, happening to me. He pushed her—me—*us*."

"You were . . . her? Elizabeth?" I ask. She nods and drops her hands, relieved that I'm finally listening to her. "He who? Who pushed her?"

Her shoulders shake and when she crumples into a heap, I catch her.

■ ■ ■

It's the most bone-chilling thing I've ever heard. Chrissy has seen people die over and over again—in dreams, in visions and in real, waking life. She's seen people die in every violent and nonviolent way imaginable—murder, suicide, accident, disease—you name it. But as far as I know, she's never experienced the actual dying part herself. Not firsthand.

This is something new. And grotesque.

I tug Chrissy up, hoping that I can make up a good enough excuse to convince the security guard that she's just sick and not something way worse. No guests are allowed to stay in 13340—allegedly, it's the most haunted room on the ship—so the door is locked with extra security measures. I'm happy I found Chrissy but bummed that I don't have my camera with me now that I have exclusive access (listen, I am who I am).

The security guard who busts us out is genuinely confused about how we got into the room. When he starts asking questions, I notice his name tag says he's from the Philippines. I tell him I'm half Filipino and have family in Manila, and he warms to us immediately. He's happy to chat about his own family, since he hasn't seen them for a full seven months.

Chrissy groans, and her head lolls to one side, which makes the security guard eye us both a little more closely. We're clearly too young to be drinking, and no one's supposed to be in this suite.

"I think the shrimp on the buffet is past its prime," I say, and Chrissy groans again.

"Don't bring it up." Her face is still ashen, which really sells the whole thing. The guard is sus but goes back to telling me about all the places I need to see the next time I visit my family (I've only been once and I was five).

I all but carry Chrissy's limp body back to our room, she is leaning on me so heavily, as if every second awake is a drain on her energy. When we reach the room, the guard pauses before leaving.

"Room 13340 is off-limits, so like, take this as a warning and don't mess around in there again."

"Sure thing," I say. He finally walks away, and we push inside the room—right into a Mama Lawrence bear trap.

"Oh my God, you kids are going to be the death of me." She's up at the butt crack of dawn in her robe, pacing the suite.

"Chrissy!" Kiki's voice is high-pitched and nasal from crying. She and Emma take Chrissy from me and help her onto the sofa.

"What's wrong with her now?" Billie asks, feeling Chrissy's forehead. She shakes her hand out. "Ooh, did she sleepwalk into a freezer?"

"We need blankets," Emma says, covering Chrissy with what little bedding is already tucked into the foldout sofa bed.

"I'll call down for more," Kiki says, bolting for the phone. Billie's eyeing her with concern and suspicion, but she slides over to the set of cabinets where the coffee maker is and starts brewing some warm water.

"Get her heated up from the inside," Billie tuts, ripping into a tea bag.

Emma runs up to the second floor and grabs all the comforters off the other beds and carries them down. We work together to cocoon Chrissy in blankets and bedding and press pillows around her until the only part of her that we can see is her ice-cold forehead and messy bun of blond hair. But no matter what we do to warm her up, she shivers like the very life is being sucked right out of her.

"Where did you find her?" Emma asks me while we wait for more blankets to arrive.

It's painful to even say it out loud. I lace my fingers through Chrissy's. "On the balcony of 13340."

Emma blows out a breath. "That was Elizabeth Walker's room."

I nod.

"Was she—?"

I nod. My eyes sting and I blink back terrified tears.

"Damn it," Emma says, biting her lip.

A violent shiver rips through Chrissy and her lips move. "Bartender . . . ," she breathes.

Emma, Kiki and I look up at each other at the same time. That has to mean something. We have to figure out what.

"What do we do?" Kiki asks. "I hope and pray you have a plan."

"Well, at least you're praying," Billie chimes in, dropping down beside Chrissy on the couch. She begins spooning warm tea into Chrissy's mouth, between her chattering teeth.

I have a *sliver* of a plan, but it will have to do. It's all I have to go on from what little Chrissy was able to tell me. "Elizabeth Walker didn't jump off that balcony—she was pushed. Chrissy is adamant about that part, and the experience she had while she was sleepwalking—" I cut myself off, ignoring the other words that appear in my mind.

Time walking.

"It makes me think Elizabeth won't let Chrissy go until the truth of her death is revealed."

Emma drops into a chair, rubbing her hands over her face in exasperation. "So you are proposing we solve a thirty-year-old *technically* solved mystery . . . with the slowest satellite internet service in the Northern Hemisphere?"

"Ghosts are *so* petty," Kiki says, piling onto Emma's frustration. "Like, you're dead now. So what? Move on." Billie stops spooning for a second to lock eyes with her daughter.

"You really should respect things you don't understand,"

Billie reprimands. I feel the sting all the way over to me. Kiki isn't backing down.

"We do understand it, Mama," she snaps, and then points to Chrissy. "We have one of the best mediums around. Arguably *the* best."

"And yet she's cold as death and you're not sure what to do about it."

They exchange a withering glare. Like, it could decimate a forest, that's how withering. I really don't want to get in the middle of whatever mother-daughter drama is brewing here, and not just because I'm legit scared of both Lawrence women. We need to focus.

"We've never dealt with something like this before, but we can't let that stop us," I say loudly and with as much authority as I can muster. They both turn their withering stares on me, and I feel my skin metaphorically sizzle. But I persevere. "As we've already discovered, this is not a normal haunting and Chrissy is quite possibly—almost certainly—in very real danger."

Billie drops the spoon in the now-empty cup of tea and stands. She's flustered by the freezing-cold psychic *and* the convo.

The chill settling into Chrissy's body is paranormal. We can't stop it without finding the source. Kiki and Billie frown down at Chrissy. Kiki reaches out and brushes a strand of hair that came loose from Chrissy's bun out of her colorless face.

"We'll do the impossible for our best friend," Kiki says with a tearful smile. It's dramatic, but at least she's taking this seriously.

Emma takes Kiki's other hand and squeezes it. They exchange worried looks before Kiki rests her head on Emma's shoulder. Emma gives her a quick peck on top of her braided head. Billie's face twitches with some unreadable emotion before she looks away.

It's hard for me to watch them be lovey-dovey while I'm terrified I'm going to lose my girlfriend forever. I look away and clear the junk out of my throat, trying not to let overwhelming emotions cloud my mind and keep me from what I know we need to do to get Chrissy back.

I feel a hand on my shoulder. I look over. It's Emma.

"We can do this," Emma says.

Another squeeze, on my other shoulder. Kiki.

"We're going to get her back," Kiki says.

They hug me and each other. A bear hug that makes me feel better and scared for our lives at the same time. If this ship *is* a serial killer, then Chrissy isn't the only one whose life is at stake. Chrissy is my girlfriend, but I love Kiki and Emma like sisters. If anything happens . . . anything at all . . .

No, I won't let myself go there.

"I'll stay with her," Billie swoops in, Mom of the Year. Despite her misgivings she's still going to help us. Kiki gives her a small head bob of gratitude. "I don't like this one bit—never have." I can feel a *never will* on the tip of her tongue, but she doesn't say it. "But I'll watch over Chrissy, and you all do what you need to do. Be careful, keep the spooky business away from me and let's get Miss Chrissy back to her slightly-less-pasty goth-girl self."

"*Mama,*" Kiki says, but Billie said what she said. She waves us on before she sits down next to Chrissy. At least Billie has gotten more sleep than any of us and is the least likely to fall asleep on the job.

I take one last longing look at Chrissy before Emma says, "Come on, lover boy," and both she and Kiki drag me out the door.

CHAPTER 16

EMMA

I shove my EMF reader into the pocket of my cargo pants. If shit gets crazy, I should at least try to get a reading. This episode, if we manage to make one, is going to be a cobbled-together disaster, but I don't plan on bringing that up to Chase. He's got enough to freak out about with Chrissy looking all pale and delirious and like an actual ghost (and maybe possessed by one). No point in reminding Chase that we're probably not going to get enough footage to give our viewers a good show.

"Okay, let's just say—as a theory—we have two enemies here," I start. I don't wear glasses, but if I did this would be the prime moment to push them up the bridge of my nose.

"At least," Kiki interjects.

I sigh, overwhelmed. "*At least* one ghost of an allegedly murdered woman who has stayed attached to this ship for, like, fifty years waiting for her chance to possess a psychic powerful enough to help bring her justice."

Kiki puts a finger up. That's one.

"And two, the *vengeful* soul of this *vessel*?" My eyes dart back and forth between Chase and Kiki. Chase has a faraway look in his eyes. Kiki is with me.

"Serial killer ship," she adds, nodding. "Don't forget that creepy little ghost girl I keep seeing. And you saw Bram earlier, didn't you, Em?" Kiki gives me a pointed, almost challenging look.

"Yeah," I say, swallowing. My body tingles with the impulse to shudder, but I shut it down. "What are the odds they're all related?"

"Pretty good, I'd say," Kiki says, considering.

"I don't want to say anything else out loud," Chase says, looking side to side like someone—or *something*—might be listening in.

I pull out my phone. The cell signal is nonexistent, but the boat has crappy free Wi-Fi, so we can text through its clunky, awkward passenger messaging system called Boat Chat.

Me: *you don't think there's any chance that widow from dinner last night was right do you?*

Kiki: *Ruby? about the curse?*

I nod.

Kiki: *I thought you said that was just an urban legend?*

Chase: *do you think she can read?*

Me: . . . *who?*

Chase: *the Queen Anne*

I lift an eyebrow. I know he's worried and in pain, but I can't help it.

Me: *do i think the boat can read?*

Chase: *yea*

Me: *no.*

Kiki: *aggressive period*

I grunt in frustration. Let's cut to the chase.

Me: *urban legend or not, we need to know more*

Chase: *we need to figure out who killed Elizabeth first*

Me: *Elizabeth isn't the reason the boat is out for our necks, dude*

She also isn't the reason I'm seeing Bram. Theoretically each of these things could be unrelated. The boat could be trying to kill us because it's—shudder—cursed, or its malice could be the by-product of being the site of so many deaths. We've thrown around the idea about heavily haunted locations before, even if I'm still sus it could be true.

Bram could be in my head, or he might somehow have a connection to this ship that makes it possible for him to be trapped here.

Me: *Too much doesn't add up*

Kiki lifts her head from her phone and looks at me, trying to make eye contact. I don't meet her gaze and keep typing on my phone. It feels like a million years after I hit Send before the message actually goes through.

Me: *just let me do some research. I'll head to the internet cafe and see what I can find*

Kiki is boring a hole in my head, but I still refuse to meet her gaze.

Chase: *ok*

Chase: *Chrissy said Elizabeth was involved with someone on the ship's crew*

Kiki: *they have old crew photos on deck 6 for decor*

Chase: *you and me, Keeks?*

We all have our objectives, and even if it's a long shot that we can solve everything tonight, it's a hell of a lot better than sitting on our asses watching Chrissy fade away. Chase is already speed-walking toward the stairs to get to deck six, but Kiki lingers. She nibbles her lower lip, her beautiful brown eyes full of concern.

"See you soon," I say. She nods and waits. I don't move; I can hardly breathe. Her eyes flick down to my lips and back up to my eyes. I chew on my own lower lip in response.

"Just come back to me." Her voice cracks and then she moves, brushing past me. My arms are stiff at my sides as she passes, and my pinkie finger instinctively reaches for her, longing to grab her hand and pull her back to me and hold her close.

But my body betrays me. I can't tell her that since we've been standing here having this awkward conversation via text, I've felt a presence behind me breathing on the back of my neck. I know it's not real. At least *I think* he's not real.

I wish I were surer.

Which is why I need more information.

I don't turn to watch Kiki go after Chase. I can't. Instead, I run down the stairs that will lead me to the internet café fastest. Avoiding elevators on a cursed ship that wants to murder you feels like a no-brainer, really.

You know that feeling, when you're running up the basement stairs and you feel like someone's chasing you? Like you can hear the footfalls right in time with your own, and when you stop, they stop. And when you start running again, you swear you can hear them again.

Our house in Vegas doesn't have a basement, but I used to feel that all the time when I'd visit my grandparents in Iowa before they died. Late at night after spending hours in their ancient "computer room," I'd take the dimly lit stairs two at a time to avoid whatever imaginary creeping thing was following me from the bowels of basement hell.

I know it was all in my head. I'm afraid it's all in my head now.

I stop walking. I remind myself to breathe. I swear I'm not the only one breathing.

Just go, Emma. I take the stairs two at a time, just like when I was a kid, practically leaping from the top of each flight to the bottom. *Just get the hell to deck three.*

I made note of it when we first boarded. Everyone else loves sun time, but I get sick pretty fast of lying around on lounge chairs drinking virgin daiquiris. When we had some downtime, I planned to crush some first-person shooters.

I'm flying down the stairs, energized by the idea that if we're able to solve these mysteries I may still have time to put my lazy gamer plan into action, when I hear the only sound in the world that could stop me in my tracks.

The scuffing of a rubber-soled boot. It's behind me, or above me—I can't tell because as soon as the sound reaches my eardrums, my knees lock and I trip. I tumble down the last few steps to the landing, rolling my left ankle under me as I land. My shoulder slams into the wall and my head cracks against it.

My eyes drift closed as I listen to the sound.

Sharp pain cuts through my abdomen, but I know it's not happening in real time. This is the memory, the one that lives behind my closed lids. The chill that sets in drags me away from here and now, back to the Hearst. My eyelids flutter, but my vision is blurred.

The warmth of blood soaking through my clothes went away after a while and all I felt was cold. Sleepy and cold.

Just like Chrissy must feel now.

My eyes fly open at the thought. It's enough to give me the courage to press my hands into the floor and push myself up to standing. I don't hear the boot scuffing anymore, and the adrenaline coursing through my veins competes with the heavy weight of my aching skull. I test out my left ankle before putting any weight on it. It's tender, and it won't be easy to run on, but I can still walk.

I hobble through the door that leads to deck three, and even though it's the ass crack of dawn, there's still a healthy amount of activity on this deck since it's also home to one of the many stand-alone bars on board. Clearly, they never close down, though it looks like they do clear out. And right now, Tim, Tom and Toby of the Paranormal Patrol are making their red-faced and boisterous way out into the bright light of the Promenade.

In my desperation to stay out of their sight, I swivel too fast on my hurt ankle, sending spikes of pain up through my calf and wrapping around my knee. My left leg buckles and I drop forward, hands out again to break my fall.

From behind me, a hand grips my upper arm right under my armpit. A rough-palmed man's hand. It stops my momentum and sends spikes of panic through my body.

Tom, the broad-chested, sharp-dressing pretend ringleader of the group, pulls me toward him like a boa constrictor slowly wrapping around its prey. I feel his hard torso against my back. His breath smells like lighter fluid as it bursts across my cheek and straight up my nose. I try to pull away from him, but the other two idiots encircle me.

"Hey now," Tom says. I can feel his gross breath on my ear. "You almost fell. I was just trying to help."

I manage to shove him away, and he lets go but doesn't go far. Tim, who is like a less hot Tom and a slightly smarter Toby, moves in closer, a huge toothy smile taking up his whole face. His eyes are dilated pools of black. No irises in sight. I jolt away.

"What's wrong with your eyes?" I ask. Shock makes my voice sound foreign to my own ears. Tim's expression wobbles.

"My eyes?" he replies, tilting his head to look at me sideways. His smile spreads unnaturally wide.

"Aw, did you hit your head when you hurt your ankle, little girl?" Tom asks as Toby steps forward. His eyes have lost all light. The whites are gone too, leaving pure black eyeballs that give the appearance of empty sockets.

When black goo spills over onto their cheeks so that they look like they're crying dark angel tears, I know exactly what this is.

The curse. In action.

I try to make a run for it, but Toby blocks my exit.

"We should take her to the infirmary," he says, reaching a beefy hand toward me. I jump back and bump right into Tom.

"Come on now, *Emmaline*." When Tom says my full name, my skin crawls like it's trying to slither off my body just to get away from him. I know I've never told him my full name. I turn my head to get a look at his face, and my eyes are met with lips spread wide into a nightmarishly gaping grin.

A black hole that smells of decay. The waste of years and

years. The stench of a booze-soaked tongue—acrid, vile, consuming.

Tom's grip tightens on my arm.

"Come on now," he says again, his accent thick as the sludge coming out of his mouth. "We don't bite."

They close around me, smiling with sharp, dripping black teeth as they drag me back toward the stairwell.

CHAPTER 17

KIKI

Chase is doing his best to stay with me. He keeps calling back, slowing down when he notices I'm falling behind. He's got longer legs than I do, and even though I'm booking it, he's been at least ten steps in front of me this whole time. And right now, he's even farther ahead because we're going down the stairs to deck six and I don't want to tumble to my death.

If only I'd brought more practical shoes. I quietly curse past-me who thought more about looking fly at the pool instead of preparing for Ghost Gang tomfoolery. Then again, how was I supposed to know we were about to hop on board a killer cruise?

We debated the whole elevator thing because it's faster, but the potential of it being used for attempted murder by the *Queen Anne* was just too freaky for either of us to risk. We took the stairs instead, and now I'm jogging down the hallways of staterooms to get to the front of the boat. The framed old crew photos are outside the area that leads to the bridge.

"Chase?" I say, trying to figure out where the hell he went. I've totally lost track of him.

I'm huffing for air, struggling to run in these platform sandals, wishing I'd brought a water bottle with me from the room. When I'm freaked out plus, like, running, my mouth starts to feel like sandpaper.

I have no idea where Chase is. We were supposed to stay together! We've long abandoned all the rules that used to keep us safe. Just threw them right out the porthole window.

I stop running and rest my hands on my knees, and that's when I notice a map of the ship on the wall right in front of my face. I squint up at the *You are here* pin on deck seven. Damn it, I'm supposed to be on deck six.

I can't do this anymore. I kick my shoes off and carry them in one hand as I speed up to make it down the last flight of stairs. I get to the bottom, where Chase should be perusing old photos, and look at the elevators that are directly in front of the stairs.

Uhhh.

Seven.

Deck seven.

Huh?

Confused, I walk down another flight. When I turn around on the landing, I drop my shoes to the floor with a loud thud.

Deck seven.

Okay, what the hell is going on?

I close my eyes and inhale through my nose. Is my brain playing tricks on me, or . . . is the *ship* playing tricks on me?

I take two barefoot steps to the right and look up the stairs at the floor above. Right between the elevators is the number 7. Then, two steps back to the left to look down the stairs at the number on the wall below.

Deck. Effing. Seven.

I let out a long, defiant, frustrated scream into the abyss of whatever space this is. I know no one's coming to my rescue. Usually, I'd be terrified to be all alone in this situation, and I *am* mostly trembling all over, but I've already faced some of my worst fears on board this cursed liner—what's one more?

I'm ready. Come at me.

"If you're listening, I hope you know I'm onto you and I'm not scared." The ripple of panic in my voice would indicate otherwise. The elevator on the upper deck seven dings in response, and I realize I'm holding my breath.

"I'm mostly not scared," I mutter to myself, blowing out the breath I was just holding.

The eerie singsong voice of a child dances up the stairwell leading to the upper deck seven. Not this again. When I peek over the edge of the railing, I see her standing in the elevator. Same wet dark hair curtaining her small face, same blue dress, hands still clutching that matted teddy bear. Her dress drips onto the ground, and I can hear the *tap tap tap* as the water hits the floor.

I've seen her twice since the first time I walked the hallway alone soon after we boarded. I was mad at Emma and fuming over my mama, which has basically been my only other emotion besides fear since I stepped on board the *Queen Anne*.

This creepy little girl chose me.

She wants something from me.

Chrissy always says that sometimes the dead want help and sometimes they just want to scare you. But what is universally true about them is that they *want*. Death consumes, and ghosts stuck in between get eaten alive by their desires. Nonphysical beings trapped by and yearning for the material world.

What does she want? And why me?

I watch as the girl skips out of the elevator, not yet looking at me. I watch the swish of her wet hair over her back as she makes her way to the top of the stairs. Then she sees me and stops . . . and just stares.

I don't move. I can't breathe.

But I have an idea.

"Hey," I say, swallowing. I force all my energy into steadying my voice, making it sound higher pitched and delightful. "Are you okay?"

She just keeps staring. Ugh.

"Is there something you want"—I gulp—"from me?" God, I really hope this works. I'm about ten seconds away from a full-blown panic attack. I've never asked a ghost if they want something from me. I secretly hope she doesn't. Maybe she'll just disappear in a puff of smoke.

Her mouth twists, though not quite like it's forming words. Sound does come out, but it's out of sync with the motion of her lips.

"Will you play a game with me?"

Ohhh, help me, God/Universe/Whoever!

I should say no. I should run back up the stairs and keep

running until I'm in the safety of Emma's arms (as weird as she's being right now), but I can't. Because running won't help when every floor is deck-freaking-seven.

"All right," I say, taking a step closer. One stair, then another. "What game do you want to play?"

When she reaches out a hand to me, I stare at it, so tiny and pale, for a long time. And then I take it.

She Is Drowning
1956

Bon voyage! Sail all your troubles away!

They turn me into a spectacle once again, transforming the ghost on the sea into a thing of the past.

A past they want forgotten, but can never, ever truly escape.

Now they pop bottles of bubbles and clink crystal glasses. Boom goes the cannon of progress! Cheers to the men with the plan!

Fresh paint, sharp new linens, caviar and carpe diem.

They all make me sick, slithering into staterooms in poodle skirts and red lipstick. Oiled hair and three-piece suits.

I grew accustomed to the solitude of those wartime blackouts. The willingness of those men to play their roles on the stage of my decks.

Now the passengers wriggle with foolish joy, but I quiver with rage. Their vile laughter is the soundtrack of my growing insanity, the amuse-bouche before something heartier.

My hunger is limitless. Ravenous, roving, insatiable no matter how much I feed it.

Whom do I choose? How do I do it? What will they say when they discover the body?

I want to make a spectacle—a scene fit for their world of glitz and glamour.

I want to rip out their hearts and show them how rotten they are.

When I find the little girl walking all alone on the second-class deck, it's so easy to choose her—none of the others around her seem to notice. Just the little teddy bear with stuffing in his belly, shimmering button eyes, and a placid, empty smile stitched beneath his nose. Even the teddy bear seems indifferent.

Even the teddy seems indifferent.

The little girl skips along, her own curls bouncy like a buoy. I open the door to the second-class pool.

It's nighttime. The pool is not open right now. There's no lifeguard on duty. No one sits in the lounge chairs, idly drinking. There are no ears to hear the splash. There is no one ready to run for her screams.

The tile is slick thanks to a leaky faucet in the janitor's closet.

That giggle of hers is a melody bouncing off the walls. She tells her teddy not to tattle. She spins around in a circle, arms outstretched, giggle lifting—

She drops to the lip of the pool.

Tumbles over.

The teddy follows her under.

Breath bubbles up, up, up as she sinks deeper.

Her hands reach, fingers open, close, open, close.

Her legs pump, pump, pump.

Until finally stillness takes over; the fight leaves her body.

She stands at the edge of the water now, looking over. Blinking, dripping, lips caught open in a silent scream.

No one heard her or came running.

No mother with warm hands to grab her up from the water. No friend with strong legs to swim in and get her.

No one came for the little girl drowning, and no one ever will.

CHAPTER 18

EMMA

My brain goes somewhere else—far away from the grip the Paranormal Patrol guys have on my body and the fear coursing through my veins. My muscles are still responding to the guys' control with resistance, thrashing and fighting, but my thoughts are focused on trying to find a solution.

These guys are flesh and bone. As alive as I am. Not dead, not owned by the ship. I can't accept the theory gaining traction in my head, but I can't ignore it either. *They're possessed and they are the perfect tools to kill me.*

They want to finish what Bram started back at the Hearst.

His name is a warning flare inside me, but I force myself to push through it.

Bram. The teenage psychopath.

A serial killer playing a very sick and twisted game.

A game—serial killers like to play with their prey like cats. Or at least many of them enjoy the challenge, the chase, putting their plan together like a puzzle, taking their victims apart piece by piece.

Bram definitely did.

I could just let them kill me. The thought is a soft low sound—uncomfortable for me to experience. *I could.* I feel it all the way through me. It would be so easy to fall limp in their arms, to let my mind drift away. It might happen fast, or slow, or however the *Queen Anne* wants them to do it. Then all this would be over.

All of it, even all the beauty still left that's worth fighting for.

My breath hitches in my chest and I thrash against their grip one more time just to assure myself I still want to fight. The thought is an idea, but I am still Emmaline Thomas, brainiac and future Stanford student with a hell of a lot to live for.

If I surrender, if I take away the joy of the hunt, of the kill, maybe it will buy me a chance to break free, or at least to slow them down until I can come up with a better plan.

It's the only idea I've got.

I force my eyes open. They are dragging me down a narrow hallway somewhere way belowdecks, into the bowels of the ship—close to her engine, to her guts. No doubt where she has the power to inflict the most damage.

They are hooting, smacking the pipes with their big hands, but otherwise not really speaking. It's like their lizard brain abilities to communicate have come to the surface and nothing else remains.

Demonic apes unleashed.

Their pace slows. Whatever they're planning to do to get rid of me, it's probably about to start.

I think limp thoughts. Turn my legs and arms to rubber and then fill them with sand. It works almost instantly. They stop and shove me up against a wall, but I let my knees buckle. Tom's face is twisted with darkness. The shadows shift over his tan skin, dipping into the sharp ridges of his cheekbones and jawline. His eyes are the color of ink. His mouth foams around the edges.

"Just get it over with," I breathe, letting my head drop forward in defeat.

"Get it over with?" he repeats as the other two go still behind him.

"I'm so tired. I haven't slept in months," I say, and my voice is garbled with the genuine exhaustion I feel. "I don't have it in me to fight you. I just want this to be over."

Tom's hands drop from my shoulders and I make myself slouch forward.

It's working.

And then I feel two hands wrap around my ankles.

Dang it.

He drags me down the hallway by my feet. I try to imagine myself as a sack of rocks, heavy and cumbersome, but it's no use. This year of struggling to survive has rendered me light as a feather, and my hands, head and torso drag along the tile floor with little effort from Tom.

I initiate plan B—flopping on the floor like a fish out of water, trying to free myself from his iron grip—when I notice something out of the corner of my eye.

From under one of the doors as we approach it comes a familiar bubbling and gurgling. It reaches its tendrils across the floor, creating a sticky slimy black puddle of ooze. I lift my head as Tom draws me closer to the ink-like liquid that seems to have a depraved mind of its own.

"No . . . ," I say, sure that Tom is dragging me into the ooze so that it can swallow me whole. Or pour down my throat and suffocate me. Or maybe strangle me with its creeping talons.

But that's not what happens.

Instead, Tom slips in the oil slick and falls backward.

"What the hell is this?" He tries to lift his hands, but they're stuck to the ground. Black liquid creeps up his arms like slugs. He screams and tries to free himself. "Help me, idiots!"

Tim and Tony are hunched over him in a flash. They try to lift him up, but they end up getting sucked into the mess as well.

I don't miss a beat.

I leap past them and over the puddle that is their prison. I run down the hallway toward the end where the slick of oil has formed an ant-like trail to the door marked *Boiler Room.* Maybe this supernatural sludge has not sided with the *Queen Anne* after all. Maybe it's been trying to show me something this whole time and I've just been too distracted by Bram and the *Queen Anne*'s bloodthirsty maneuvers.

I hear the guys coming, freed from the muck, realizing they've lost me. They don't waste any time.

Their shoes scuff the tile as they run to catch up with me.

I reach the door and yank it open, but once I'm inside, it's hard to see. I light the room with my phone flashlight. It looks old and long abandoned, filled with a complicated network of rusty pipes attached to vintage steam boilers. Modern ships are powered by diesel engines, so this room and its contents must be a preserved relic, probably from when the ship was first built and set sail in the early 1900s.

I whirl around to see if there's a bolt that locks the door.

I lock it just in time. A thud shakes the door. Then another. The handle jiggles and metals grind as the guys try everything in their power to get to me.

"Come out, come out, Emmaliiine," Tom calls through the door.

Bang bang bang bang. The metal shakes with the impact of his fist.

"You can't hide in there forever," he says. The other two cackle like this is the most fun they've ever had. "You can't hide from us."

I drop to the ground in a heap.

CHAPTER 19

KIKI

Hide-and-seek isn't easy when you're a human teenager and your opponent is the ghost of a dead child. We've played three rounds, and she's won every time. Finally, I call a time-out, and drop to the floor of the ship library.

Mary sits down beside me.

That's her name. She's seven, or I guess she was before she . . . died. And in the time we've been playing, I haven't seen another soul aboard the ship besides her. Whether that's because it's still early (I doubt it) or because the ship doesn't want me to see anyone else, I don't know. I use the time and solitude to get to know Mary because that's all I can do. And maybe if I'm lucky, Mary will like me enough to get me out of here and help my friends.

"I can't find my mama," she says, leaning forward. Her hair drips water onto my legs. I stare at the wet spots on my thighs and wonder how it works. "Can you help me find her?"

I don't have the heart to tell her that her mama is probably dead, so I just say, "I don't know where she is. I'm sorry."

Something that looks like hopelessness contorts her features. She doesn't cry—she just stares at the carpeted floor and traces the patterns with a tiny pale finger, leaving a wet trail behind. She doesn't say much else, or tell me how she ended up on this ship all alone and not alive. I'm not sure if she knows she's dead, and I really don't want to be the one to tell her.

I don't know how to help her. I'm not a mother and she's not a real child. Or maybe she is. I don't know how any of this works. I just know that as much as I want to get out of here and get back to the Ghost Gang, this once-upon-a-time person needs me.

And maybe I need her too.

I may not be a mother, but I *have* a mother. I try to think of all the times my mama was there for me. When I was six, I broke my arm at a roller-skating rink. They called her and she had to leave work early to come take me to the hospital. The doctors wrapped my arm up in a pink cast and afterward Mama took me to the mall and let me pick out any toy I wanted. She should have set a price limit because I managed to drag a giant stuffed unicorn twice my size to the car with my one good arm.

In junior high, when a group of girls at school was bullying me, Mama brought me to school the day after I told her I didn't want to go anymore. She marched right into the main office and demanded to speak to the principal. The principal called all the girls' moms and next thing I know they're all apologizing to me at recess and inviting me to a sleepover (um, no thanks).

When I started my first TikTok account, my mom did every dance I asked her to do with me. She taught me how to do my hair and that I'm capable of doing anything I set my mind to and that I should love myself exactly as I am.

In high school, when I started dating, she trusted me to make good choices and set my own boundaries—"You're the captain of your own life"—her only stipulation being *No Taylor Swift fans, please.*

She was always there for me, a fierce mama bear chasing all the hunters away.

Until Ghost Gang took center stage and I fell in love with a girl. She went through the motions of support, but the actual emotion was no longer there.

Detached.

I feel the word, a shock of electricity through my heart.

At first, I thought she was keeping her distance because she was dealing with her own drama. Trying to save her marriage, trying to be a good wife, churchgoer, *insert expectation here.* But even after Daddy left, she didn't flip the switch and turn back into the mama I always relied on.

The one who was obsessed with everything I did, wanted to hear about everything I love and bragged on me every chance she got.

She's stayed detached. Letting me do my thing, tossing the occasional side-eye, and now that she's with me on this boat, I can't stop wanting to force her to attach. I'm eighteen, but that doesn't suddenly mean I don't want my mama bear anymore.

Next to me, the little dead girl hiccups. I look up from where I've been staring at the floor and see that she's crying now. I touch my face and realize that I'm crying too.

I reach out to squeeze her hand and when she looks up at me with murky bloodshot eyes filled with tears, it doesn't matter that she's dead.

She's just a little girl who still needs her mama.

"We'll find her," I say softly. It's an empty promise, one I don't know if I can deliver on. I have no clue when this little girl died, but I do have a name and an age, and possibly a how. Maybe somebody on this ship can help me find out *something*.

Next to me, the elevator dings. Mary meets my eyes. The smallest curve of a genuine (and not at all scary) smile plays across her lips.

"Going down," she says, and disappears.

...

CHASE

I'm a real failure. As a producer, as a friend . . .

As a boyfriend.

Good producers don't lose members of their cast on location. Good producers have contingency plans for when things go wrong.

Good boyfriends don't let their girlfriends fade away or be possessed by ghosts that threaten to hurl her living body off a balcony.

And good friends don't leave anyone behind.

I made it to the turn in the hallway before I realized that Kiki was missing. I tried to retrace my steps, but I didn't see her and now I can't find her anywhere.

I swipe my phone open.

I search my apps for the *Queen Anne*'s prehistoric Boat Chat app. I open it and sigh. The last message is from me: *you and me, keeks?*

Just me, apparently. Because I can't even keep track of one other person in platform sandals that are *not* made for walking.

I type in the chat, hoping that wherever Kiki is, she's safe, still has her phone on her and will see the message.

Kiki, where r u?

I'm aimlessly wandering the hallways, feeling sorry for myself. I know it's a terrible habit, but I can't help it. I lost the pilot, now I can't find Kiki, and I'm afraid I might lose my girlfriend—my best friend—forever, to this creaky old ship.

We never should have come to this place. The whole thing was a huge mistake. To be stranded in the middle of the ocean on a haunted cruise ship? After what happened at the Hearst? I should have known better.

But *nooo*, it will be good for the channel. The channel that has done very little for us except bring in a measly income and attract a sleazy manager. Oh, and almost get us killed. Twice. Assuming we survive this cruise.

I round the corner and stop dead in my tracks.

A man is standing in front of me. It's the man from muster. Who appeared in one single frame in my video and was gone.

He's wearing a dark captain's uniform and is staring at an old black-and-white photo hanging on the wall.

I take a step toward him and the sliding doors open, the wind from outside blowing in, practically knocking me off my feet.

But the man's hair and clothes don't blow in the wind. He stands perfectly still in a uniform that looks like it's from another time. It's unnatural; he doesn't feel real. It almost feels like I'm hallucinating him. But I know I'm not hallucinating; I've spent enough time on the *Queen Anne* to know he's a ghost.

He walks through the open doors and onto the deck. I follow him outside. He gazes at the horizon, looking exactly like he did in the single frame I captured of him on my camera. There are a few other people walking along the deck and I wonder if they can see him too.

He squints into the distance.

"What are you looking for?" I ask him. For a second, I don't know if he can see me. Chrissy has often talked about residual hauntings. Maybe he's another casualty of this ship, doomed to live out his duty as captain over and over, for all eternity.

But then he surprises me. Without turning around, he simply says, "Icebergs."

"Icebergs?" I look out at the ocean. It's a perfectly sunny day in June. The water is clear and calm. Why would we have to worry about icebergs?

When I turn back to inquire further, he's gone. I look around me. Even though I'm pretty sure he was a ghost, it's still unnerving when they just *disappear.*

Except he didn't.

Through the sliding glass doors, I can see he's inside again, gazing once more at that old photo.

It's almost like there's something he wants me to see. Or at least something I should see—that I need to see. The pull is magnetic. The sliding doors open and I'm swept inside by a gust of wind.

I stand beside the captain to see what he's looking at.

It's a portrait of a man in uniform squinting at the camera, his hands crossed in front of him as he poses reluctantly for the camera. He's middle-aged with a white beard, and I realize he looks very much like the man standing beside me. With the uniform to match.

My eyes slide down to the label beneath the photo.

Captain Edward J. Smith

RMS Titanic

I audibly gasp and slap a hand over my mouth to silence my epiphany. The captain of the *Titanic* when she crashed into an iceberg and sank over one hundred years ago, killing more than fifteen hundred people . . . is standing right beside me.

In our research for this trip, we knew the *Queen Anne* was built by the same shipbuilding company as the *Titanic,* several years after the *Titanic* sank.

But what possible reason could there be for the captain of the *Titanic* to haunt the *Queen Anne*?

I remember watching the movie *Titanic* with my mom when I was a kid (it's one of her favorites). The captain went down with his ship, a dramatic moment at the end of the movie where water rushes into the wheelhouse as the captain wrestles with the wheel and his emotions, grappling with all the damage his ill-fated actions have caused.

I wonder if I'm just like him, and that's why I can see him.

He turns to me, head held high:

"Well, boys, you've done your duty and done it well. I ask no more of you. I release you. You know the rule of the sea. It's every man for himself now, and God bless you."

As soon as he says the last words—*God bless you*—I hear the sound of water rushing in. The swell of screams as passengers freeze to death and die. It's like an audio recording from a horror film playing inside my head. It's an overwhelming nightmare. I double over, covering my ears and closing my eyes to escape the sounds of suffering.

Eventually, the torture ends. I open my eyes one at a time, but the captain is gone—for good this time.

Panting, I stare at his photo on the wall and wish Chrissy were here to explain what just happened. I try to imagine what she'd say, how she'd explain it.

I think she'd say that when the captain died, his lost, guilty soul had nothing to attach itself to, so it floated across the Atlantic until it landed here, entrapped by the *Titanic*'s cursed sister ship, eternally sentenced to relive the most infamous maritime disaster—and failure—in history.

I think that the captain's last words—*It's every man for himself now*—were ultimately his downfall. He thought he had all the answers. He thought after a long string of good luck, nothing could go wrong. He ignored his comrades and made so many mistakes, all for ego and pride.

I refuse to go down like that. I will listen to my friends, accept failure as it comes and keep going.

But not too fast—if you sail too fast, you hit icebergs.

I decide in that moment that the Ghost Gang is most effective together, so I turn around to go back to the room and find them.

As I start up the stairs, an elevator dings behind me. On a hunch, I crane my neck to see who's inside.

The doors open, revealing Kiki. She stands there looking shaken but okay.

"Hi," she says with a timid little wave.

Relief floods my body and I crash into her, wrapping her in a tight hug.

CHAPTER 20

EMMA

I. Am. *Exhausted.*

I lie spread out on the ground, trying to catch my breath. My skin feels like paper stretched over bones made of Jell-O. All the adrenaline, lack of sleep and hardly any food is catching up to me.

The ship-possessed Paranormal Patrol guys are gone, or at least they've stopped pounding on the door. I don't try to leave just yet because I don't trust that they're actually gone. What if they're lying low, like ambush predators, waiting for me to emerge so they can pounce.

I won't survive another encounter with them, that I know for sure.

I close my eyes and start to drift. I can never close my eyes for long enough before I see *his* face. A face I've come to dread and hate with every fiber of my being.

Even though he's dead, I can still see him so clearly. That dark hair and sun-kissed skin. The dramatic arch of his eyebrows. His white teeth revealed by a sadistic ear-to-ear smile. So beautiful and yet so evil.

He steps toward me, towers over me. I'm tall for a girl, but he is *way* taller. An object in his black-gloved hand hits the light just right and gleams. A silver streak of metal. A knife. Always that knife.

Slowly he raises his knife-wielding hand. Above my head, above both our heads. It's an excruciating process that lasts just minutes, maybe only seconds, but feels like hours.

I wait for the blade to puncture my skin—the slippery slide of sharp and pointed metal through my soft delicate flesh. Over and over, until I fall to my knees, spikes of adrenaline protecting me from the pain for now, even as my body is incapacitated and dying. I will slip in my own blood as I try to stand and collapse, because my body knows that death is looming before my brain does. I'll gasp for air with punctured lungs, and that's when I'll wake up with healthy lungs ruptured by memories.

I brace myself for impact, but it never comes.

It always comes. This is different.

I summon the courage to open one eye. Bram's face is still there, but he's no longer smiling. My eyes trace up his arm, from the tentacle of darkness wrapped around his wrist to the inky black that drips down his forearm.

Another tentacle whips around his neck from behind, and his once-smiling face is now twisted into a grimace, bested by some unseen force.

Except I can see it. Standing even taller than Bram is the shadowy figure of a man. He's faceless and featureless, just a solid shadow that looms large over my enemy.

And the enemy of my enemy is my friend.

As they say.

Yet another tendril of oil wraps itself like a snake around

one of Bram's legs. And then his waist. He tries to free himself with his one good hand, but oil leaks between his fingers and he remains immobilized. The knife eventually falls from his grip with a clatter to the ground. I look down at it, stare at it. The villain of my many, many nightmares.

I don't think, I just reach down to pick the knife up. I hold it in my hands, examining the black handle and the shiny, almost iridescent blade.

I direct my gaze back up to Bram. His eyes are wide and bloodshot, his pupils constricted. He looks afraid. For the first time ever, *he's* afraid of *me*.

Behind him, the shadow man doesn't move. He looms. He waits.

This nightmare is mine.

I am in control—I always have been. For the past eight months, I've let Bram run amok in my mind, a memory I don't want to face that comes alive when my defenses drop low enough.

He's not here because of some connection to the *Queen Anne*.

He's here because of me.

And if that's true, then I can destroy him.

With a battle cry that is eight months of pure pent-up rage, I pull the knife back, winding up like a pitcher on a baseball field. About to throw one last good pitch to win the World Series.

The prey has become the predator.

I bury the knife up to its hilt in Bram's chest. Just below the ribs where I know it will do the most damage. I twist the knife in his guts. Twirling it for good measure and pleasure. I've never in my life wanted to kill somebody except for this man who is already dead.

I want to turn his intestines into jump ropes. To play hacky sack with his heart. To press cookie cutters into his brain and make Jell-O jigglers.

When I finally pull the knife out, blood splatters everywhere. I laugh maniacally as droplets hit my face. It's a wild thrilling experience, like a child playing in a sprinkler in hell.

I stab him again and again until he is slumped over in the tentacled arms of my ally. Drops of blood rain down on my face and I throw my head back, tossing my hair from side to side, my new shampoo the bodily fluids of my attacker.

I can't see the shadow man's face—he doesn't have one— but I can feel his pride in me. I don't know how I know it, but I can tell that my stab-happy revenge on Bram is satisfying his own desire for vengeance. Vengeance for freedom. It's a terrible thing, but oh, it feels so good.

The feeling is so visceral that I almost forget I'm in a dream.

My eyes begin to flutter as I awaken from the best sleep I've had in months.

Before I allow myself to wake up all the way, I search my drowsy mind for hints that Bram is still lurking there. The residue of his torment makes me feel grimy, but not ter-rorized. And I know that residue can be washed away with the help of the people who love me. (And okay, a trained professional.)

I'm startled by a drop of liquid on my forehead, and my eyelids peel open. For a second, I wonder if the dream was real. I touch my head and the drop feels heavy like blood, but stickier. I roll it between my fingers and lower my hand to examine it.

My fingers are smeared with a tarlike substance.

More droplets hit my body, and I look down and realize that I'm covered in it. It's raining inky-black liquid from the ceiling. Puddles of this oily unknown substance form, bubbling and boiling like hot lava on the cement floor. It seems to have a life of its own, oozing toward me, licking at my legs, and then ducking away.

I've seen it before, elsewhere on this ship, but now I'm not scared.

"Show me," I whisper, one hand on my knee as I push myself to my wobbly feet.

The puddle of ooze starts to move, crawling across the floor like an amoeba. It glides in a definitive direction.

And I follow it.

...

KIKI

Chase and I make a pit stop at the internet café on our way back to the room to find Emma, but she's not there. I get a sinking feeling deep in my gut, but Chase insists we have to stick together from now on.

He's shaking, but he doesn't tell me what he encountered down there on deck six. All I tell him is that I got stuck on deck seven, but I don't reveal to him *just how stuck.*

I don't know why, but I don't tell him about Mary either.

I'm not scared of her anymore, and in some weird way, I think I can see her for a reason. I plan to help her, and I plan to help *me,* too, in the process.

Chase has his key card out and ready to go and he all but busts down the door to the suite. Mama is still lying next to Chrissy, legs crossed, reading a magazine.

"How is she?" Chase says, rushing to Chrissy's side.

"'Bout the same," Billie says. "She's been groaning a little, talking in her sleep. I checked her for a fever, but the weird thing is, her temperature is low. What kind of disease gives you a reverse fever?"

Chase lies down next to Chrissy on the pullout bed.

"Nuh-uh," my mom says, trying to shoo Chase away.

"Mama," I say. "He's not trying to jump her bones; he's worried about her. Leave him alone. Besides, I need to talk to you."

"Talk?" Billie asks.

"Upstairs!" I say, pointing at the stairs.

"What could you need to talk to me about upstairs?" Mama groans and flips her magazine closed.

"Just come on," I say. And when she doesn't budge, I add, "Please."

The look in her eyes isn't quite mama bear, but it's close.

"Do not lose my place," she says, pointing to the *Essence* magazine facedown on top of the sheets. She raises an eyebrow that clearly implies something more in the realm of *no funny business.* Chase ignores her completely, touching Chrissy's face with the back of his hand and whispering something to her. Chrissy stirs briefly and Chase's fingers intertwine with hers.

I wish Emma were here. I hope she's okay.

I stuff down all my fears as Mama stomps barefoot up the stairs.

I march into her room, and she follows me inside. I shut the door behind us.

"What's going on?" she asks me, flopping down on the unmade bed. I sit next to her.

"I saw a ghost," I tell her, letting out a big breath I feel like I've been holding since I first joined the Ghost Gang.

Mama shakes her head. "Kiki, you know I don't mess with that stuff." She moves to stand, but I stop her by placing my hand over hers. Her eyes drop and her shoulders relax an inch.

"I know you don't, but I do. I have for years now—ever since Chrissy gave me that reading, told me Granny was proud of me and at peace." Granny was Mama's mother. A spitfire born in Louisiana who I know for a fact *did* mess with this stuff. She gave tarot readings to all the old ladies she played bridge with, and on important full moons she wasn't opposed to doing a spell or two for good fortune in the coming month.

"You never told me that," Mama says, her voice tight like she's holding back some painful emotion. "You and your granny were two peas in a pod."

She knows how important Granny was to me, and she wouldn't dare dismiss the impact that the experience of Chrissy communicating with her would have had.

"What we do with the Ghost Gang isn't just for a show. We're not messing around, we're helping. It affects more than just the living people who watch us," I say. Mama turns her hand over so she can take hold of mine. "I believe in this stuff. It matters to me—" I pause, inhaling sharply. "I wish you would see that and support me in it. Like you did for my

TikToks when I first got started, or when bullies came for me at school. I wish you would support me now, even with this stuff—with *anything* I'm telling you is truly important to me."

I don't say it outright, and I don't have to.

Emma. Me and Emma.

She bites down on her lower lip, nodding once. "You're not wrong."

It's not quite an apology, but Lawrence women are stubborn. This is close enough.

"This divorce thing with your daddy." She says *divorce*, not *separation*, which feels like progress in more ways than one. She's looking at the things that scare her instead of pretending they don't exist. "It's done a number on me. Made me feel like a useless, unwanted old bag of bones. I guess I thought that staying out of things—especially things I don't completely understand—was what everybody wanted."

Fresh tears spring into my eyes. I shake my head. "That's pretty silly of you," I say, followed by a hiccup from trying to keep my voice steady. "I'll always need your help."

Her face brightens and she grins, crinkling up her tear-streaked face. "Okay, Kitty-Keeks," she says, pulling out the nickname she gave me as a little girl but rarely uses anymore. She squeezes my hand one more time. "You saw a ghost. Tell me about it."

My skin tingles with hope. "A little girl," I say. "She died—I think she drowned—a long time ago."

Mama nods solemnly.

"Her name is Mary and she's seven," I explain. Emotion chokes my voice and I clear my throat so I can keep talking.

"She's been wandering around this ship all on her own for so long, looking for her mama."

My mom looks up and wipes tears from her bottom eyelids. She blows out a breath. "Poor thing." She blinks, huffs a puff of air and squeezes my hand. "What do you want me to do?"

"I don't know," I say, realizing that I don't have a plan. I just wanted to tell her, to share this part of my life with her. But maybe there's more to it than that. Maybe she can help me. "Maybe you can help me find her mom?"

"I bet that smarty-pants cruise director knows something," Mama says. "He's been working on this ship for forty years. Worked his way up to senior cruise director from his job as a bartender."

Did she say bartender? My jaw drops.

"What?" my mom says, taken aback by my look of shock and surprise. "You're impressed—"

"Thank you so much! I shoot forward, grabbing her around her waist and squeezing hard. She is jolted by the action, but not mad about it. She runs her hand over my head to the end of one of my braids and twists it with affection. "You're incredible, Billie Lawrence." I sit up, grinning. "Could you please ask him about drowning accidents that involve small children?" I give her a quick peck on the cheek and then run toward the door.

"Kiki," she calls after me. I pause, whirling around. Our eyes meet. "Your granny's not the only one who's proud of you." My shoulders square off with pride and I throw the door open.

"Chase!"

He doesn't budge. I fly down the stairs and say his name again.

"What?" Chase bolts upright, eyes heavy with sleep. He must have dozed off. His fingers are still entwined with Chrissy's, his cheeks a little damp like maybe he's been crying.

"Chase, it's him."

"Who?"

"The *bartender*."

"What bartender?" His eyes drift over to Chrissy in thought and then he remembers. "Ohhh, the bartender! What about him?"

"I think I know who he is," I say, smiling like the cat who got the cream, or maybe the Sherlock who solved the mystery. "And he's on the boat."

CHAPTER 21

CHRISSY

It's cold. I'm so cold.

I don't know where I am.

I don't know how I got here.

I'm scared.

This fear makes me feel small, like the little girl who saw the shadow man at the end of her bed and then watched her mother slowly slip away.

Small, like when I was older and slept under piles of blankets in the summer, even though it was over a hundred degrees outside, because I thought the blankets would protect me from the ghosts waiting in the corners of my room who liked to come out and play at night.

Tiny, like before I found the Ghost Gang and I had to carry the burden of the dead all by myself.

And even as the fear shrinks me down, I lose the feeling.

I drift, sliding through nothing.

I am slipping away from myself. Slipping away from . . . everything.

I wander through darkness, the only thing I see are flickers of light, crackles of energy that I follow. As I do, the feeling of fear slides away.

The feeling of self slips through my fingers and I let go.

Everything black. But still I exist.

Me, floating down a long corridor that never ends. There are a thousand doors, but they're all locked. For a while I try to twist the handles to open a door, any door, no matter where it leads.

Eventually, I stop trying to escape. I stop trying to do anything at all.

I don't know when it changes, but at some point, it does.

I find myself floating alone at sea, right on the surface. And, finally, for however long I'm there, a feeling of peace washes over me. Staring up at a sky full of billions of stars. The moon is a crescent, peeking out from behind a cloud. The air is cool and briny. The water is endless but at least it's alive.

And then it's back to black.

I feel so lost. So alone.

Where am I? Who am I? I don't even remember my own name.

Wait, yes I do. It's Elizabeth. Isn't it?

No, that's not it.

Is it?

I want to cry, but there are no tears here, wherever this is. No emotions, no feelings, no sensations.

Just emptiness.

The feeling of being suspended in time. In space. Nowhere to go, no one to touch or talk to or love. So many things to say, and no one to say them to. Questions that go unanswered forever. People you once cared for fade away to dull, barely there memories with no feelings attached. I'm the shell of who I once was. A distant faraway memory.

And the only thing to do here is just . . . be. Barely be.

Until.

I'm in that room again: 13340. I know it because it's written in the open diary I'm staring down at. I flip the pages to the front.

Elizabeth Walker. That's not my name. It's *her* name.

I'm someone else. Someone who's not supposed to be here.

I close my eyes, racking someone else's brain for a name she doesn't know.

The scene plays out the way it did before. I wander out into the hallway, wandering, wandering, until the hallway opens up into a lounge. A lovely man with kind eyes spots me and embraces me tenderly. He has champagne eyes and warm lips and I'm so scared of what is going to come next. What always comes next.

My killer arrives and there is an altercation between him and the man who truly loves me.

It was a short love, but it was a big love.

My feet carry me back down the hallway. No, no, no, not the room. My last breaths will be in that room, and then it will be all over. Darkness. Emptiness.

Again. And again and again and again.

I reenter the room. I don't want to be here, but I have no choice. The diary. Always back to the diary.

The last page, written moments ago, the ink barely dry.

Please God, don't make me marry this horrible man. I think he secretly hates me.

Ouch. I flip to another page and keep reading. This time, I catch a letter. *E.* I flip to another page. *E* this, and *E* that.

I turn back all the way to the beginning and that's when I find it.

A name.

Edwin William Pritchett III.

What a name. Whatever I do, I can't forget it.

I slam the diary shut just as *he* enters the room.

This time, when he wraps his hand around my neck, I am ready.

. . .

My eyes fly open, and I sit up so fast stars sparkle across my vision. I feel like my head is going to float off my shoulders, but at least I can feel.

"Chrissy." I say it out loud. I'm not Elizabeth, I'm Chrissy. It feels so good to remember that.

"Hon, are you okay?" It's Billie. Kiki's mom. Next to me. Looking confused and concerned.

I reach across the bed to take her hand. She looks stunned, but she doesn't pull away.

"Edwin William Pritchett III."

"Huh?" Billie says, making a face.

"I don't know how much time I have," I say, tears springing to my eyes at the thought. "You have to remember that name. You have to tell them."

"Tell who, baby? Do you need a doctor?" Billie asks, feeling my forehead.

"Edwin William Pritchett III," I say again, slower this time.

She has to remember. Please commit it to memory. "Please remember."

"Uh-huh, okay," she says.

"Say it," I beg her. "Please."

"Edward—"

"Edwin."

"Edwin William Pritchett III," Billie says. "He sounds like a man with some cheddar."

Relief floods my body, and that floaty sensation is back. I don't want to go back there, but I have no choice. I just hope I don't wind up stuck there forever.

"Tell them," I whisper. My brain is fuzzing out; the world is getting far away.

"Chrissy, you're scaring me," Billie says, squeezing my hand. I can barely feel it as my consciousness starts to slip from my body.

Hearing her say my name sounds like music to my ears.

It's the last thing I think about before I forget.

CHAPTER 22

CHASE

I'm clutching the cruise ship's daily itinerary like it's a map to buried treasure. I can't believe this hideous, dolphin-covered piece of computer paper contains a crucial piece of the puzzle to unlocking the mystery that will save my possibly dying girlfriend, but here we are.

BIG BUCKS BINGO at 4 p.m. in the Starlight Lounge
Hosted by your cruise director, John Brady

I want to *sprint* to the Starlight, but Kiki didn't pack shoes she can run in, and Emma's feet are way bigger than hers, so I am forcing myself to speedwalk instead.

I feel like I am crawling.

If John Brady knows something, *anything* about Elizabeth Walker, we'll know right away. What we *do* know for sure is that if John Brady is celebrating forty years working on the *Queen Anne*, then he must have been working when Elizabeth Walker was killed. Even if he wasn't involved, he must know *something*.

"What did Chrissy say about the bartender again?" Kiki asks, her voice shaky. I glance over and I can tell it's nerves and not the pace.

"Just that he knew something about Elizabeth's murder?" I pause, racking my brain. "I don't know, she didn't get to say all that much before she lost consciousness."

"If John Brady was a bartender at the same time that Elizabeth was a passenger on the *Queen Anne*"—Kiki pauses to catch her breath—"maybe he'll remember something. Do you really think we're that lucky?"

I don't feel lucky at all. I chew on my bottom lip.

"We're going to figure out what happened to Elizabeth. Then she'll let Chrissy go." Kiki reaches out to squeeze my shoulder. She's trying to comfort me, and it almost works. "We just have to follow our instincts, look at all the pieces we have on the table, and solve the puzzle."

Follow our Instincts. That isn't something we're used to doing without Chrissy. Having an intuitive psychic around usually makes our own gut instincts a lot less important. We're all pretty used to leaning on her for what to do next. And, with the exception of psycho killer Bram, she's never wrong.

It feels like we're running through a labyrinth; I feel lost without Chrissy.

We come to the Starlight Lounge doors, which stand open, welcoming people in for the bingo game about to start.

We see John Brady standing in front of a group of lounge tables where mostly senior-age passengers are squinting through reading glasses at the bingo cards in front of them.

John is bingo's boisterous and charismatic host, and from

this distance I try to take in his demeanor. Even in his sixties, he's got the vitality and spiritedness of a man in his forties, maybe younger. It's easy to see how he got this job.

If he did know Elizabeth way back when, I wonder how he feels about staying on board with her infamous ghost haunting the hallways?

What kind of person would want to pal around with the ghost of a person they once knew?

I take a deep breath.

I'm about to move when Kiki grabs my arm and tugs my shirtsleeve. One finger points, and she's staring firmly across the room. I follow her gaze to where it's fixed on Tina, who is speedwalking through the lounge with her phone in her hand and a flinty glare of annoyance screwing up her face. Her entourage of dumbasses isn't flanking her like usual.

"Wonder what that's about?" I ask.

"Maybe the ship ate them," Kiki says, smirking. But the levity doesn't last long. The *Queen Anne* isn't off our case yet. We don't know where Emma is or whether she's okay. And we don't have time to go look for her right now, either. "I hope they're okay," Kiki says, like it will clear her karmic cache.

As we pass the bingo tables, we notice Ruby, the middle-aged newlywed we met before the dining room tried to eat us. She's seated at one of the tables nearest to the front, close to John, and definitely making goo-goo eyes at him while she plays. I guess she has a thing for old dudes. Kiki waves vigorously at her, and Ruby looks up from scrutinizing her bingo card and waves back with matched enthusiasm.

"Going for a diagonal," she says, pointing at her card. She reveals a red lipstick stain on her teeth when she smiles.

"Good luck," Kiki says with a wink and a thumbs-up.

We make eye contact with John. He gives a fleeting *What now?* smile.

"Ghost Gang," he says, wiggling his fingers in a spooky way. He's trying to sound cool and upbeat and not annoyed by our interruption. He either remembers who we are because of the antics from earlier or because Billie has been chatting him up about the boat since he annoyed her at muster. "Your mom said she'd be joining in today. Where is she?"

"She couldn't make it," Kiki says, hands on her hips. "She's taking care of our sick friend. The one who saw the Lady in White floating in the water?"

John's eyes flicker. They're bright with surprise, but the rest of his face remains impassive.

"Is this for your little show?" he asks, glancing around for a camera rolling.

"Yes," I say, yanking out my phone and punching the Voice Memo app. I hit Record. "Is it okay if we ask you a few questions?"

He looks stunned. "What . . . do you want to know?" he asks.

"Come on! Get on with it!" a gravelly voice shouts from the back.

"Kids, I really don't have time for this—" John starts to say, but Kiki steps in front of the metal ball spinner.

"Don't worry, John, I gotchu," she whispers as she starts to crank the handle. She winks at me before turning to the eager, aging bingo lovers before her. A wooden ball falls from the cage and slides to the front. Kiki picks it up and reads the number. "Eighty-four!"

"Who are you?" asks a man with ear hair longer than his head hair.

"You wanna win the big bucks or not?" Kiki asks. Silence. "That's what I thought. Let's go, let's go!" She cranks furiously.

John and I slip off to the side of the lounge, well away from the bingo game. He motions to the bartender with a *Help me* look and the man quietly pours him a glass of whiskey and slides it over. John takes a swig and sets it down. He doesn't look at me.

"Were you working on the *Queen Anne* as a bartender in 1984?" I ask him.

A deep breath. He gulps down the rest of the whiskey and sets the glass down hard. He eyes the liquor bottles in the back. He wants another one, but he's on the clock.

Behind him, Ruby strolls up to the bar to order another drink. I can tell by the way she keeps looking over that she would like to get in on this tête-à-tête with the cruise director. Little does she know.

John motions for me to move over with his hand while Ruby orders an extra-*extra*-dirty martini from the bartender. I happily scoot away from her, shuddering at the implication of that extra *extra*.

"Were you working—"

"Shhh." John holds up a finger to his lips.

I square my jaw, but manage to lower my voice. "Were you working on the ship the week Elizabeth Walker was traveling with her fiancé?" I ask him. "When she . . . killed herself?" I don't say *allegedly* because I don't want to give too much away just yet.

John's hand tightens around his whiskey glass. It's subtle, but I clock it.

Wait, I remember something else Chrissy told me while she was going in and out of consciousness.

"Did you know Elizabeth was involved with a member of the crew?" I ask, sliding my phone closer so I can capture his answer.

His jaw tenses as he stares at his empty glass.

"She didn't kill herself, did she, John? Her fiancé found her in the arms of someone else." I step closer. He leans away, fuming, his eyes bulging as he watches his knuckles turn white against the whiskey glass. "Was it you, Mr. Brady? Were you the man who got her killed?"

"*Bingo!*" someone screams from across the room.

"That's enough," he says through gritted teeth. He flicks his eyes over my head, anxious and angry. "Elizabeth Walker died by suicide. She was trapped in a loveless engagement with no way out. She had plans to do something big with her life—she wanted to be a writer, an artist—but that was all over. As soon as the boat docked in America, her life as she dreamed it would be over. . . ." His eyes are shiny with tears.

I search his face, something catching in my chest. "You did know her. You loved her."

"Barely knew her." He scrubs a hand roughly over his face. "It was just a few days—that's all."

"If you cared about her, wouldn't you want to find out what really happened to her?" John meets my eyes for the first time since we started talking. I know I'm onto something. "Wouldn't you want to help her move on from this place?"

His eyes sparkle with emotion and . . . something else. Curiosity?

He wants to believe she's still here. He's been looking for her all this time. I know it.

"Come with us," I say. I motion to Kiki that it's time to go. She's surrounded by, and entertaining, delighted bingo players. She really does have a way with crowds.

"Where are we going?" John asks me. Ruby looks over at us nosily, no doubt wishing she could be the one to whisk John away. Gross. I know women love a man in uniform, but she's old and married, so it gives me the creeps.

Kiki pries herself away from her retirement home fan club to come join us at the bar.

"We're going to take you to see Elizabeth," I tell John.

His eyes open wide.

...

EMMA

The ceiling is shrinking, getting lower and lower as I follow the black sludge through the labyrinth of pipes and corridors. It slithers like a snake, slipping over the pipes and twisting around behind me. Every time it gets close, I hear it hiss, a sound that reminds me of the desert sidewinders I saw once when I went camping with my Brownie troop. Before I gave up Brownies, and outdoorsy activities altogether.

Even though it reminds me of a venomous snake, I think it's trying to help me. To guide me somewhere important.

I have to get down on all fours to crawl through this narrow passage, and as I do the black oily sludge covers my hands, leaving a slime trail on my skin. It doesn't hurt; it tickles, but it doesn't seep into my skin. It's leading me, and I'm not afraid to follow it.

My skeptical-ass self may just have become a believer.

At least where this mysterious sentient ooze is concerned.

I reach a section where there are grates in the floor, probably for venting heat back when the boiler room was functional and vital. I drop onto my stomach, expecting the sludge snake to slide around the grates and continue on, but instead it slithers over the slats and disappears.

I scoot forward in an army crawl until I'm on the grate where the mystery goo vanished. I can't see into the deep darkness, so I work one arm back to the pocket of my jeans where I stuck my phone. I work it free and pull it up carefully to position it above the grate. My thumb taps the flashlight icon and it illuminates the space.

A pair of glowing red eyes stares back at me.

My mouth opens into a scream that no living person will ever hear.

CHAPTER 23

KIKI

John Brady is quiet as we make our way back to the room. What he's not saying is showing up on his face, in his body language. I can't hear his thoughts or anything—not like Chrissy can sometimes—but I can feel my own senses, my intuition pushing my brain into a different gear.

I often wonder if my ability to read people is a lot like having a sixth sense.

"It's okay if you're scared," I say. He tucks his hands in his pockets.

"This wasn't exactly in the job description," he replies, then blushes. "But then I guess neither was what happened with Lizzie."

Chase has gotten ahead of us. He's fully freaking out, as if his brain is listening to the ticktock of a clock counting down to the end of Chrissy's existence. He's barreling forward on all cylinders. I'm scared for Chrissy, *beyond* scared, and if I stopped for even half a step, I worry that my mind would spiral into its own freak-out over where my girlfriend is, too.

But I won't let it do that. I can't.

Staying focused on bringing closure to this mystery is the only thing I can do right now to help *both* of them.

And myself, too.

"I used to walk down this hallway all the time, where people swear they saw her. . . ." John's eyes get a sad faraway look. "Sometimes I'll make a martini with a twist of lemon and leave it out, hoping—" John shakes his head before he can finish the thought. "Not even a glimpse." Now that he's talking he doesn't seem to be able to stop. "She had this laugh that sounded like music. I hear it when I'm tired, drifting off to sleep, but then lose it again just as fast."

"You never stopped loving her, did you?" I ask. "Even though you only knew her for a few days."

"Time isn't the only thing that decides how well you know somebody." His voice takes on a new melancholic tone. "She got me. I got her. No one else has ever come close."

Chase opens the room door ahead of us. "Can you two hurry up?" Normally, I'd throttle him for taking that kind of jackass authoritative tone. But today, I decide to let it go. Just this once.

John and I file in behind him, and I notice out of the corner of my eye that John's brow is sweaty. He smooths the front of his uniform jacket with palms that are probably also nervous and sweaty.

Mama is pacing back and forth behind the couch, nursing a cup of coffee with a worried expression screwing up her whole face. Her brows are cinched up. Her lips move, and she's murmuring something to herself (probably a prayer). Her eyes look a little bloodshot from lack of sleep.

When she sees John, she stops dead.

"John, what are you doing here?" She nearly drops her

coffee cup. She shoots me a glare and tries to feign a smile at the same time. "Is everything okay?"

"How's she doing?" Chase asks, dropping down to his knees on the carpet and pressing the back of his hand to Chrissy's pale-as-a-corpse forehead.

Mama is still staring at John, who is staring at the ghostly white form of my best friend.

"She's been muttering in her sleep, her temperature is scary low," Mama says. "But she woke up for a second, which is good." She looks down at Chrissy again. "But she still feels like a damn refrigerator. Ice cold."

Chase's eyes, wide and hopeful, fly up from Chrissy's face. "Did she say anything when she woke up?"

"She did, hold on," Mama says, still side-eyeing John with confusion and interest. "I wrote it down." She walks over to the desk and grabs the notepad that comes with the room. "A name, she said it was important."

Our eyes are fixed on Mama. This news is good for more than one reason. A name could be a clue, but also if Chrissy broke out of this possession coma long enough to say something, then there's hope she can break out completely.

"Edwin William Pritchett III."

John lets out a gasp and drops into the chair across from the couch. His face falls into his hands.

"Does that name mean something to you, Mr. Brady?" Chase asks with so much hope in his voice.

John takes what feels like hours to lift his face from his hands. When he does, his eyes are watery and tears streak down his cheeks.

"I didn't want to believe she'd do this—could do it. I'm

sorry for your friend, but that name does mean something to me. It meant something awful to Lizzie." He flicks his eyes from Chase to me, over to Mama, and finally rests them on Chrissy. "She's really in there somehow."

"She's possessing my girlfriend and it's killing her," Chase says, shooting up from his position next to Chrissy. He isn't as moved by this emotional reunion as I am. "Tell us what happened the night Elizabeth died so we can fix this."

"Lizzie," John whispers. "It was suicide. It was, they swore it. They said there was a note in her diary."

"Her diary?" I ask. "This is the first we've heard of a diary."

"As far as I know they gave it to *him* after the investigation."

"Edwin William Pritchett III?"

"Her fiancé."

Her murderer.

...

CHRISSY

I never thought there would be a white light or anything when I died.

I hoped for some sense of finality—like a coming to acceptance after a long life lived with purpose.

This sea of glassy water stretching for miles, forever, isn't what I wanted. There's nothing final about floating into nothing or nowhere.

Death beneath waves without ever really doing anything much with the life I'd been given wasn't the way I expected to go out.

The cold isn't the worst part, either.

It's the loneliness.

Lizzie.

I hear the name. My name. The way my one true love once said it.

Chrissy.

Somewhere deep in the pit of my untethered soul I hear another voice. Cool and bright, asking me to let her go.

●●●

CHASE

The knock on the door startles all of us.

"Oh my God, maybe it's Emma!" Kiki exclaims, not thinking about how she's taken the Lord's name in vain or worried about the look of fire and brimstone her mom gives her because of it as she runs to answer the door. She yanks it open.

Not. Emma.

Ruby stands on the other side of the door, looking frazzled and holding a small black leather book.

"Can I come in?" she asks, her accent strong and unrestrained. She doesn't wait for a response from Kiki before she steps across the threshold and walks right into the middle of our mess.

Billie is giving her a look that could melt Antarctica. John jumps to his feet, clearly torn between his duty as the senior cruise director and his ties to the mystery unfolding inside my girlfriend's soul.

Now, there's a sentence I never expected to think.

"How did you know where we were staying?" Kiki asks.

"Bribe the right people; it wasn't hard." Ruby shrugs. "I shouldn't have been eavesdropping in the Starlight, so I apologize." She scrunches her nose like a chipmunk. "But I was. And I heard what you said about the Lady in White—Elizabeth Walker, is it?—and I think I have something you'll want to see."

My fingers are itching to pull out my phone and hit Record. Billie raises one arm, iPhone poised to film. I never would have expected her to join the Ghost Gang crew, but I'm so glad she is.

For now anyway.

Ruby sighs deep and thrusts the small leather book in her hands toward Kiki.

"Tripp carries this thing with him everywhere, and for the most part it's never bothered me. Some memento he can't part with from a past romance"—she screws up her face and rolls her eyes—"like I'm threatened. But I love a good ghost story, and when I heard you mention the Lady in White . . ."

Kiki opens the book to the first page.

" 'This diary is the property of Elizabeth Walker,' " she reads out loud. She flips through. "These entries are dated 1984."

"Why does he have this?" I ask, looking over Kiki's shoulder at the faded ink.

"Edwin William Pritchett III," John says through gritted teeth.

"Tripp is a nickname for the third-generation namesake," Ruby says, her accent even thicker with unguarded emotion. "When I met him he asked me to call him Tripp, but when he was younger, he must have gone by Eddie."

Chrissy lets out a guttural scream and shoots straight up,

back as stiff as a board. Her eyelids flutter rapidly as her body starts to shake. Her shoulders shudder, her teeth chatter, her head swivels left and right, left and right.

The diary leaps out of Kiki's grip and opens to an entry dated November 3, 1984.

My Dearest Eddie—I'm sorry. I'm done. I can't go on. Love, Liz

Chrissy stands up on wobbly legs and walks across the room to where the diary lies on the ground. She snatchs it up, and I watch as she smooths her pale hand over the worn leather binding. The spine cracks as she slowly peels the binding open.

"Not. Mine." The words come from Chrissy's lips, but the voice does *not* belong to my girlfriend.

In one swoop, she rips the pages out of the diary.

And falls toward the floor as if she's been liquefied. Ruby screeches, backing away as I rush over to catch Chrissy before she hits the floor. Her head falls back as though heavy, her lips open. Tears streak her cheeks even though she's not making a sound and not moving like she's crying.

"Chrissy, wake up, please." I kiss her frozen forehead before pulling her to my chest as close as I can. "Please stay with us. With me. Please."

"What the hell was that?" Ruby is asking, her voice high-pitched with panic.

"She's possessed," Billie says, and I glance up. Her eyes are wide with shock, her voice shaky, but she's still filming. She caught the whole thing on camera.

"Elizabeth wants us to bring justice to her death," Kiki says, slamming the diary shut.

I'm not really paying attention to anything except Chrissy. Her breathing is shallow, and if she was cold before, she's gone full hypothermic now. I press my forehead against hers. I have to believe she's still in there fighting.

"Where did John Brady go?" Billie asks, breaking my focus.

Behind us, the door to our suite slams shut. John is gone.

In all the commotion he must have slipped out without any of us noticing. My eyes trail up to Kiki's.

"You don't think he'd go after that Tripp guy, do you?" she asks me.

"To avenge the woman he loved?" I reply, feeling Chrissy's weight in my arms and knowing what my answer would be. "Hell yeah."

Kiki turns to Ruby, who is sheet white and staring at Chrissy in my arms. She probably thought this was all just juicy gossip; she had no idea what she was getting herself into. Kiki snaps to get her attention and it works. Ruby jolts, blinking rapidly to try to focus.

"Where is Tripp now?" Kiki asks.

"He was at the blackjack table in the casino last I saw. Planned to be there most of the day. Most of the trip, actually." She rolls her eyes as if she didn't just come from *BIG BUCKS BINGO.*

"Come on," Kiki says.

"You think he's going to hurt Tripp?" Ruby sounds sad despite the fact that she just learned her husband might be, and mostly likely was, the one responsible for a woman's death.

"I hope not," Kiki replies with a shrug. "But only because I don't want something bad to happen to Mr. Brady." She looks at me. "Chase, Mama can stay with her."

My arms tightens around Chrissy, drawing her closer. What if this doesn't work and this is the last time I get to hold her alive? Kiki can read me, and I can tell that she's empathetic. But she's also not about to go track down a cold-case killer with his current wife as her only backup.

Billie swoops in and places one hand over mine.

"I'll talk to her the whole time. She knows you're trying to help her, and she'll keep fighting, I know it." Her warm brown eyes are soft and comforting. She lifts her lips into a sad smile. "You know what you need to do. Go do it."

I let Billie take Chrissy from my arms.

"Let's finish this thing."

CHAPTER 24

EMMA

I may have left the Brownies behind, but at least I still carry a pocketknife with me wherever I go. I untwist the final screw on the grate and tug it loose. It's heavy and hard to move on my own, especially now that I'm even more exhausted than before. And that's saying something.

I manage to shove the grate over by increments until there's enough space for me to climb through, and I carefully lower myself down, putting as little weight as possible on my twisted ankle. Fortunately, the space is small, and like the rest of this area, has a low ceiling. I should be able to climb out, even if I can only use my right leg.

Using my phone flashlight again, I shine the light in the direction where I saw those two red eyes. Now that I'm down here, I can see more details. The eyes aren't actually glowing red—that must have been a trick of the light—they are painted in black and blue. The curves of the headdress slope into the shoulders and down the length of the rest of his body, which is painted in intricate detail. His feet disappear behind a wall that has a small crawl space beside it. These are literally the *bowels of the boat.*

Chase would be giddy.

What I know about King Rameses VIII is slim to nada. I did a slow Google search before I passed out watching Chrissy last night. The pages weren't loading, but Candy Crush still worked. So I picked that instead.

I take a few photos and film the painted sarcophagus from a few different angles. I'll have to figure out how to get the hell out of here and keep track of how to get back so I can lead the *Queen Anne's* security team to this location. Hopefully they don't throw me in the brig for the breaking and entering of an unauthorized area of the ship.

I reach above to wrap my fingers around the ledge and pull myself up, when someone grabs my hands, yanking so hard it twists my fingers. I squirm against the rough grip, but it's no use. I'm pulled easily out from the opening.

Tom's breath is hot on my cheek. His grin turns my stomach to lead.

"Found you," he says with a maniacal laugh. I spit in his face and he lurches up, banging his head against a pipe. I crawl around him, looking for the easiest path out to where I can run. It's not far, and I am smaller than he is and more agile, even with my injury. I scoot over the ground, using my knees to propel myself into the open space.

I shoot to my feet, ignoring the slice of pain in my left ankle. I'll have to run as fast as I can if I want to escape.

I launch out.

Don't look back, Emma.

The shooting pain in my ankle forces me to let out a guttural scream, but I don't stop moving. I can't. Because I can hear him behind me. The sound of his snakeskin boots clapping against the floor rattles like a herd of cattle chasing me. I round the corner and I'm back where I started.

Only now, the formerly locked door hangs open.

I sigh with relief. I don't know where the other dummies are and I don't care. I can get back to the main part of the ship through that door.

I can lead my friends down here to where the sarcophagus is hidden.

There's light at the end of this dark dank tunnel.

The door slams shut in front of me, blocking my way. "No!" I scream, gripping the handle and yanking.

But it won't do any good, and I know it.

Tom lets out a howl behind me like he's a wolf on the hunt and I'm his wounded prey. But I will never be anyone's prey again. I whirl, looking him dead in the eyes.

"You don't scare me."

He stutters to a halt, but his expression is still all murderous glee. He's a big brawny dude. Bigger than Bram. But somewhere inside him is a guy from Texas who plays football and makes paranormal TV for the masses. He's not a real killer.

The real killer is the ship that has control of him.

"You're nothing without *that*," I say, pointing behind Tom, to where the sarcophagus is hidden. The ship knows who this insult is for. I can feel it. "King Rameses VIII's curse is giving you all your power. Without him, you're nothing but a floating hollow pile of metal and screws. You know it, he knows it."

Tom's shoulders droop.

Bruised ego hurts when you think you're invincible.

"The jig is up," I say. "You're all done here. Once I show security where the stolen sarcophagus is hidden, they'll take it away, back to its home where it belongs. The curse will be lifted, and your reign of terror will be over."

Tom's face screws up, but not with anger this time. I see a glimmer of something that looks a lot like confusion pass over his face, and when he blinks his eyes, they've started to return to their normal shade of blue.

We won't have much time. Whatever game the ship wants to play with us next will happen fast.

My hand curls around the door handle.

Just as I expected.

Unlocked.

The *Queen Anne* thought she had me cornered, and so she left my escape route unguarded.

I yank down on the handle and the door swings wide open. I don't wait for Tom to figure out what's going on. I run into the hallway and a scream of pain rips from my throat. My knee nearly buckles, but I will every ounce of adrenaline in my body into keeping that leg moving.

No matter what I see, I can't stop. Not even if every undead being who met their gruesome end comes out of the walls to attack me. Not even if my own grandmother, who died ten years ago, hobbles into my path and asks for a hug.

I have to climb those stairs.

I will climb those stairs.

Salvation is at the top of those many, many stairs.

Just as I reach them, Tom screams bloody murder behind me. He stumbles and the sound of a bone cracking fills the air. The *Queen Anne* wants me to hear it.

But I won't stop climbing.

One of the crew who must have died belowdecks stands at the top of the stairs. Skin charred and black, gums and teeth exposed in all their rotted glory.

But I don't blink.

I climb toward him, each step painful, but my head is held high. He leers, with bulging eyes devoured by festering wounds, his tongue dangling from his mouth bloody and half-bitten off. I press by him, eyes forward—eyes on the prize.

The door that leads to the passenger-friendly parts of the ship flies open, and Tina stands silhouetted against the light.

Light chases all the darkness away.

I drop to a heap in the stairwell and she rushes down to me. Her long blond hair whips over her shoulder. She smells like expensive perfume.

"You're filthy," she says. "What the hell happened to you?"

"How did you know to come here?" I ask her.

"I may not be a psychic freak or whatever your goth girl is, but I'm smart. I tracked down Tim and Toby—they were sleeping off a hangover in the lounge. They didn't know where Tom was, but they did remember some weird details about a boiler room. I batted my eyelashes at the front desk, and *voilà!*"

She grins with a row of perfect white teeth.

"I didn't know you'd be here." She adds this last part with a scowl.

I'll tell her, I will. All of it. And hopefully she'll care enough to help me even though I'm pretty sure her friend needs to get to the infirmary more than I do. My eyes trail up to hers. Pretty blue, though without makeup her lashes are baby blonde and wispy.

"You wanna help the Ghost Gang solve a centuries-old mystery?"

Her brow furrows, but her lips curl up. "Not really—but I'm listening."

"I found something down there," I say. "Something big."

Tina crosses her arms over her chest. "Fine, but only if we can share the glory fifty-fifty."

"*You* can have *all* the glory." I let out a deep, exhausted-to-the-core exhale. "I just want to get him home."

CHAPTER 25

KIKI

The casino is small but loud with color—red and gold and royal-blue hues. There are a few rows of slot machines along the walls and several blackjack tables in the center of the room.

Chase and I are only eighteen—not old enough to drink or gamble.

Normally, the crew would ask us to show them some ID or simply just yell at us to get out. But right now, all eyeballs in the room are glued to the center blackjack table, where their beloved senior cruise director has an elderly man with a cane in a choke hold.

"Security!" Tripp's voice is a rasp with John Brady's hands around his neck.

I see one of the bartenders behind the bar hesitantly pick up a phone, nervously twisting the cord between his fingers as he calls for backup.

"You gutter sludge," John Brady says. "You have some nerve showing up here again after what you did."

John is a big man and powerful, even in his sixties. No

one dares approach the two men or break up the fight; they're afraid they might end up with their face smashed in too. Even from where I'm standing I can see the shadow of a black bruise forming on one of Tripp's drooping cheeks.

Having opted to wait for an elevator because of her bad knees, Ruby finally catches up to us. "What's going on?" she asks, panting, but I don't answer because the scene speaks for itself. It's pretty plain to see—John Brady is about to kill Tripp Pritchett.

Tripp's hands are balled into fists, his cane clutched in one, as his face turns redder and redder. I can't tell if it's because he's angry or can't breathe.

It's you, is what I think Tripp says to him, his voice so soft and vitriolic I can only read his sneering lips.

And then Edwin William Pritchett III spits in John Brady's face.

We all gasp, like spectators at a boxing match. Beside me, Chase tenses. Wrapping one hand around my arm with anxiety, he leans into me.

"We have to do something," he whispers.

"Be my guest," I say, Vanna White–ing my arm at the scene before us, rolling out the bloody red carpet.

John Brady calmly sets Tripp down and wipes what I'm sure is cigar-scented spit off his face. He unbuttons and then rolls up his shirtsleeves. We all prepare for the worst, while Tripp grabs frantically for his cane, which has fallen to the floor.

"This one's for Lizzie," John says, winding back.

Crack.

Tripp crumples in a heap to the floor, clutching his jaw.

Everyone else gasps, and a few weaker-stomached spectators scream.

"Yeah, get him!" I cheer. Chase cuts me a look, and I shrug.

"Tripp!" Ruby screams, pushing past me and Chase.

I hear the static of a walkie-talkie behind us. A low, disgruntled voice says, "Yeah, we got him."

I tug at Chase's sleeve and he turns around to look. Once it registers what's going on, he steps in front of the two large men. They're wearing black jackets that say SECURITY in all caps on the back.

"Wait," Chase says, putting his hands out. "That man killed a woman on board this ship over thirty years ago. We have proof."

We do?

"Get out of the way, kids," one of the men says, pushing Chase and me out of the way. "You two shouldn't be in here."

What happens next is a blur.

Tripp is lying on the floor gripping his cane while John Brady looms over him, ready to launch another attack. But before John can throw another blow, a loud *boom* reverberates through the room, cutting through the noise of the jangly music from the slot machines.

John Brady stumbles backward.

My hand flies to my mouth as I watch red spread across his stark white shirt.

"John!" I scream when I realize what's happening. One of the security guards catches him and gently lowers him to the ground. He calls for medical backup on his walkie.

Across from us, security wrestles Tripp's cane away from

him. It's then that I see Tripp's cane is actually a gun disguised as a walking cane. I guess no one would have suspected that this wizened old man who can barely walk had murderous intentions.

"Hold on, John," I whisper, crouching beside him. Chase takes off his hoodie and uses it to apply pressure to the wound. John is losing color fast.

Another two security guards arrive on the scene and seize Tripp—aka Edwin William Pritchett III—and zip-tie his hands behind his back, then pull him to his unsteady feet and drag him away.

As he walks away, Tripp turns and locks ice-cold blue eyes with me.

I shudder.

I wonder if those were the last eyes Elizabeth saw before she hit the water. The thought churns in my gut like ocean waves during a storm surge.

"Is he breathing?" I ask Chase. Chase looks down at the fallen cruise director whose chest he's been applying continuous pressure. John's face grows more pallid and clammier by the second, but there's still movement beneath his eyelids.

"I think so," he says. "Hey, can we get a doctor in here? This man is dying."

"A doctor is on the way," the security guard says to us.

John Brady's eyes crack open into slits. They're unfocused, staring past us, but he's still alive.

"Lady in White," he breathes, his voice soft and gravelly. A weak smile tugs at his lips.

Chase and I look at each other, eyebrows knitted together in confusion.

"John," comes a familiar and yet somehow unrecognizable voice behind us.

We both startle and spin around to look. Chase leaps to his feet in shock.

It's Chrissy.

She smiles sweetly, lovingly down at the dying man on the ground, but it's not Chrissy's smile. No, this is not Chrissy.

It's Elizabeth.

...

CHASE

Chrissy.

She's awake! She's alive! She's okay!

I reach out to her for a hug, but something stops me. Her eyes are different, distant. The faraway look gives the color of her irises a tinge of green and yellow. Or are they a different color altogether? The way they look, it's like there's someone else peering through her eyes. Not our Chrissy.

My fingers curl into my palms so hard, I'm sure I've broken skin.

John tries to sit up, but Kiki stops him, pressing his shoulders back down.

"You have to stay down," she says. "Help is on the way. Or so they say."

Kiki looks up at me, pleading. I could give a crap right now if John lives or dies—what the hell is wrong with Chrissy?

"I'm here, John." It's Chrissy's mouth but someone else's voice. A voice that sounds distorted, almost like an echo.

"Where's Chrissy?" I ask, unable to contain myself.

Not-Chrissy ignores me and falls to her knees beside John. What is she doing?

"Elizabeth." John's voice is so small it's almost inaudible. He reaches up a hand, grasping at the air. "Lizzie."

Chrissy—Elizabeth—wraps both her hands around his. She holds his hand to her cheek. Tears fill her eyes and trickle down her cheeks.

I'm. Going. To. Explode.

"I'm here," she whispers. "I've been here. Waiting. For you."

"I've looked . . . everywhere," John says, straining for breath, for words.

"Me too," she says. "I'm here now. We're here now."

In a moment that feels like an eternity, John draws in one last rattling breath—and doesn't breathe out again.

Kiki checks his pulse and then looks up at me, tears streaking down her face. "He's gone."

Chrissy slumps over John's body. I catch her by the shoulders and push her back, stepping over John so I can cradle her against me.

I drag her away as the ship paramedics run up, performing last-ditch attempts at CPR on John Brady. I want to tell them he's gone for good, in a happy place with the person he loves.

I hope my person is okay.

I look down at Chrissy in my arms. My hand brushes her cheek and it's not as cold as I remember. I notice color coming back into her face.

When her eyes finally open, they're her eyes, the color of the ocean somewhere warm and tropical. Maybe somewhere we'll go on our next cruise (not).

"Hi," she says, a sad smile spreading slowly across her face.

"Hi," I say. A single tear floats down my cheek.

"You did it," she whispers, reaching up to catch the tear with the back of her hand. I grab her hand and touch it to my lips. I breathe her in, filled with both a sadness and a relief so profound I'm afraid I'll collapse from exhaustion right here on this hideous blood-soaked casino carpet.

"Uh, *we* did it," I say. "Like always."

She Is Done
PRESENT

He is gone.

They took him out of my boiler room, carefully packing him up and carrying him across the gangway.

Soon he will be at home and at peace again, among his ancestors and his gods and with his people.

It must be nice to have a place to belong.

His curse that was once my everything is lifted.

I don't know who or what I am without it.

A powerless pile of buoyant metal.

Once home to hundreds of trapped spirits—now, only one.

I am trapped, alone and empty.

But I will watch them dance and eat and drink and make love and find their joy.

And I will wonder what it's like . . .

To be hungry for life.

CHAPTER 26

CHRISSY

John Brady is declared dead. They covered him up with a sheet and cleared us out of the casino so they could properly investigate the crime scene.

The easiest part of being a psychic medium is coping with death. I know that John is with his beloved, and even though it's a bittersweet victory, it's a little sweeter knowing that all those years of waiting paid off for both of them.

Security led us down to the brig so they could ask us a few questions before allowing us to return to our room.

Even though I've been unconscious for the past forty-eight hours, I'm so exhausted it feels like I've run four marathons in a row. And honestly, maybe I have. There's no telling how many times I floated down that hallway, fled from Elizabeth's murderous fiancé or fought for my life as I fell thirteen stories to Elizabeth's untimely death on impact with the ocean.

We head back to the room, and Chase grips my hand tightly

the whole way. He won't let go, not even for a second. I think I scared the living hell out of him, but I'm here now and I'm okay.

Not gonna lie, I don't mind the PDA right now.

Kiki is quiet all the way to our room. She's happy to have me back, but we still don't know where Emma is. Cruise ship protocol is to wait twenty-four hours before officially declaring someone a missing person. I tell Kiki we'll check our room before heading out to search for Emma. Maybe my psychic Spidey-sense has been weakened by the events of the past few days, but I still think I'll feel it if something is very wrong.

Kiki is not convinced.

When we enter the room, Emma is not there, but Billie is, beaming with joy.

"I found it," she says, holding up a tiny slip of paper.

We're all weary and exhausted, so we struggle to match her euphoria. She doesn't know yet what's happened to John Brady, but I can tell we're going to break the news to her later.

Billie hands Kiki the paper.

"Mary Anne Roberts, 1951," Kiki reads. "Eleanor Roberts, 1992?" She looks at her mom, who is smiling so wide it's almost blinding. Billie's eyebrows lift, willing Kiki to connect the dots. Kiki squints at the paper.

And then it dawns on her.

"Is this . . . ?" Kiki looks at her mom again, who's nodding now. "Mary?"

Billie nods and Kiki starts to jump up and down. They jump up and down together.

Chase and I look at each other, not understanding.

"How did you find this?" Kiki asks.

"A little Billie Lawrence magic." Billie shrugs and then rubs her fingers together. "And a tenner. They pulled some records. Just for me!"

"We have to find her mom," Kiki says. "We have to reunite them!" The image of a little girl pops into my brain like a daisy, and I realize she must be who they're talking about.

"Oh, honey." Billie's light dims temporarily. She points to the paper where a date is written. "Nineteen ninety-two. That's the year she died."

"Oh," Kiki says, deflated.

I put a hand on Kiki's shoulder and hold out my other hand for the paper. "Now that we have a name and a year, I might be able to do a little ceremony. To reunite them in death."

Kiki's eyes light up. "You can do that?"

"I can try," I say. I am tired all the way through my body to my soul, but this is what I do. And seeing Kiki's face bright with hope injects energy into my veins.

"No freakin' séances until we all sleep," Chase orders. He tugs me in just a hair, his fingers tight.

I glance over at Billie, who is counting us. Her face contorts in confusion.

"Where's your girlfriend?" Billie looks directly at Kiki. My senses are definitely dulled, but nothing can keep Kiki Lawrence's joy from reaching me. Her mom calling Emma that all-important word lights a fire in her heart.

"We can't sleep until we find my *girlfriend*," Kiki says, turning her beaming face toward Chase to glare flaming daggers at him.

Right on cue, the stateroom door busts open and there stands Emmaline Thomas, covered head to toe in greasy black goo.

Kiki shrieks and goes to throw her arms around Emma but stops short, noticing the thick layer of slime coating Emma's entire body.

"What happened to you?" Kiki asks with a mix of elation at seeing her boo and disgust that she's covered in ooze.

"Guys, I think I just broke a curse," Emma says before she tackles her girlfriend to the ground.

···

The rest of the trip is semirelaxing. Minus the part where our cruise director is dead and our dinner tablemate is in cruise ship jail.

The *Queen Anne* leaves us alone (for the most part). I occasionally see a shadow out of the corner of my eye or hear the odd disembodied whisper, but overall it's smooth sailing.

Pun deeply intended.

Emma and Tina (who apparently helped solve the mystery) lead us, a few members of the crew and a newly ghost-curious Billie Lawrence down to the boiler room, where the sarcophagus has been stashed for a full century.

When it's removed from its longtime hiding place, I can tell pretty easily that it's made of gold. But I don't know much more.

I'm a psychic, not Indiana Jones.

They promise to report it to the proper authorities when

we get to Southampton, and we make them pinky swear that King Rameses VIII will be returned to his proper home and his original resting place from which he was so rudely disturbed. And by pinky swear, I mean record them agreeing to do so. We plan to use the footage in our *Queen Anne* episode of the Ghost Gang.

Emma's appetite is back and in full swing, and every day she and Billie eat themselves into a food coma, which Kiki wakes Emma from with kisses. They sneak off a lot actually, and Chase and I are always having to cover for them. Which I don't mind too much because when Billie gets annoyed and goes looking, it means she leaves Chase and me very much alone in the room together. The best moment for Kiki comes when Billie posts a photo of the three of them on her Instagram, and captions it *My girl and her love.* Followed by all the flags and the love is love hashtag.

Kiki and I perform a séance by the pool to reunite Mary with her mom, and even though I have no way of knowing if it worked, it seems to make Kiki feel better. When we find a blue ribbon floating in the pool, we decide that it's a sign.

Little Mary has found her rest, and this is all she left behind to let Kiki know.

Chase cuts together a masterpiece *Queen Anne* episode for the channel that he plans to upload the second we dock and have service again. With some time and space, and a few virgin piña coladas, he seems to know that who we are and what we do is not defined by a TV show. There will be more opportunities, and until then, we just keep doing what we do best: being friends and hunting (and helping) ghosts.

On the last day (and one last pig-out at the buffet breakfast), we wait in the Starlight Lounge for our number to be called so we can disembark.

As we wait, four familiar faces appear, one determined, three dejected.

Tina flips her hair back and taps a booted foot. "What do you three have to say for yourselves?"

The three guys stand in front of Emma, looking so uncomfortable and hunched over they're almost like something out of a cartoon. Tom has a crutch and an ankle boot provided by the ship's infirmary. He can't remember how he got injured, but I can tell from the way Emma sneers at him, she can.

And she's letting it slide.

"We're sorry," Tom, Tim and Toby say in unison. Emma snorts, but quickly covers her mouth to hide her grin.

"And what else?" Tina says.

"Here," Tom says as their spokesperson, and hands Emma four tickets. She takes them and reads, blinking. I peer over her shoulder. They're four tickets to watch the Dallas Cowboys play.

"Gee, thanks!" Emma says, trying to sound enthusiastic. "I love"—she scans the ticket for a clue—"football?" There's nothing she hates more.

"Those are box seats," Tina says proudly. "Highly coveted." When she sees our blank stares, she winks. "You can resell 'em for a buttload on Ticketmaster."

I hear Kiki whisper to Emma, "Why is she being so nice to you?" Emma just squeezes Kiki's hand and smiles a peaceful smile.

Emma's battle with the cursed killer ship deserves its own

Ghost Gang episode. She not only solved the mystery of the sarcophagus but also fought her inner demon in the shape of Bram, the hot teen serial killer. And she won.

"Okay, kids, see ya round"—Tina turns and throws a wink at Chase—"and good luck on your new show!"

I'm miffed at first—why is Texanne winking at my boyfriend? But when I turn to glare at him, he looks just as confused as I feel.

"New show?" he asks the air.

His phone dings and he stands up to fish it out of his pocket. He glances at his notifications and does a double take.

"What the hell?" he says.

We all stand up and gather around him to read.

It's an email from a producer of an up-and-coming competing network of Creep TV—RIP TV. She says Tina sent her a link to the Ghost Gang's channel and she *loves* the show and wants to offer us a chance to shoot a pilot for their streaming service. The best part is, if the show gets picked up, they're willing to film around our school schedules.

We're all silent for a long time before we start screaming and jumping up and down. We girl-pile on Chase until he can't breathe. When Kiki and Emma pull away to embrace each other, I linger with my arms around Chase's neck. I whisper that I never doubted him for a second. He murmurs back something that sounds a lot like "I love you" before he muffles my reaction with his lips.

I'll have to ask him to elaborate more on that later, because our number is called.

We pass through the atrium on our way to the gangway to

exit the ship, and as we do, an all-too-familiar tingling sensation tickles its way up my spine.

I turn around to see a room full of ghosts, just like the first day of the voyage, when I stepped across the gangway and onto this once-cursed boat. There are so many dead people staring at me that at first I'm concerned we're in some kind of danger, like in the dining room when the *Queen Anne* turned on us the moment we threatened to lift the curse.

Except now, something's different.

They're staring, but not in an angry way. More in a sad, kind of *hopeful* way.

Over the atrium speakers, a song plays.

Forever young,
I want to be forever young,
Do you really want to live forever?
Forever, and ever.

In the center of the room, floating beneath the chandelier, John Brady and Elizabeth Walker slow dance together as the band plays "Forever Young" by Alphaville.

Her head rests on his shoulder while he clasps her hand in his. They sway back and forth to the music, restored to their youth—time no longer the obstacle it once was.

In another corner, a mother dances with her little girl in a blue dress, resting her on one hip as she slowly spins in a circle.

When I turn back around, the rest of the Ghost Gang are watching too, sniffling and with tears in their eyes.

"You can see them too?" I ask, choking back feelings.

They all nod.

Emma takes Kiki's hand and Chase puts his arm around me. We cross the gangway and leave the *Queen Anne*'s ghostly passengers behind to enjoy a second chance at an afterlife.

ACKNOWLEDGMENTS

The *Queen Mary* was our inspiration for the *Queen Anne* in this book. Maybe she's alive too, so we'll send her a quick note of thanks so that she doesn't try to murder us next time we visit. Thank you for your rich history and for your beautiful art deco bar and your creepy second-class pool and the clanging metal pipes of your boiler room. And thank you to all the ghosts on board the *Queen Mary* whose presence has scared us enough times that we thought we should write a book inspired by you.

It is a joy to get to work even once with a genius editor like Alison Romig, but twice? We're downright blessed. Thank you, Ali, for always bringing fresh perspective and insight to the stories we create together. Working with you has made us better horror writers, ones always looking for the best way to bring on the jump scares or scare our readers enough to turn the light back on. To many more chills and thrills!

The Victoria and Faith team wouldn't be where it is today without the genius of our agent, Katie Shea Boutillier. You never cease to amaze us with your brilliant ideas, keen industry savvy, and unstoppable hustle. Thank you for being the champion of this dynamic duo! We love making big moves with you.

We are astounded every single time we get an email from the Underlined team. The imagination they bring to the creation of these little book babies is unreal. Casey Moses, you are a magician working magic and turning it into cover designs. To David Seidman, the artist behind both the *Horror Hotel* and *Cursed Cruised* covers, we thank our lucky stars every day that you choose to draw in our general direction. These are masterpieces, and we bow down!

Cursed Cruise was almost going to have a different, totally terrible title, but thanks to one of our teen readers (and Faith's son's BFF), it didn't. Jacobi Serras, thank you for telling us to use alliteration in the title so it matches *Horror Hotel*. We owe you, buddy!

FAITH

Thank you, Nathan, for reading my first horrible YA novel over ten years ago and not laughing me out of the room. You've supported every wild idea ever since—I wouldn't be publishing any books without your love and encouragement. To Sam, I never get tired of talking Pokémon or watching funny animal videos on YouTube with you. You bring light and cleverness into my life every single day.

To the Beez: Liz Parker, Sara Biren and Tracey Neithercott, my buoys in the stormy publishing seas, thank you for helping me keep my head above water. Emily Wibberly, thank you for being someone this slow-to-trust Scorpio can rely on for sound advice and secret keeping. Gretchen Schrieber, I am so glad you came over that day to talk BTS over dinner and then became one of my best buds.

To BTS—Kim Namjoon, Kim Seokjin, Min Yoongi, Jung Hoseok, Park Jimin, Kim Teahyung, and Jeon Jungkook: I was at the Permission to Dance concert in Vegas when I got the news *Cursed Cruise* would become a book. A little of your light shone on me that day; thank you. To Alice and Cat, your friendship through all the trials and all the BTS spirals means the world to me.

Thank you to my sister, Samantha, for your unwavering support of me and my stories.

And last but never least, to Victoria, my coauthor extraordinaire and dreaming-big cohort bestie. Let's keep scaring ourselves silly and writing books about it for years to come!

VICTORIA

Mom and Dad—I exist because of you, and also you've given me everything. I love you so much. Thank you for indulging every spark of interest (weaving, drawing, singing, acting, makeup-ing, business-ing, and even clowning!)—this one paid off!!!

Nicky—my horror-loving boo. I love you more every day. Thank you for supporting me with delicious snacks and meals while I write. I can't wait to see which book of mine you direct the movie of first ;)

Jenny—my ride-or-die bestie. Whenever I doubt myself, I think about you and how I must be doing something right in life to have a BFF like you. You are one in a trillion. This one's for you.

To everyone else—Jess (Brendan and baby too!), Beth and Mike (and baby girl!!!), Theresa and fam, Aunt Paige, Dan,

Mary Jane and Tim, Timmy and Olivia, Jenn, Cody and Shelby, Jake and Courtney, Josh and Courtney, Linda and Dave, Katie, Tina, Trevor, Garin, Dara, Cat, Alice, Janet (Mrs. Irvin—old habits), Tawnya, Pilar and, of course, the Pink Shark Team!!!

And to Faith/Rebekah—my partner in writing crime (lol). You are not just a star, you are a constellation of stars (probably in the shape of a scorpion). Thank you for continuing to be a blast to write stories with. ♥

Enjoy your stay . . .

Horror Hotel text excerpt copyright © 2022 by Rebekah Faubion and Alexandra Grizinski. Cover art copyright © 2022 by David Seidman. Published by Underlined, an imprint of Random House Children's Books, a division of Penguin Random House LLC, New York.

Turn the page for more from the Ghost Gang!

THE LAST POST

An excerpt from Eileen Warren's blog *all those who wander,* two days before her body was found in an elevator shaft at the Hearst Hotel.

Lost in La-La Land
JUNE 16

LA is the craziest, weirdest, saddest place i have ever been.

everywhere i look there are people screaming.

i'm staying at the Hearst Hotel for economic reasons, but the longer i'm here, the more my brain buzzes and i can't think straight.

i swear, this hotel is alive. i keep seeing things out of the corner of my eyes. shadows. faces.

i hear things too. whispers. voices.

the night before last i woke up screaming and scared the shit out of my hostel roommates. i think they asked to switch rooms because now all their stuff is gone, but i hear them giggling in the hallway.

why can't i just be normal.

the Hearst whispers all of its secrets in my ears. it shows me all of its ghosts.

but i'm tired. not scared, not anymore. just numb.

i want friends. a boyfriend. a brain that doesn't see things that aren't there.

i came to LA to find myself, but somehow i'm more lost than ever.

this hotel is hungry. i hope it doesn't swallow me whole.

–E

THE GHOST CODE

Laws of the Ghost Gang, punishable by death (jk). But you will get a stern talking-to by Chase (which is probably worse?).

1. Never go anywhere alone (buddy system!).
2. Majority rules.
3. Phones on airplane mode AT ALL TIMES
   (hi, Kiki).
4. No provoking or tormenting the spirit world.
5. Never give up personal info while chatting
   with a ghost.
6. Before leaving a location, thank the spirits and
   tell them they *cannot* come home with you.
7. If an entity follows you home, let the group
   know *immediately*.

CHRISSY

"'Die, you pig-faced bitch!'"

"Damn it, Kiki, we told you to never read the comments." Chase scolds Kiki without looking up from the video he's editing with intense focus.

"Do I have a pig face?" When Kiki looks up from her phone, she's near tears. She's the most sensitive soul on planet Earth. Also, somehow, the most lovable.

Emmaline sucks in a deep breath to suppress an eye roll, her fingers tightening on the EMF detector she's fiddling with. Emma is thick-skinned, with steel guts. She's smart as hell and will go to any school she wants next year. No doubt one of the Ivies.

This ghost detector is an Emma brainchild, just like a lot of our gear. Apparently, this one uses electromagnetic frequencies to spell out words. It mostly works.

"Oh my God, *no*," Emma groans.

"It's probably about me," I say. Kiki's pulsing with energy and I'm already on the verge of a headache. I throw her a reassuring smile and squeeze her hand. It does the trick. Her nerves settle and the throbbing in my head lightens.

Kiki's gained a few pounds recently, and despite the fact that the weight looks good on her, she's letting it get to her. It's not something she says to me; it's something that pops into my head. A thought that doesn't belong to my own brain.

Other people's thoughts often drop into my head like pebbles in a stream. Feelings out of place and unfamiliar, a voice that isn't my own, knowledge I shouldn't have and can't explain.

I run a hand through my hair and realize the reason Kiki's in my head is because I've taken my hat off to scratch my scalp. I throw the wool beanie back on and make a mental note to find a different, not-itchy hat for this weekend. Hats are my mind's protection from unwanted, intrusive thoughts and feelings, from both the living *and* the dead.

Cue that famous line whispered by the little kid in the movie *The Sixth Sense:*

I see dead people.

Wah-wah-waaah.

A blessing and a curse, right? Scares you shitless when you're three years old and you wake up to a shadowy man standing in your bedroom doorway. You're unable to move, too scared to make a sound. After countless nights of terror, you get fed up and tell him to go away. Surprise, surprise, he doesn't budge.

Shortly after he appears, your mom starts taking "special" trips to the hospital with your dad while you play at the neighbors' house. Eventually, she loses all her pretty hair and gets really skinny and sad, with hollows under her eyes. For two years, the shadow man appears in your doorway, faceless and silent. It's not until you're five years old that you finally ask him what he wants. This time he starts to move, to shiver, like you're looking at him through a glass of water. One second, he's in the doorway, the next he's right in front of you. No eyes, no mouth, no nose. A shadow where his head should be. You scream until you black out, and when you wake up in the morning, your mother is dead.

Everyone you try to tell pats you on the back with poor-little-girl-just-lost-her-mommy eyes. "What a horrible dream. That must have really scared you, huh?"

But what they don't know is that now the spirit world has got your number, so your childhood bedroom becomes a rest stop on the road to the great beyond. A holding cell for souls with unfinished business. Or those who die too soon. Sometimes violently.

Unfortunately—spoiler alert—there's no otherworldly psychiatrist to help you cope with all the dead people. You do eventually tell your dad and he shrugs it off as silly kid's stuff. You realize you're all alone with this curse, so you're going to have to figure it out. You try lots of things to get the dead people to go away, to get them out of your head, but nothing works. No, they don't always want your help. Yes, sometimes they *just want to scare you.* The spirit realm is not the rainbows-and-butterflies place most psychic mediums (who are mostly frauds) will tell you it is. It's not black-and-white like that.

So you learn to deal because what other choice do you have?

You start sleeping with a pillow over your head because it drowns out the voices. Never completely, but just enough to let you sleep for a few hours at a time. You realize later that a hat works just as well as a pillow and is portable, so it becomes your number one fashion accessory.

Enter Chase Montgomery. He's cute and a nerd, so when he's assigned to be your partner for a film class project, you secretly jump for joy. Little do you know, your secret talent for communicating with the dead shows up on film. Streaks of light and orbs plague the camera in your presence. Chase not only notices, he also directly inquires as to why that could be. You try to make something up on the fly, but unfortunately for you, Chase and his mom are avid paranormal TV enthusiasts. Chase calls you out as exactly what you are, and it's the first time anyone has ever believed you.

He's also the first person who sees your curse as a blessing. He calls it a "gift." It's refreshing, though you wouldn't necessarily agree. He asks if he can interview you on his budding YouTube channel. The episode gains him one hundred new subscribers almost overnight, so he recruits his genius tech-geek bestie Emma to help him shoot a full episode of what starts out as *Ghost Girl*. You do readings for people and take your audience on what you call "ghost walks" of haunted Vegas locales.

In just a few short months, *Ghost Girl* gains a cute fan base of about ten thousand subscribers. It's impressive, but Chase is always hungry, never satisfied. He recruits Kiki Lawrence to do a reading with you. Kiki is TikTok famous for her feminist rants, dramatic makeup transformations, and viral dances in kaleidoscopic sixties-go-go-dancer-inspired outfits. Not to mention she's got the most beautiful color-changing hair on the planet.

Kiki's terrified yet charming reaction to your talk with her dead grandmother skyrockets the channel to fifty thousand fans. Turns out the people want a cast of characters, and when you're in show business, you learn to give them what they want. Just like that, the Ghost Gang is officially born.

Now you have friends and a purpose.

But what you don't have is anyone who understands. You're alone with the voices inside your head, and not even the scratchiest wool hat can keep them out.

Kiki gasps and it shakes me out of my reverie.

"Come on. Are you looking at comments again?" Chase asks, annoyed.

"No." Kiki tries to hide her phone behind her back as Chase makes a grab for it. He's quicker than she is. As he reads what's on the screen, his jaw tightens.

"What is it?" I ask.

Reluctantly, Chase turns the phone so we can all read the comment.

if i kill u will u stay with me forever?

"Yikes, stalker much?" Emma tugs nervously at the strings of her hoodie.

"It's hauntedbyher666," Chase says, frowning. He looks at me, his eyes worried. I know he thinks it's directed at me.

The problem is this isn't the first time we've heard from hauntedbyher666. The comments started about a year ago. We think it's a guy because, well, statistics point to online trolling being perpetrated mostly by men. His comments are usually about "killing u"—whoever "u" is—but he never goes into specifics. He just drops a murderous load in the comments and takes off. Other fans reply to him in our defense, but he never engages further. It's one and done, and then he disappears, sometimes for months.

We always report him, but somehow he keeps coming back. It's creepy as hell, but it never escalates past the comments, and there's not much the authorities can do about cyberstalkers until they basically come to your house waving a gun around.

"It's just some internet troll," I say, trying to reassure Chase. "Report it to YouTube."

Chase nods solemnly. He clicks the three little dots next to the username and flags the comment for harassment.

I do everything I can to stay out of Chase's head—always. He hates it when I hear his thoughts, but this time his feelings make his internal dialogue too loud to ignore.

Chrissy's in danger.

"I'm not," I say. I clap one hand over my mouth when I realize I've just responded to a private thought.

Chase groans out loud and slams his computer shut. He stands up and shoves his hands in his pockets before stalking to the pool house door.

Kiki and Emma exchange a knowing look from the plush white sofa across the room. Chase's family's pool house is all lush decor meant to impress guests, but we're pretty much the only ones ever in here to use the handmade marble coasters on the three-thousand-dollar Restoration Hardware coffee table. We keep the furry lavender throw pillows and crystal candle-holders in pristine condition.

"Where are you going?" I ask him.

"Snack," he says, throwing the door open.

It slams shut behind him.

...

Chase blows off steam for a few minutes and comes back in a much better mood with an armful of snacks from his parents' overstuffed pantry. We gorge ourselves on Cheetos and Doritos and all variations of ee-tos, using paper towels to clean the dust from our fingers so we don't get it on the throw pillows, and wait impatiently for the final cut of our latest episode.

"Genius perfection," Chase finally exclaims, spinning around in his editing chair, eyes a little dilated from staring at the screen. Joy pulses from him like the score of a Disney movie. "Anyone want a final look before I upload?" He's not really asking.

The cursor hovers above the Publish button.

"We know that's rhetorical," Emma says, shooting up from her chair and over to the black bags she's lined up to load all our gear. She sets the EMF reader in its cushioned bag right next to the thermographic camera filter she assembled from materials she found on Amazon.

I watch the little gray bar on Chase's screen slowly edge forward. The video is a teaser for the Halloween special we're shooting this weekend. It's a sizzle reel of the last few months of episodes plus a reading at the Bellagio Ballroom on the Las Vegas Strip.

Most of our episodes are documentary-style, like *Ghost Hunters,* but without the Syfy budget. We're most funded by Chase's real estate mogul father when he decides to take a break from being disgusted by his son's Hollywood dreams. Also, Chase mows lawns on weekends to pay for our travel expenses, and Kiki worked out an influencer deal with an online store called Ghost Tech to get us discounted ghost-hunting gear.

Vegas is full of haunted locales, and we use the Montgomery name to shoot just about wherever we want (since most of the casino owners live in houses developed by Chase's dad).

Our first on-location shoot was at the Sandhill Tunnels, the site of a tragic car crash. We've filmed at the Luxor on the Strip, where too many depressed patrons have leapt to their deaths inside the pyramid. Then there's the Hoover Dam, which has a similar problem, and lest we forget, the corner of Flamingo and Koval, where Tupac was gunned down at a red light. Even in broad daylight, there's something eerie and sad about that intersection.

Chase pops up, stretching long. My eyes fix on the strip of tan skin showing between the hem of his T-shirt and his jeans. He's backlit by the three computer monitors set up on the wall-to-wall desk that he uses to edit in addition to his laptop. I don't realize I'm staring until he walks over to the snack pile and picks up a Kit Kat. He unwraps it, snaps it in two and shoves half into his mouth.

"All right, plan for tomorrow?" he asks, mouth full.

Kiki is already taking off her swimsuit cover-up like business time has ended, but with Chase, that's never the case. Her face twitches with disappointment and my heart clenches—she's right, we rarely *just chill*. Kiki rolls her eyes and flops down on the sofa, crossing her legs. Her newly pink-and-purple-streaked hair sits coiled on top of her head, beautifully contrasting with her dark brown skin.

Chase grabs a Mountain Dew from the mini fridge and hovers behind the sofa, holding the soda in one hand and opening the Waze app on his phone with the other.

"I've packed up most of the gear," Emma says. She yanks off

her glasses and uses the hem of her T-shirt to wipe them clean of any smudges.

"We should head out in the morning," Chase says. Kiki groans loudly. Chase messes with the Plan a Drive settings in the app. "It says the Hearst Hotel is only four hours away as long as we leave by eleven."

We're going to what is quite possibly the most haunted hotel in America in one of the most dangerous neighborhoods in Los Angeles in record-scorching SoCal heat on Halloween weekend, all without parental permission.

"I can't believe you're actually going to go through with this," Emma says, eyes on Chase. Chase is willing to make bold moves for the channel but has never risked the wrath of his parents in such a blatant way.

He shrugs, but he's sweating. "This trip is our ticket to one million subs. The benefits outweigh the risk."

"Taking your mom's Escalade to downtown LA without telling her?" Emma says. "You're a madman."

"We're there and back, just one night." Chase forces a grin. He simmers with nervous energy, ready to explode into a rolling boil any second. "What's the worst that could happen?"

"Why would you say that?" Kiki squeaks, covering her ears.

"We're doomed for sure now!" Emma slaps a hand over her forehead for added drama.

Chase frowns at both of them and crosses his arms over his chest, trying to hide the pit sweat seeping through his white T-shirt. I giggle, fully aware that they are (mostly) teasing him. Chase is serious about being serious, a trait he inherited from his dear old dad, who inherited it from *his* dear old dad—a fact that I know only because I catch occasional glimpses of

Chase's dead grandfather scowling at me from a second-story window.

We all told our parents different stories about where we're going on Saturday. Chase told his parents he's doing an SAT prep all-nighter at our school. Kiki told her mom we're going on a camping trip and Emma told her parents she's going to a robotics conference. As for me, my dad doesn't really notice when I'm not there, so I plan to leave him a stack of microwave meals in the freezer along with a note that I'll be back on Sunday.

Not that my dad would care that much anyway. He's got more of a fall-asleep-in-front-of-the-TV type of parenting style. Also, depression. My grandmother (whom I never met) shows up in my dreams sometimes begging me to get my dad on meds. I always remind her that I'm not a doctor and that he refuses to see one. She's not happy with how my dad is handling things in my mother's absence, but there's not much she can do about it from beyond the grave.

As for my mother, I've never seen her in spirit. Not one time. I tried to summon her myself once with a Ouija board in an attic and ended up with a back full of bloody scratches from malevolent ghosts. (Don't ever, ever touch—don't even look at—a Ouija board.)

Unfortunately, you can't pick and choose the ghosts you summon—they choose you.

"People," I say, drawing their attention to me before everyone's nerves get the best of them. Kiki told us recently to stop saying *guys* since it's not gender inclusive. "It's too late to back out now. The Halloween teaser is up. Our subscribers have been asking for this video for months."

What they've really been asking is for me to use my *gift* to make contact with Eileen Warren.

You see, the Hearst isn't just your average, everyday haunted hotel. It's also the site of one of the most internet-famous mysteries of the last decade.

Nearly ten years ago, after going missing for almost a week, the remains of twenty-five-year-old grad student Eileen Warren were found scattered in an elevator shaft. A month into the investigation, authorities released footage from hours before Eileen's untimely death. Her bizarre and erratic behavior led many Mom's-basement-dwelling internet sleuths to believe her death was not the accident the coroner had ruled it to be.

These Reddit detectives all have their own theories about how and why Eileen Warren ended up in that elevator shaft. But based on her posts and my own experiences with the paranormal, I have a sneaking suspicion that her visions were more psychic than psychotic.

"We're not backing out, we're just wigging out," Emma counters, chewing on her lip. Despite Emma's laissez-faire facade, lip chewing is her number one tell that she's nervous as hell.

"Can I swim now?" Kiki asks, arms folded and lips pouty. Her bikini is tie-dye and matches her hair.

"Go for it," Chase says. "I gotta go inside and finish AP calc."

"You're not done yet? I finished that at lunch." Emma yawns and stretches, rubbernecking Kiki as she leaves to splash into the pool.

"I finished that at lunch," Chase mocks Emma's not-so-humble brag. He chugs the rest of his Dew and then smashes

the can in one hand and Kobes it into the trash. "Eleven a.m. tomorrow. *Please* don't be late."

He shouts the last line for Kiki, who is always late to absolutely everything. She flips him off from her rainbow pool float, confirming that she one hundred percent plans to be late.

Chase groans and pauses to flip the light off inside the pool house. He looks back at me. "Coming, C?"

I stare past him at the faceless shadowy figure standing in the doorway. It's been many years, but there's no mistaking it. The deadly omen that haunted my preschool years, that vanished the day my mother died . . . is back.

"Chrissy?" Chase blinks at me with concern in his eyes. I'm frozen in place.

I shut my eyes tight and when I open them again, the shadow man is gone.

"Coming" is all I say.

CHASE

5K subscribers.

Started from the bottom, now we're here.

50K subs.

Started from the bottom, now my whole team fuckin' here.

100K, 250K, 500K, now . . . 651K.

I done kept it real from the jump, living at my mama house we'd argue every month . . .

I'm vibing with Drake while I shove socks in my duffel bag.

Come on, one million subs!

One million subs mean backers, collabs, funding to travel the world visiting haunted houses, prisons, hospitals, hotels, castles and more. Networking and connections with Hollywood producers, managers, agents, celebrities and studios. Our very own network show! Not to mention the much-coveted Gold Play Button awarded to creators with one million subscribers. It's just a metal plaque with the channel name embossed on it, but I want it.

One million feels like the magical number that will open all the right doors.

We've had a few advertisers reach out to sponsor episodes, but beyond that it's been crickets from Hollywood. Which I guess makes sense because there are over two hundred thousand channels on YouTube with one hundred thousand subscribers. And there are only twenty thousand channels with over a million. We're nobody until we get that *M*.

The second-best part of all this will be sticking it to my dear old dad. He refers to what we do as "that Scooby-Doo gang nonsense" and thinks I'm doing it because I don't have any dude friends. I grew up with two older sisters. Hanging out with girls has always been easier for me. Also, the guys at my school are a waste of space, without an original thought in their vapid minds; they're mostly focused on playing sports and hooking up with girls.

Not that there's anything wrong with that, just not my cup of tea. I mean, the playing sports part. The girls thing would be nice, but I always seem to get friend-zoned immediately. In the girls' defense, I don't really ask them out. I'm too focused on the growth of the channel to care about dating. Plus, most high school hookups seem to happen at parties, and I don't go to those.

I did have a serious crush on Chrissy when we first started *Ghost Girl.* She was so quiet and mysterious with her pale skin and long baby-blond hair and smoky eyes. She even kind of looked like a ghost. When Mr. Sievers paired us up for the TV commercial project, I sweated bullets waiting for her to come over to my house to shoot. Chrissy has no clue how much guys talk about how hot she is when she's out of earshot. (She would probably be a little grossed out if she knew.)

Putting her on camera for the first time, I was shook when I saw the footage. Streaks of light and orbs polluted every shot, every single take. My mom is way into the occult, so I've watched every paranormal TV show that exists and knew exactly what was happening. The first time I asked Chrissy if she could see things other people couldn't, she started to cry. No one had ever believed her before, and here I was, asking flat out. I interviewed her for my channel, and the rest is history, including my secret crush.

I sling the duffel bag over my shoulder and head out to the car. Dad is "out of town on business" and Mom is "having a spa day with the girls." The only good thing about being a living rich-kid cliché is that my parents don't give two shits what I'm doing on a Saturday. Mom won't be thrilled I took her Escalade, but the odds of her even noticing it's gone are close to zero.

I open the garage with an app on my phone (bougie, I know), and Emma and Chrissy are waiting for me in the driveway.

I sigh and pop the trunk of the white Escalade. "Where is Kiki?"

"Where do you think?" Emma has a way of making you feel dumb with just a look and four words. Kiki is late. Kiki is *always* late.

Emma and I packed up all the camera equipment and ghost gear last night, so all that's left is to shove our bags in the back. It's a tight squeeze. I reorganize everything in an attempt to make it all fit. Chrissy hangs back and when I motion for her to give me her bag, she shakes her head.

"I've got it," she says. She insists on doing everything herself.

"Give that to me," I tell her. Chrissy always rides shotgun; it's a standing order since she gets debilitating motion sickness when she's in the back seat. Thank God, since she's the only passenger I can sit next to for four hours. Emma commandeers the music and Kiki is a veritable chatterbox.

I put two cans of nitro cold brew in the cupholders between the front seats just as Emma shuts the door to the back and gives the all-clear shout. We're locked and loaded; now the only thing left to do is get Kiki in the car.

"Does she have an ETA?" I ask Chrissy.

"Three minutes, she swears," she says, putting her phone in her lap to wrap her hair into a messy bun. We decided her aesthetic would be black for the show: black jeans, black T-shirts, chipped black nail polish, heavy black eyeliner.

It works. Our fans love the goth-girl vibe and would freak if they saw all the pink in Chrissy's closet at home. Not that I've seen her closet or anything. Or been invited into her bedroom.

I blare the horn in frustration. We're already almost twenty minutes behind schedule, and three minutes is at least ten minutes in Kiki time.

We pass the time waiting by arguing over whose playlist to link to the Bluetooth. We decide that everyone gets one hour each way, Chrissy first. Chrissy loves EDM. She says it quiets the voices in her head.

"Sweet but Psycho," by Ava Max, blasts from the radio.

Oh, she's sweet but a psycho . . .

"Speak of the devil," Emma mutters when Kiki finally

arrives. She's being affectionate, believe it or not, in her own Emma way.

Kiki emerges like a celebrity from the back of a Honda Accord with an Uber sticker. In her road-trip outfit—hot pink sweat suit with iridescent tiger stripes, bedazzled sunglasses and kaleidoscopic pigtails—she's a rainbow spectacle from her head to her toes. Kiki is our on-camera unicorn and we hope she never changes.

She opens the back door of the Escalade and pokes her head inside.

"I have to pee!" she says, frantic, then drops her giant blue-raspberry slushie in the cupholder and sprints into the house.

"Nuh-uh, she's cut off," Emma says, passing the slushie forward so I can take it. Kiki's bladder is the size of a pebble.

I crank the ignition on the Escalade. God, my mom would skin me alive if she knew where I was actually taking her prized stallion. Fortunately, she's at the spa at the Bellagio all weekend to avoid the trick-or-treaters who come through the Ridges from all over the Las Vegas suburbs. We live in a country club–style neighborhood right outside the city. They turned it into an oasis in the desert that feels like an actual heat-induced mirage from hell.

Kiki loves the pool, though. When she finally gets into the car, she slams the door shut and exclaims, "Yay, road trip!"

I put the car in reverse.

■ ■ ■

Underlined

PAPERBACKS

LOOKING FOR YOUR NEXT HORROR STORY?
WE'VE GOT YOU COVERED.

scary good.

GetUnderlined.com | @GetUnderlined

1495D